THERE'S SOMETHING WRONG WITH AUNTY BETH

A COLLECTION OF HORROR

MARK TOWSE

D & T
PUBLISHING

CONTENTS

I am again dedicating this to my mother, my first editor and someone I've bonded with enormously throughout this writing journey. For that, I will be eternally grateful.

THERE'S SOMETHING WRONG WITH AUNTY BETH (AN ODE TO NANA)

THE PLATE of biscuits always looks promising to George, but he's made that mistake before. Pink wafers with no crunch, chewy gingernuts, and even the thought of the Chocolate Bourbons induces a little bit of sick in his mouth. He wonders how anything in the house could be damp with the heating turned up so bloody high.

His Aunty Beth leans in, half her mouth curled into a smile, and the other half doing something completely different. A question's coming; he knows it. The sit-off ensues. Nothing yet, just eyes drilling into his. He squeezes at the flesh under his legs and drives his back further into the softness of the chair.

Her breathing is nasally, as if something is rattling around inside her nostrils. She moves closer still, giving him a close-up view of white chin fluff, and even worse, the half-a-dozen thick black hairs emerging from a globule her mother once told him was a beauty spot. To George, it looks more like a spider crawling out of a shit nugget.

Unable to bear the sight any longer, he turns his gaze to the orange and red carpet. He can feel her stare still on him. He wills himself not to look up, but the carpet is beginning to move, patterns rotating and merging, getting faster all the time, and he's starting to feel dizzy. So damned hot, too. Thoughts turn to his friends, Zac, and Lachlan, no doubt lounging in the comfort of their cool and dimly lit rooms, snacks spilling onto their desks, controllers in hand, and not a care in the world, focusing only on shooting as many motherfuckers in the head as possible.

He glances to his mum for support, but she's talking to Uncle Rodney about how much petrol they get to the gallon. The loud clock on the mantelpiece, sounding like a ticking bomb from an old movie, tells him they've only been there for seventeen minutes. It feels like a lifetime.

Totally not fair, any of it.

Aunty Beth opens the left side of her mouth to speak, the other side puckered and dead. She sucks in some saliva before it escapes. "How's school going, Georgey?"

Fourteen years old. He wonders whether he'll still be answering to Georgey when he's thirty. "Good," he replies, the same answer he gave the last three times she asked. He looks over to his mum again, but *the bitch* is still talking.

"You have to speak up, dear. I'm a bit hard of hearing in my left."

"It's good. School's good."

"That's good. Good." She moves in a little closer, her left eye performing a series of twitches as though someone is tugging at the bottom lid with invisible cotton. "Let's see those beautiful eyes, boy." Another sloppy recoil of spit. Her words come out slurred these days, but he's getting better at picking them up. "Don't be shy, Georgey. Let's see those peepers."

Never again. Never, ever, ever, again.

He pinches his skin harder as he turns towards his aunty. A stroke, according to the doctors, but he overheard Uncle Rodney say they were "very airy-fairy about the details." One thing's for sure; the old Aunty Beth never made his skin crawl.

"Beautiful," she says, wiping the other corner of her mouth with a bit of tissue. "Such a handsome devil." Her eyes continue burning into him.

Stop talking, Mum. Stop talking! He swallows hard, offering Aunty Beth a half-assed smile. It's the worse day ever, even beating the time his mum caught him in the back living room, pants around his ankles, strumming one out to the weather girl. "I forgot my car keys," she had said, grabbing them from the fruit bowl and rushing out as though the house was on fire. The next time the urge came, he made sure it was in a more controlled environment.

"Such strong legs, too."

His school shorts are suddenly riding far too high up for his liking. He thinks perhaps Aunty Beth might be overdoing the vitamin tablets.

"Bet you have all the girls after you."

It's too much to bear. The musty smell of the house, the stifling temperature, the stray hairs, the slurpy mouth, ladders in both tights, thick legs akimbo, offering a dark void that is melting his brain. "Have you got any soda, Aunty Beth?" he manages to croak.

It's as if she's in a deep trance, lost in a world full of youth and smooth skin. "Huh?"

"Soda."

Remaining perched on the edge of the chair, she nods, glistening eyes still targeting him.

"He's asking for a soda, love," Rodney utters.

"Shut up, you prick!" Aunty Beth screams back without looking at him.

It's a hard one to follow. Rodney's eyes are wide and moist; he looks like he wants to say something but instead shuts his thin lips. Probably best. In contrast, his mum's mouth falls open, but she doesn't look like she has any intention of saying anything.

The silence is unbearable. It's going to take a hero.

"Is it in the fridge?" he says, finally pulling his hands from under his legs and readying them on the arms of the chair. "The soda."

She shakes her head as if bringing herself to, and with a groan, heaves herself to her feet. Already, George feels better, his eyes no longer needing to avoid the black hole that seemed to be eating its way towards him.

"Cola or fizzy orange, pet?"

"Cola, please."

He waits for her to disappear through the doorway before adjusting his position in the chair. Moist with perspiration, the leather underneath offers a little fart as he plops himself back down again.

"How are you doing over there, buddy?" Uncle Rodney asks. His mum turns for an update, too.

"Good, thanks."

"Changed a bit, hasn't she?"

Not feeling ready for a smile just yet, George nods. *Understatement of the fucking year.*

"She's still Aunty Beth. Just a few gremlins in her head, so to speak."

George nods again. *Shut up, you prick.*

Uncle Rodney looks on the verge of tears. "How's school?"

"Can I use your bathroom, please?"

"Of course. You know where it is. Upstairs, second on the left."

It feels good to be out of the chair, walking. Bought himself a bit of extra time, and he's pretty pleased with himself. He wonders how long he can stay in the toilet without raising suspicion. If only his mum would have allowed him to bring his phone. *Ten minutes too long?* He grabs the banister and pulls himself onto the first step, observing his reflection in the hallway mirror.

"She's getting worse, Joan."

As he's about to take the next step, George softly plants his foot back down and arches his neck towards the doorway.

"What do the doctors say?" his mum asks.

"They just feed me the same old crap. Nothing we can do." George thinks he hears Rodney's voice crackle a little at the end. "Yesterday, I caught her giving me the middle finger from the kitchen window while I was hanging the washing out."

"Poor Beth. And poor you."

"I don't know what to do, Joan. This morning she was uttering some rubbish about things being in her brain. She started hitting herself on the side of her head, over and over again. I don't mean a gentle tap; I mean proper going for it. I tried to stop her, but she started on me next."

"You need help, Rodney."

"She said she was going to kill me in my sleep."

"Jesus Christ!"

"I hate myself for it, Joan, but I give up; I can't do it anymore. The doctors gave me the name of this—"

It all goes quiet. Taking his cue that Aunty Beth is back with his drink, George bounds up the stairs like a ballerina, grimacing as they offer a moan halfway up. He swings himself around using the top railing and shuts the bathroom door behind him, breathing a sigh of relief as he leans against it. On the opposite wall, there's a plaque reading *The Best Seat in the House*. Right now, he couldn't agree more. He reaches for the bolt but only sees screw holes where it likely used to be before Aunty Beth got batshit crazy.

The dark brown shag of the toilet mat absorbs his feet as he takes his place, providing warmth and a whiff of disturbed urine. A small price to pay if it means avoiding the stare of those watery *peepers* for a while. He drops his pants and begins thinking about Vanessa Taylor from gym class this morning, the droplet of sweat running from her neck towards her—

"Georgey."

You've got to be fucking kidding me.

With Vanessa now only a distant memory, he suddenly feels quite nauseous at the thought of holding his pecker with Aunty Beth and her black hole on approach. He recalls reading something about their gravity field being immense.

Black holes, not old ladies that is.

"I've got your drinkypoos!"

Fuck off, you crazy old bat.

Accompanied by Rodney's sheepish calls in the background, the inevitable squeak of the stairs brings a further tightening of the knot in his stomach that arrived since first arriving at the frosted glass front door of Aunty Beth's.

"Georgey!"

"I'm on the toilet, Aunty."

The knock on the door sends his heart thumping and blood pumping in his ears, creating a feeling of overwhelming dizziness. His world was so different only an hour ago, safe and familiar, something he promises to himself he'll never take for granted again.

Another knock.

Double maths and now this. It's just not fucking fair.

"Do you need any help, little Georgey?" Another tap. "Geeoooorrrgggeeeyyyyyy."

"I'm doing a poo, Aunty!"

In disbelief, he watches the handle begin to turn. *You've got to be kidding me.* He thrusts himself from the supposedly best seat in the house, fumbles his pants back up, and begins working frantically at the zipper. "Aunty, this is not cool."

"Come on." As her head pokes around the door, she lifts a finger to the centre of her lips, a marker for two very different faces. "I've got something to show you."

"I think Mum's calling me." But her fingers are already coiled around his, leading him towards where a sliver of dull yellow light tries to escape from the darkness.

Shit on a stick.

Before he's even through the door, the smell hits him—a noxious concoction of cheap perfume and something far worse. A double bed takes up most of the room, pink sheets almost sickeningly garish enough to draw attention away from the patch of black on the left wall that seems to be spreading from the ceiling down. Almost.

"Bit pongy, isn't it? Rodney, the silly old bastard, said it's mould." Aunty Beth shuts the door behind her, prompting George to edge away towards the window, the room suddenly feeling more than a little claustrophobic. He follows the trail of thick black from the coving of the ceiling towards the antique mirror where it begins to thin out, disappearing behind the large oval frame that's supported by two ornate posts.

"I thought it was too, at first, but I know better now," Aunty Beth says, reaching for the necklace hanging over one of the supports. She slips it around her neck and offers George a wink with her good side. "Beautiful, isn't it? Found it in lost property at the community centre over on Newhaven Crescent." She digs her chin into her neck, running her fingers over the globe pendant as she approaches. "Got a cleaning job there once they finished the restorations and reopened after that awful incident."

Words begin to rush over George. A quick glance over his shoulder to the world on the outside, and he imagines the smell of fresh air and the touch of the breeze. Another world.

She continues moving towards him, shimmying from left to right, one finger circling the pendant, the other trailing across the duvet. "It told me things, Georgey," she utters.

George backs up until the window ledge presses against his spine. An awful thickness dwells at the back of his throat, and images burn into his mind that he knows will haunt him for weeks to come, possibly years.

Only inches away, she leans in close and sucks on her spit. "Now it's inside me, spreading as it did up the wall, revealing all its secrets. I'm going to kill him before he kills me, Georgey. Put some powder in his whisky tonight and run the breadknife across his neck." It's hard to tell, but George thinks she's smiling. "Over and over and over and over and over."

There's nowhere else to go, trapped in a nightmare—the bed, black wall, the smell, Aunty Beth's leaky mouth and glassy eyes. He looks to the ceiling, eyes on the meringue-like swirls. He opens his mouth, but only a rasp emerges.

She shuffles forward. *What the fuck?*

Cold hands clamp his face. "It's what I wanted to show you." That nasally rattle, the *beauty spot*, and—her eyes—filling with black ink.

Before he has the chance to find a scream, her dry lips are on his, thrusting and squirming. Spiders' legs tickle his soft cheek as big hands pull his head into hers. He grabs her shoulders and tries to wrestle her off, but she's a fucking powerhouse. As something cold tries to work its way into his mouth, he clamps his lips together as hard as he can, but he's losing the battle. She brings him in closer still, and he feels her cold flesh pressing against his. She lets out a little moan—and—she's in!

Fuck! Fuck! Fuck!

It's no tongue. George can feel tiny worm-like tendrils searching his mouth, wriggling their way towards God knows where and creating a bitterness that layers the back of his throat. He swallowed a fly once, but this is much worse. Veins pop as he pushes against her, but she outweighs him at least two to one and isn't going anywhere. Unable to breathe, he starts thinking this is the way he's going to go; french-kissing his Aunty Beth. Iciness begins running through his veins. A dizzying sensation brings black floaters to the edge of his vision.

"Pickle, where are you?" The squeak of the stairs offers George hope.

It feels as though their heads may merge into one, bound by whatever vileness leaks from her mouth to his. He lets out a shudder at the thought, or it could be the images that are starting to flood his mind.

Only as the door begins to open is he released, pushed back into the window ledge with force, Aunty Beth and the bed offering a deep moan as they meet.

"What the Devil?" Rodney says as he pokes his head through.

"He tried to touch me." She says, half her bottom lip jutting out.

"I didn't! I didn't!" George croaks, beginning to cry.

She snaps her head back towards George. "Yeah, you did! You wanted a big ole slice of Aunty Beth's cherry pie."

"That's enough!" Roger screams.

With that, Beth begins writhing on the sheets, hiking her dress up. "Get it while it's warm, gents."

As George is escorted from the room and down the hallway by Uncle Rodney, he hears his aunty begin to giggle, which turns into a guffaw, which turns into a choking rasp.

His mum is waiting for him at the bottom of the stairs. "Everything okay?"

"She's had another turn, Joan," Roger mutters as they reach the bottom, shaking his head with exasperation. "I think it's probably best you leave."

"Are you sure? Can't we help in any way?"

To the soundtrack of Aunty Beth's raucous laughter, George can feel himself trembling. He feels so damned cold. "Mum, I want to go home. Please can we go—"

He stops mid-sentence to swallow his saliva.

"George, that isn't funny." His mum's face twists into a scowl, eyes wide in that *wait until I get you home look.* "There's something wrong with Aunty Beth. Mimicking her like that is really low."

George turns to the mirror to see his downturned mouth. Part of him wants to scream, but a greater part of him wants to *scrape his mum's eyes out with a spoon and feed them to the dog* for bringing him here.

THE FRUITS OF LABOUR

THE HOUSE BECAME mine on 12th December 1978. Over a decade ago now. I'd just come out of a marriage that lasted longer than it should have done, a lot less affluent but a damn sight happier. I wanted to move on, make a fresh start. A city dweller all my life, the country seemed like the perfect place to reset and breathe life into my writing career.

Climbing mountains, playing in old castle ruins, telling ghost stories surrounded by fog—all treasured memories from family holidays in Dartmoor. I wanted that air of mystery back in my life, to channel my inner kid. It wasn't so much a whim but a feeling. As soon as I rolled up the driveway to the third house on my list, Sanctuary Place, the hairs on my neck bristled, and I had that same feeling.

My search was over.

You've heard the tale before, the too good to be true price, the nearby cemetery, the rumours around town, all the warnings of classic horror, but when you're smitten, it's hard to see through the mist. Hell, at the time, those factors likely only made me want it more.

Even mother approved of its stateliness, only diluting her enthusiasm with thoughts of it being far too big for a single man. Bitterness towards the end of my marriage with Denise was something she carried around for quite some time. "People give up too easily these days."

The weather was abhorrent the day I collected the keys, at least that's what I recall. I suspect memory often adds desolation to winter seasons gone, extra layers over time, British melancholy with a touch of ever-present pessimism. Roads were gritted, but the snow was winning, especially on the country ones. I took it slowly, but it only added to the anticipation. By the time I rolled up the driveway, gravel crunching underneath the soft white coating, I could hardly contain myself. Songs crackled from the radio as I sat in the warmth of the car, admiring my new home. I could have stayed there for hours, taking it all in—weathered but proud, vibrant green ivy wrapping around crumbling golden stone and grounds filled with a variety of songbirds.

Everything about it was grand. Outside and in. Double doors opened to a magnificently ornate staircase that split the house in two. Impressive but dusty cobweb-covered chandeliers conjured scenes of music and laughter. But its sheer size also induced a feeling of inexplicable sadness, as though the good times had been and gone.

I wanted to resuscitate it, give it meaning again.

Before arranging for the removal van, I often drove down just to familiarise myself with the house and its surroundings. Hours were spent mulling around the place, inspecting its bare bones, looking for secret doors, or shifting walls. Did I mention I was a writer? Etched into the corner of the main dining room floor, I found a heart, the initials MT, KT, and ET scratched out in the centre.

In the middle of the countryside, buried between sloping hills, the nearest house at least half a mile away, it was so quiet, so serene. The orchard in the expansive backyard would give me the most pleasure, though, and soon become a second obsession.

The back bedroom became my study, and I filled it with books and furnishings to make it as comfy as possible. Overlooking the then skeletal fruit trees that subtly turned to rolling countryside, marked only by a rusty collapsed wire fence, it was the perfect place to write. Even though I could see my breath, I was already picturing the blossom and could almost taste the perfumes wafting through the open sash window.

Denise would have said I was stark raving mad, but she was out of my life, and my time was my own. The first couple of weeks went by quickly, days taken up by painting endless walls, attempting to fix things, and sitting in front of my typewriter. The moans from the old pipes, the creaks from the walls, and the trespassing wind that whistled its haunting tune were yet to inspire, but I knew it was only a matter of time.

The first spring arrived bang on schedule, and my backyard transformed into a wonderland of colour almost overnight. No words came, but plenty of fruit did over the coming months—a bounty of ripe apples, pears, plums, and peaches, to name just a few. Best fruit I ever had. Perfection. Only two trees failed to provide anything but leaves, and they stood side by side at the edge of the dam. They looked sad, out of place.

Friends from all locations flocked to Sanctuary Place in those first few months. Depending on the weather, you would find us in the main hall or courtyard area, drinking, singing, dancing, laughing. I guess it was my way of trying to reignite the flame.

And then there was Frank, a friendly but stubborn oaf I'd known since boarding school. Constantly trying to matchmake, he would insist on his *current* date bringing a friend along. He never knew when to give up. I must admit that I was tempted once; Nancy, an artist who gushed over the house as much as I first did.

One of many things I will live to regret.

Slowly but surely, the honeymoon period wore off, and by the time winter came around again, the familiar feeling of disappointment knotted in my chest. Friends had lost interest in making the long drive. The orchard looked sad.

Blank pages taunted me.

The following spring, things would change. It was an unseasonably warm start, bringing premature blossom and an array of wildlife to the algae-stained fountain. Hope washed over me again, and although I'd written no words, they felt close.

Then one morning, I looked out the study window and somehow knew from that moment things would be different. Blossom had bloomed on the two trees near the dam, paling the other flowers into relative insignificance. Spectacular shades of red and pinks demanded attention, almost looking too vibrant to be real.

It was as if they were calling me.

The small patch of grass between the two trees soon became my new favourite spot—the view of the house, the tranquillity, the perfumes—it all had an energy that the house didn't. That's where the first few words spilled from the dusty catacombs of my mind onto paper.

The two trees soon started to bear fruit unlike any other. Perfectly round, skin like peaches, but paler and even more tender, as though it could break at the slightest of knocks. I picked one from the tree, the one that looked ripest, and held it to my nose. Its scent was extraordinary, a cocktail of perfumes that induced contrasting melancholy and happiness. I wanted to laugh and cry at the same time. Bursting with magnificent redness, it was all I could do not to gorge it down, but I made the experience last for as long as possible. Heart pounding, I rolled the fruit across my lips, inhaling its beauty, before finally sinking my teeth into its silky skin.

The pop induced a heady sweetness that made my legs buckle. The treacly substance carried tangs of the ripest pomegranate, grape, pineapple, but so much more. Even the slightly bitter after-taste at the end was far from unpleasant. Each bite made me want it more. There was an unmistakable high that went with it, too, an induced separation from the real world, unlike anything I'd experienced from the questionable substances Frank used to bring.

They were the only two trees I netted; I let the birds have the rest.

Two thousand words found their way to paper that evening.

Time passed, and the fruit continued to ripen, becoming even larger and bursting with even more colour. And then something began to happen. I noticed the fruit starting to change. The taste was still heavenly, intoxicating, but there was no doubt the roundness was developing into more of a pear-like shape.

My manuscript was at twenty thousand words. It was my best work to date.

The next day, I turned up with my basket to find the slightly narrower half of the fruit had developed two small bumps adjacent to each other. I'm not talking a single piece; I mean all of them, identical. Something else, too. There was a series of small but unmistakable wrinkles where the two now distinct-looking shapes joined, like a—neck.

I remember giggling as I made my way through countless pieces but also feeling some disquiet. The bitter aftertaste was getting stronger, but so was my need for that sweetness.

Words flowed.

Excitement for my next bestseller was undeniable. The following day, I couldn't get out of bed quickly enough. The morning sun poured through my window as I walked and stretched my way towards it, eager for a dose of nature's smelling salts. Squinting into the brightness, I surveyed my orchard with considerable pride, and even as my eyes fell on the two trees that were impossibly full of fruit once more, I took it as a good omen. The house and grounds were alive once again, bursting with creativity and hope.

A third bump appeared, slightly larger, like a nose, and below it, a crease resembling a smile. I got through four pieces that morning and went back to my study to write six thousand words before lunch.

As fast as I could eat the fruit, it was growing back. Ears next, two bumps on the outer edge of the upper half. The fruit was no doubt getting bigger, heavier, but still, the branches refused to let it fall to the ground.

The following day, four stubs appeared, which, by dusk, had

matured into lengths that could have passed for short limbs, albeit missing hands and feet.

I needed more to sustain the high. I couldn't get the juice down my throat quickly enough. Five thousand more words found their way onto paper. I denied what was happening, put it down to arboreal aberrations, but each day the trees bore new fruit, and each time, the resemblance to a human baby became harder to blame on mother nature alone.

Fingers and toes appeared shortly after.

The metallic aftertaste got stronger every day, bringing back memories of scraped knees and disinfectant. It didn't stop me gorging on the fruit, though, and not wasting a drop of that opulent redness.

Most days I was in a haze, alternating between time behind the typewriter, and time under the tree, refilling my creative juices.

Sixty thousand words. The final few chapters. Home straight.

The wail woke me up at 2.06 am—a muffled screaming that dragged me to the study window. There was movement in the trees, the ones adjacent to the dam.

Even before I had my dressing gown on, I knew what I'd find.

As I approached the treeline, eyes on the crying sexless babies, arching branches attached to their midriff like umbilical cords, I remember wondering if the moon had ever seen anything like it before. As with their appearance, the noise they created was identical—high-pitched and deafening—just as nature designed it to be, but their boneless limbs flailed in a way that would make even the Devil blush.

My stomach growled as I observed their movements. It was just fruit, I justified, a deviant of mother nature. Ears ringing with their unbearable screeching, I picked the first one from the tree and sank my teeth into the neck, ripping the head away in a violent spray of red. One after the other, I stuffed my mouth with their juicy boneless flesh, draining their sweetness, basking in the innocence of the moonlight. I was insatiable. The taste was even sweeter, a further improved blend of fruit, earth, syrup, all with perfect acidity that made the tongue sing and the belly crave more. And that familiar after taste, of course.

Finally, the tree was empty, and I retired to my bedroom to sleep soundly.

The following day, the fruit had replenished. In its early stages, yes, but I knew within twenty-four hours, it would be singing to me. I ran my tongue across my top lip in anticipation.

Another six thousand words that day—only two chapters to go.

2.06 am.

The chorus woke me, slightly louder, but the same muffled cries as though through stitched lips. Even tucked so far away into the country, I was afraid someone would hear. I rushed outside, naked as the day I was born, and I started picking the toddlers from the tree, shoving their juice-filled limbs into my mouth as quickly as I could in a ravenous frenzy of popping, tearing, and guzzling. Only when the tree was empty did I stagger back, belly full and eager for the sun to rise.

I slept like a baby, waking up just after nine. New fruit was already growing on the two trees by the dam.

Five thousand words. One chapter to go!

As I said before, obsession is blinding, much like love. Reality takes the chair behind, patiently waiting for the front seat to become free again.

In the early hours of the following morning, and like clockwork, the chorus began. But this was different, more of a synchronised moan than a cry. I jumped out of bed, my belly giving out a huge groan, and I scrambled through the darkness towards the source, ignoring the chill that seeped through my bones. The fruit that hung from the tree resembled small children now—all identical, all sexless. I ate every one of them and was still hungry for more.

The bitter but pleasant aftertaste still lingered at the back of my throat when I woke just after seven that morning. Hairs bristled with excitement at the thought of finishing my second novel, and I almost skipped towards that study window where my typewriter sat.

As I took in the rolling landscape, habitually cracking my fingers, I let out a garbled moan as my eyes fell upon the two naked trees by the dam. I didn't want to believe it; I wouldn't let myself believe it. The trees looked—bare. With tears in my eyes and grumbles from my belly, I ran, only to find it true. In a heap, I crumpled between them, clawing at the ground, pleading for them to offer their fruit just one more time. I was so close.

But days grew shorter, and evenings got colder. The book remained unfinished. I could hardly summon the energy to get out of bed, never mind thoughts of writing. I wasn't eating. The fruit from that tree had become my only sustenance, the only taste tolerable to me.

Time went by painfully and slowly. Autumn days also proved poor nourishment for the house. Cold draughts sneaked through decrepit frames, taking with it all remnants of residual energy and leaving sadness once more. Even the birds had grown quiet, their songs few and far between.

Occasionally, the telephone would ring, but I ignored it. I just lay in bed, shaking, knowing it wasn't the cold causing such a violent physical reaction.

I don't know how many days went by before the knock on the door came, and the distant but familiar gruff voice of Frank broke the deafening silence. "Thomas!"

"It's not locked," I croaked back.

"Thomas!"

More knocking followed. "Are you there, Thomas?"

I knew he wouldn't come all this way and just walk away. It wasn't in his nature to give up. Finally, the door clicked, and I heard his footsteps thundering up the wooden staircase. "Thomas?"

"In here."

"Thank God, I was beginning to—"

I saw the change in his face immediately. Some things you can hide, get away with, but shock is like a sucker punch that takes your breath away.

"Thomas, what the hell?" he asked, rushing over to the bed, forehead creased.

I hadn't seen my reflection for weeks but had run my fingers over my face and could trace too easily the shape of my skull. My arms, too, were scrawny, skin hanging from the bone.

"I've not been well."

"I tried to ring, Thomas. My God, look at you."

"Nearly finished the book."

"Never mind the goddamn book; you need a doctor! Can you get up?"

"I don't know."

He helped me to my feet and all but dragged me out of the room to the top of the staircase. "When was the last time you ate?"

I couldn't remember.

"You look like death, my friend. I thought country air was supposed to be good for you?"

I smiled at him politely. "Does anyone know you're here?"

He shook his head. "You need to come back, though; people miss you."

"I think I'll be okay now, Frank."

"You sure?" He looked me up and down, sighed, and shook his head again. "I'll lead, you follow, just in case those sparrow's legs you're borrowing give up the game."

As soon as he walked in, I could smell it, hear it even, rushing around his body, hidden beneath the pale and overripe flesh. I knew the taste wouldn't compare to the freshness from the branch, but nerve endings tingled regardless at the prospect of feeding again.

He got one step down before I pushed with what remaining strength I had.

I remember him reaching out as though trying to grab an invisible bar. The fall was clunky, noisy, quick. He let out a long moan at the bottom, his limbs twitching and jerking in a contorted heap.

Adrenaline surged, but using the banister, I forced myself to take things slowly. I kept thinking how tragic it would be to fall, especially being so close to finishing the book. I owed it to Frank, too, for his suffering to not be in vain. My belly grumbled loudly and relentlessly as I approached him. Dormant for weeks, it was awakening, and so was I.

I crouched towards him, observing the fear and confusion in his eyes. The scent was mesmerising. Blood pounded in my ears as I lifted his arm and sank my teeth into his toughened skin, allowing the bitterness to pour into my mouth. I could feel my strength replenishing as though being reborn.

He took a long time to die, stubborn to the end.

I wrote four thousand words that evening. The book was finished.

It sits here, in my study drawer now; has done for many years. So lost in the haze, I didn't realise the possible implications of its release. It is, after all, more confession than fiction and may well raise unwanted attention.

The book will have its day.

Since then, I've written two novels, both well received and profitable enough to do some upkeep around the place.

He's out there, Frank, in the orchard, with the others.

Each spring, the trees near the dam provide their fruit, but when the colder days draw in once more, that's when I go hunting. I can smell it from miles away these days; hear it pumping in my ears. I'm good at it now, much less clumsy in my efforts.

Sometimes I visit the town pub, *The Fox and Hen,* just to blend in, pass off as normal. It was there that I recently met Richard Brannigan, an old English professor from the Grammar School. Interesting chap with even more intriguing stories, including the one about Sanctuary Place. It turns out he was good friends with Michael Turner, the owner. Although born into money, Richard said Michael was salt of the earth, one of the nicest chaps you could hope to meet. His wife, Katherine, was just the same, so welcoming, not an ounce of malice in her. They often held soirees for the locals, partying until the early hours. "Everyone loved them."

The pair were obsessed with each other, wanting to extend their family. Michael confided in Richard that they'd been trying for children for months, even chosen names—Elliot for a boy, Elizabeth for a girl. Alas, no matter what they tried, the gift of children evaded them.

"And then that. Such a goddamn tragedy!" he told me with tears in his eyes.

It was a robbery gone wrong. Two of the locals that attended the previous week's shindig had decided Michael and Katherine's hospitality was not generous enough. They came back in the early hours of one morning, hyped up on cocaine, and broke into Sanctuary Place.

"Unfortunately, Michael woke up." Richard's hands were shaking as he told the tale, knocking back countless whiskies.

Michael and Katherine's bodies were set on fire, their charred remains found at the edge of the dam.

"Nobody deserved that, especially those two."

The place fell into the hands of Michael's brother, Dylan, who tried selling it, but nobody wanted to go anywhere near the place. People said the house gave off negative energy; made the hairs bristle but in the wrong way. Over time, rumours faded, interest waned, and Dylan finally decided the time was right.

And that's where I came in.

Although my hunger is stronger, I do have a heart, and thinking of the pain Michael and Katherine must have endured over the years, especially after only offering goodness to the world, certainly pulls at its strings. I have nothing but admiration for how they managed to grow through the hardened soil and stone, persevering through winters of freezing cold temperatures and summers of dry heat, stubbornly refusing to give up on each other, even in death.

One could be mistaken for thinking it was only their love for each other that kept them going from ashes in the soil to their ultimate cross-pollination. But the fruit those trees bear; the children they could only spawn after death, well, they're bursting with bad blood for sure.

What happened to them, not to mention being buried under soil for all those years, would be enough to turn anyone to vengeful hate.

I'm an off-season killer with a thirst for blood, a conduit that shares the *Turner* family home. Nothing compares to the freshness of the branch, but "Beggars can't be choosers," as Mother often says.

She came for a visit last week; still disapproves of my single status.

"This house needs a family, Thomas," she said. "It's so cold and empty."

"Yes, Mother," I replied.

"It's been over ten years since you and Denise split."

"Yes, Mother."

"I'm ready to be a Grandma, and babies don't grow on trees, you know!"

MY NAME IS MARK KELLIS

I DON'T PLAY SPORTS; I prefer word and number games, particularly anagrams.

Last week for my seventeenth birthday, my parents bought me an annual subscription to Puzzlers Weekly because that's how I roll. As you can imagine, I'm not a big hit with the ladies, but that's fine, once bitten and all that. Besides, girls are crazy and unpredictably chaotic. They give me a headache.

Unlike most mathematical problems, life doesn't have a single solution, no secret formula, and because of that, I'm not very good at it.

My name is Mark Kellis, and I'm on the spectrum. More than one, might I add. I'm also OCD, bipolar, and allergic to peanuts. People call me high functioning, but that's debatable as I don't believe I've ever served any real function.

I look for numbers, create equations, look for letters and make words. Not exactly a dating profile, is it? Number plates, people's names, road signs—doesn't matter what—I'll blink and see new formations. It's habitual. Muscle memory.

Let me give you an example. Take Archie. Archie Levenson— knocked down a few weeks ago outside number eight Peartree

Drive on his way back from the inter-college soccer game. Hit and run. No witnesses. They found the car abandoned two streets down. Let's take his name, or more specifically, what people called him: Arch. Arch is an anagram of car with a leftover h, and h is the eighth letter of the alphabet. Can you see where I'm going with this?

Coincidence? Manipulation?

Let me give you another. Ranjit Khatri. Ranjit was a bright, intelligent Indian boy who used to sit behind me in Maths class. Some people gave him a hard time, just because, but I liked him. A train. Tenth platform. T-r-a-i-n and j—the tenth letter of the alphabet. Put them together and mix them around. Ranjit.

And there's my previous psychologist, Doctor Lowen. They found his body parts in the shallows of the lake behind the Jackson property, wrapped up in bin liners. Five, to be precise. I made the mistake of once calling him by his first name, Ian, and he didn't like it at all.

Can you not see it yet?

I guess this one's a bit trickier but stay with me.

Dr. Ian Lowen. *Drown in a*—still with me? Take the *l* from lake. That just leaves e—the fifth number of the alphabet—five bin liners.

Get it?

Kinsy Taylor. Nickname at college, 'Slinky,' on account of her skill at gymnastics and general flexibility. She was my friend. She said so.

They found her on waste ground behind the college, twisted into an *l*-shape, with most of her face missing and twenty-five stab wounds to her chest. *S-k-i-n*. *L*-shape. *Y* is the twenty-fifth letter of the alphabet. Mix them around. See it now? Slinky?

You're thinking I'm crazy.

I'm on different medication now. It helps a little. The new psychologist is nice enough, but it won't take her long to see through me, just like Doctor Lowen did.

Kinsy brought some calm for a while, but it boiled my blood when I saw her flirting with Archie. She was supposed to be *my* friend, my *'girl' friend*. I was there at that game, right to the end and through to the celebrations when they—kissed. I followed them home in an old Ford I stole from the car park, trailing behind them until Kinsy broke off to take her usual shortcut across the field. Then I rammed that smug fucker, Archie, into the wall of number eight. Caught up with her, too, and gave her a piece of my mind using the steak knife I stole from Ranjit's house. Twenty-five fucking times.

I couldn't concentrate on much else after that. My college work was being disrupted, too. Nail in the coffin was Ranjit beating me on the last maths exam. I liked the kid, but he was so smug that day. "Let's celebrate; go into town," I said. And he bought it. We never did make it on that train, though. Well, some of Ranjit did.

If things don't fit in their box, how am I supposed to keep my life tidy?

The irony is they all ended up in boxes.

I can't tell you how long it took me to cut through Doctor Lowen's flesh and bone. Bloody hard work, and messy too!

Why?

Good question. And tough to understand if you're lucky enough to be normal.

I needed an answer to the chaos, the jealousy, the envy, all the emotions that churned me up, a single solution that would make everything linear once again. There was no scribbling on pen and paper; the letters and numbers appeared to me, just like they do in Puzzler's Weekly. And I knew what I had to do. They were just problems to solve.

I can kid myself that I'm too smart for them. As best I could, I covered my tracks, but I guess things will eventually catch up with me. I don't intend to be around for that, though.

Did you see it yet? The clue's right in front of you.

Mark Kellis. M-a-r-k-k-i-l-l-s. E is the fifth letter of the alphabet. Mark Kills 5.

The new tablets help me rationalise things a little, but it's too late, and the damage is done. Besides, I have no empathy, no compassion; I'm numb to it all and this world to me.

I've left a note in my bedside drawer confessing to all.

This knife is sharper than the one I used on Kelsy, and it will run across my skin like butter.

Before I go, did you see it, though? The initials of each victim?

Archie Levenson. Initials, AL.

Ranjit Sethi. Initials, RS.

Ian Lowen. Initials, IL.

Kinsy Elliott. Initials, KE.

Mark Kellis. Initials, MK.

Mark Kills 5.

I didn't see it until this morning. A complete coincidence? Perhaps life is more mapped out than we think.

Thanks for listening.

Yours,

Mark

MAMA'S BOY

I'M GUILTY.

Guilty as all hell.

"Move it!" Two warders on either side and two more behind for good measure, the grip on my arm unnecessarily tight as they lead me towards the horde.

This ain't no confession, trying to get on your good side or something like that, but I want you to know I'm glad they finally caught me. Mean that, too. Countless good folks suffered at my hands: men, women, young un's, not even talking age some of them.

No, couldn't give you a number, not even thereabouts.

Oh, Mama, I'm sorry.

Through watery eyes and over the sea of heads, I spy the wooden frame in the distance. The rope now, too, swaying in the breeze, next to the rounded shoulders of the hangman.

My legs buckle, but momentum keeps me going. Feels like my heart is working too hard for its own good.

"Burn slowly, fucker!"

Please help me, Mama.

"Hang, you dumb fuck!"

At church every Sunday, I was. I don't have many friends, see.

Got bullied an awful lot for being a bit slow and different. "Mama's boy."

"I hope you choke for days you evil bastard!"

I was just looking for someone to listen—a bit of company, other than Mama. And when the voices started, I thought it was *him*.

"Waste of fucking skin!"

We talked for hours, and he listened, and even though it was all inside my head, I didn't feel so lonely anymore.

"All those children. You're a fucking monster!"

I let *him* in.

Mama was so pleased; she knows I've been through a rough time and was so happy that I was talking to God. She told all her friends and other folks, too.

"Fucking Devil himself!"

Over time, the voices began to change, though, saying things 'bout people. Said they talked behind my back, making fun of dumb ole' Frank and his imaginary friend. Didn't want to believe, but why would God lie?

Dumb ole' Frank!

"Rot in hell!"

Started saying things about Mama, too. That she wished she'd let me bleed out that time she found me in the barn with the knife in my wrist. I was an embarrassment. A failed act of blasphemy that she had to carry around with her for all to see.

Told me I was a burden to all and that he was my only friend.

"Death's too good for you!"

It got to be as soon as my eyes closed, the voices would start and wouldn't let me rest. I didn't know what was real anymore, but I'd already begun to suspect it wasn't the good Lord in my ear.

"Fucking rat filth!"

They started to drive me insane, wouldn't let me be in the end, even after the sun came up. It grinds on you. Takes you to the very edge until you'd kill for it to stop.

"Just bairns, they were!"

I can still see Mama's face, eyes wide and confused, as I recited the Lord's prayer through to her very last breath. So sorry, Mama. Please forgive me.

It looks like the entire town is here for blood, elbowing for the best spot in front of the gallows, cackling and heckling. The vendor is having a field day. Line must be twenty deep at least—people handing over hard-earned money for food and drink, likely not even to find its way into their mouths. Hungry for something else, this lot.

Less than forty yards to go.

It's in the air. The smell of death, that is. It's as though the crowd is disturbing bad dust, tainted earth that has seen more than its fair share of evil and misery. The opposite of hallowed ground if you like.

Oh, Mama. Oh, Mama.

Less than twenty yards now between me and the steps. The crowd's getting louder, restless.

Voices stopped when I went down as if they were never there. Made me question myself, for sure, but at least I started to feel some way to normal again. Well, as close as one can with so many sins resting on their shoulders.

I even started re-reading the Bible. I'm a slow reader, but I had time. Prayed for salvation every night and twice yesterday because the voice came back.

Something flies by my left ear, but a tomato strikes a direct hit, leaving a sting on my cheek and a string of pale red down the burlap suit they dressed me in. Other things hit me on my back, chest, the side of my head. They all hurt, regardless of the level of pain.

"I hope you feel their agony, you fucking ugly bastard!"

He told me he was coming for me. Nothing from the good Lord, but I have to hope.

Something splashes across my neck; catches one of the warders, too.

"Don't get paid nuff for this," he hisses.

I'm at the steps, looking up at the man that will send me to hell.

Mama, I'm so scared. Mama.

"Get up there!"

There ain't no coming back. The top of those stairs is the end of my story. Ain't no coming back.

I just wanted to set the record straight. I'm not a monster. Yes, I did bad things, and those children—those poor children.

"Too late for tears, you dumb fuck!"

But he made me do it! He tricked me. Then when he got in, he spread through my mind like mould.

Halfway up, silence falls across the crowd. Not a drop of saliva in my mouth. Blood pounds in my ears, and my legs feel like lead weights.

Three more steps to go.

Mama.

I bite down hard on my lip, just like Mama told me to. "Don't let them bullies think they're getting to you."

Final step.

Lord, I beg for mercy.

My right leg gives way, but the warder is quick and drags me back up.

This is it—the end.

They drag me towards the noose in full view of the crowd. I can see it in their eyes, impatiently bloodthirsty, ready to get on with the rest of the day in the knowledge the *monster* is no more.

Why me and not one of them? Because you're fucking dumb; that's why.

Nothing but the Devil's puppet.

There's a mix of emotions on their faces: fear, hatred, excitement. Some look like they don't know how to feel.

The hangman steps forward, a small piece of black cotton fabric in the chubby fingers of his right hand. I look into his eyes, but he gives me nothing, as if I'm already dead, just a body to be discarded.

Just a burden.

He stretches out his thick arms and begins pulling the fabric over my head, but just before darkness prevails, I see *him* in the crowd.

I know it's *him*. Grey cloak, no face in sight, just a hooded shadow that has come to collect.

Hands are on my shoulders, twisting me around.

My breathing is fast and erratic. Lord, please help me.

I feel the harshness of rope against my neck.

"Mama."

Warmth runs down my leg.

The rope tightens.

The cool breeze finds its way through the fabric. Never again will I feel its touch.

Save me, Lord. Save me, Mama.

Silence, only the swell of blood pumping in my ears.

Don't let him take me.

I swallow hard, feeling coarseness against my adam's apple.

Do it! Do it now, please.

Mama, are you with me?

I hear the lever go, and my stomach drops. Eyes screwed shut, I brace for pain.

Brace for pain.

Nothing.

Ahead, and to either side, the sound of choking emerges—pained gargles from above.

"What—what's going on?" I feel the rope, but my words are not strained.

The breeze rushes across again, strangely warm. Death taints the smell of food, but even more so now.

Mama, what's happening?

Bloodcurdling rasps slowly begin to quiet until finally, silence once again prevails, a deafening and never-ending quiet.

Warmth around my wrists and neck.

My arms fall to my side, no longer bound.

No tightness around my throat.

I feel the damp gravel beneath my toes!

What is this? A reprieve? My prayers answered.

I rip the fabric from my head, squinting around the wooden

beam and into a sky I never thought I'd see again. But something is different, broken, and it takes a while for my brain to catch up. Momentarily, I think I'm in hell, that he snatched me as I fell, but the place looks the same as before, bar the floating bodies. All suspended in air, discoloured heads lolloped to one side, some with tongues protruding from pale lips. It's as though someone has picked each of them up by their necks, squeezed the life out of them, and left them there like ghosts.

Someone.

The soft thud to my right snaps my head around. Another to the left.

One by one, they begin falling to the ground, lifeless sacks of bone that were heckling only moments ago. Sunlight finds its way to my face again as the bodies continue to fall around me.

Heavy rain.

Guess this ground got more than its fair share of death today.

I respect the dead, just as Mama taught me, weaving my way through the bodies, taking nothing from them. The vendor's cart is different, and I don't feel bad for raiding the stuffed metal tin. Grab some food for the journey, too.

I ain't ever had this much money in my pocket at one time. Should see me through for a while.

Don't know where I'm heading yet, but I know he'll be with me, and it's only a matter of time before the voices begin.

I'm sorry, Lord. I'm sorry, Mama.

AN OLD ROMANTIC

FROM THE TOP of the Ferris Wheel, the place looks even emptier.

I miss her already.

The town pops and sizzles for a few weeks of the year, an animated collage of colour, laughter, and hope. Sets the scene, and it's impossible not to fall in love, a little summer romance, encouraged by the smell of saltwater and skin.

And her smile, her laugh.

She arrived just over a week ago. I knew she was the one.

A droplet of rain splashes across my nose, inducing an exaggerated shudder. Damn sight colder today; my knee won't stop tapping, and the icy breeze stings my eyes. Hard to believe people yesterday were walking up and down the strip in shorts and bikinis.

Town changes at the drop of a coin, see. One could hardly see the sand yesterday, folks after one last bit of fun and sun before returning to their mundane jobs and lives. But clouds rolled in like clockwork this morning, turning the blue sea to grey. Black in some places even. Calm water turned rough and is all but empty. Yellow warning signs alerting to strong rips suddenly seem more than just for show.

As if the town's heart slows when the tourists leave, life dampens

AN OLD ROMANTIC | 33

to a pulse, and we wait patiently for their return and another spike of adrenaline.

Be tough to match the high that Kate brought with her, though. It sounds so cliché, but I was smitten from the moment I laid eyes on her. That's her name; short but inexplicably beautiful. Nothing else would suit.

Kate.

Rum and raisin; her favourite ice cream. Always in a cone. She'd pull a napkin from her handbag, wrap it around the base and turn it slowly into her tongue. Only when she finished the entire thing did she wipe the moustache away.

All in.

My Kate.

Kate.

Only yesterday, she was seated in this exact carriage, her laughter carrying on a much warmer breeze, and her scent, the essence of summer itself; wildflowers and summer fruit, filling my nostrils.

It's like a knot twisting in my stomach that only she could unravel. The softness of her skin, the glimmer in her eyes, the way she carried herself, even the way she ate her ice cream. Christ, it hurts, like being let out of prison, allowed to live life, feel things, really feel them, only to be locked back behind the iron door a few days later.

After Jenny, I used to think I'd never have such feelings again, that I'd used up all my love on her. We moved here ten years ago, gave up our jobs in the big city in search of a different lifestyle, a sea change. We bought a place and still had enough money in the bank to semi-retire, neither of us even thirty at that stage. We even talked of marriage. How gullible we were to think our needs were so perfectly aligned; that we were different, better than our peers.

For Jenny, the bubble burst quickly. "I'm not happy here," escalated to "We want different things," eventually giving way to "I just don't love you anymore."

With a jolt, we're on our way back down, but this time to wet pavement and the smell of petrichor over street food. The music sounds so much harsher today, without the harmonising sound-track of laughter and soft plunk of arcade machines.

Kate. My sweet Kate.

Yesterday, I could have stayed up here all day, listening to her talking about everything and nothing. The perfect pasta at Valentino's, the cocktail she wanted to try once more before leaving, the way the heat made her walk that little bit more slowly.

Even though I knew our time was coming to an end, I'd envisaged our life together multiple times, an extension of a few memories, but nevertheless, a glorious cinematic storyboard of happiness.

The guy opens the carriage. Albie? Alfie? He always looks at me like I'm crazy but doesn't object to the extra notes I slip him to hold us near the top. Likely wouldn't know true love if it took a bite from his sandwich.

"Cold enough for you?" He'll ask a slight variation of that question for days to come; he always does. I nod politely and make my way towards the café. Empty now, of course, apart from a single staff member, Doris, a chain-smoking blue rinse who can talk about two things only, the weather and what's on the Specials Board. She sure makes a meal of it, though. Before she can even open her mouth, I order a cappuccino and retreat outside to one of the tables.

I can picture her now, legs crossed, smiling that smile, lens-covered eyes darting from person to person as she spoke. A people watcher, just like me, feeding off their energy, inhaling their hope.

My Kate.

The breeze cuts through me once again, but no shudder this time, only a nostalgic melancholy at the thought of her dry auburn hair dancing in the air like kite strings.

"Here you go, Petal."

"Thanks, Doris."

I know better than to take a breath until she's at least twenty seconds away. Ten is a definite no-go. Fifteen seconds and you still risk a few tainted air molecules.

And Inhale.

A splash of rain creates a ripple in the puddle of brown in the saucer, and I can't help but liken it to Kate—dropping into my life in such an explosive way but ultimately fading to nothing, just like all the other raindrops. I don't even like coffee. The smell of it, though, and the memory of her lipstick on the side of the cup.

It's getting faster, the rain. Dark clouds threaten worse, too. I leave the money, including my contribution to Doris's lung cancer fund, under the saucer and head towards the beach, tucking my chin into my neck to try and escape the brunt of the wind.

As if trying to earn their bread, the seagulls dance but eventually declare me a lost cause, turning their attention back to the litter bin. I make my way down the sand-covered wooden steps, eyeing the curling waves, kaleidoscopic shades of grey that finally echo to shore, bringing seaweed and adding to the existing foam. As if she is here, her laughter carries on the breeze. I envision her prints in the sand as she moves in and out with the tide, giddy like a child each time it threatened to swallow her feet.

Love.

Love is visible, invisible, wanting but not being able to have, having but wanting more. Love is all-consuming. Love is passion. Love is tenderness. Love is sunlight bouncing off the skin, not being able to eat, reminding yourself to breathe. Love is flying.

Love is drowning.

I still wear the ring that Jenny bought me all that time ago. She taught me what love is, after all. Then she ripped my fucking heart out. We used to take late evening strolls on the beach. Even the night she told me she was leaving, deserting this town with the tourists, I insisted we share one last walk together.

Almost ten years to the date.

"Don't go, please. We'll work it out."

"We've tried, Jeremy. The move couldn't save us. We were foolish to believe it could!"

"Please, Jen."

"I'm going back," she eventually said after my endless pleas, eyes full of tears. "I need to pack."

I started walking towards the blackness of the water, gripped by fear, but more from the thought of losing her than immersing myself in the ocean.

"Jeremy!"

Up to my waist, freezing cold, endless black ahead cut in two by a sliver of moonlight, but I kept wading. I should have been terrified, but it felt so right.

"Jeremy, what are you doing?"

Up to my shoulders, nothing ahead but an empty void.

"Jeremy," she screamed after me, knowing I was unable to swim.

Love is drowning.

Even as I submerged my head and the pressure on my lungs became immediate, I only felt a kinship with the water. I sensed its sadness, felt its emptiness, and its need to be loved, and it felt mine. We shared our pain, a captive audience for each other. I nourished it with thoughts of Jenny, the sparkle in her eyes, the crackle of her guffaw, and the wind plastering her hair to her forehead. As I inhaled its softness, empathy, and compassion, the ocean filled me with memories of recent days—the glimmer on its surface, children's laughter, kites jerking in the warm summer breeze.

And just like that, we were one.

As I continued walking across the ocean floor, weighed down by sorrow, but at the same time, experiencing overwhelming affinity to the peaceful melancholy, I felt a hand on my shoulder. I turned to see my love, her eyes wide and face tight with panic.

She'd come back to me.

I grabbed her wrist and dragged her towards me, watching the bubbles spill from her delicate lips. We embraced until her struggles stopped, and she finally gave in to me, reunited once more in the presence of something powerful but just as vulnerable as I.

They found us in the early hours, washed up onshore, twenty yards apart. The doctor said he'd never seen anyone survive who had swallowed so much water—wanted to run further tests, but I declined.

From that day onwards, I became poor old sad Jeremy, the guy whose wife drowned trying to save him. "Accidental death," they called it, blaming the rips that had taken the occasional tourist before and no less than one a year since.

We thrive and grieve simultaneously. We are one; the sand, the foam, the clouds, the morning mist rolling in from the sea, the guy in the café observing his new love sipping on a coffee. The ocean and I are just two romantics, basking in each other's sadness and nostalgic memories of happier times. Memories fade, though; can only sustain us for so long, and by the time the holidays come along, we pine for new love.

Without love, we are just bodies, living, breathing, but not feeling.

I don't age, but nobody notices; after all, how much do people pay attention? Only someone close to one's heart might comment on the absence of any lines and skin as smooth as a pebble rolled by waves. I am a ghost, sharing a heartbeat with the ocean. You can see me, touch me, smell the saltwater leaking through my pores, but you can't love me. I belong to the ocean and the ocean to me. Together, we love from afar—dreamers, sentimentalists, optimists, pessimists, voyeurs.

Romantics. We fall fast, and we fall hard.

I still visit *the* house sometimes. There's little sustenance to be had now, though, even the dusty photographs of Jenny and I evoking little emotion these days. My *home* is in the ocean now, and I rise with the morning mist and retire once the town goes to sleep, trying to soak up all the energy and love in between, enough to nurture over the off-season.

Since Jenny, others have taken a place in my blackened heart, but Kate is something special. The way she smiled at the café, from her table across to mine. Sitting atop the Ferris Wheel, listening to her on her phone in the carriage in front, or the restaurants, gushing to friends about how much she's enjoying alone time for once; the food, the wine, the weather, mundanities seeming less so after leaving her soft lips. Standing behind her in the queue for an ice cream, breathing in the mix of saltwater, fried foods, and delicious perfume that I can still taste now. It felt like I'd known her forever, the woman I named Kate.

It suited her perfectly. Kate. Christ, just the mention of her.

Alone and scarred from past loves. Kindred souls.

We knew she'd come to say goodbye on her last night. She took her shoes off, left them in the sand, dipped her feet in the water while staring at the moon. A romantic just like us.

"Help," I cried from blackness. "I can't swim."

She came to us, just like the others. And we finally embraced.

It's a moment that will help nourish us through the off-season until the memory of her fades and love comes to town once again. For now, it's time to head home, to wallow for loves lost, and to dream of loves to come.

MOTHER DEAREST (A NOVELLA)

IT DIDN'T MATTER HOW HARD LANCE PULLED, THE SIGN WOULDN'T budge, as though in the short time it had been there, the ground had laid claim to it. "Come on, you fucker!" Sleet had made the front strip boggy and slippery, traction nigh on impossible, so it made no sense for the sign to be so stubborn to his efforts. Veins popping in his arms and neck, he finally doubled over, hands on his kneecaps, sucking in the crisp air.

"You fucking fucker!"

Beyond the sign, the house stood tall and impossibly gloomy, a contrasting sight to the stately grounds reflected in the pictures when they first listed the place, almost two months to the day. Back then, trees were in full bloom, the front lawn lush but dry, and the house basked in the last of the summer sun. Autumn had well and truly arrived, though, ominous clouds preventing any softness from touching the walls. Each flaw stood out, no longer hidden behind layers of foliage or clematis vines once sporting purple and yellow flourishes but now looking as dead as the previous owners. Every cracked board was noticeable, every filthy window, some with cracks running top to bottom. But it was the way the house was, for want of a better word, *looking* at Lance, that made his skin prickle. Never in all his years had a property made him feel *funny* before, but something about this place didn't sit right with him. Not to mention the smell wafting on the breeze.

There were rumours about what happened, tittle-tattle and whispers mostly, but Lance was a great believer in the no smoke without fire theory. The mother had been diagnosed with terminal cancer; he knew that much to be a fact. She withered away at home until her last breath finally gave her a reprieve. Soon after, the husband allegedly snapped, those that had occasion to stop by the house, family mostly, giving accounts of a broken man with a vacancy behind the eyes. Visitors after the event, made up of delivery folk and concerned work colleagues, attested to seeing something beyond the man's blankness, something manic. Something 'dark.'

The daughter, Iris, was pulled out of school well before the incident. Lance knew that, as he was to marry Becky, 'Miss Harman' to her class, the following summer. Iris was a quiet girl, by all accounts, but always pleasant enough. She became increasingly withdrawn when her mother fell ill until it got so she was as timid as a mouse, easy bait for the other students. Nobody saw her much after that, even less so when cancer finally claimed the mother.

It wasn't long after that Lance saw it on the news. When Becky pointed to the screen, he'd just sat down with a bowlful of snacks and a cold beer. "That's Iris," she had said, turning up the volume. The newscaster reported the child's body was discovered underneath her bedroom window on the concrete path that circled the house. They found the father, Frank, gently swaying from the ceiling of the adjacent barn. That's when the rumours and theories took legs, but nobody knows what really happened or what went through those folks' minds in those final moments.

"Come the fuck on!"

After another futile effort, Lance gave the sign a healthy kick, cussing under his breath as reverberations shot up his right leg. The bottom of his pants speckled with mud, and his clothes becoming notably heavier from the fine rain, he decided to call it a day and return with tools when time and weather permitted. Before walking back to the car, though, he made the mistake of offering the house one last glance, enough for his mind to take an everlasting snapshot. The faces faded quickly, but Lance was sure of what he saw, enough for his fingers to remain tightly coiled around the steering wheel all the way home.

He saw them that night, too, while his wife lay sleeping next to him, the girl's face in the top left room, mouth forming a scream, and the man's through the first-floor bay window, eyes as dark as coal, mouth curved into either a smile or snarl. Haunted him for nights to come and sometimes during the day when his mind wandered. He never did return with his tools, figuring the house just wanted to be left alone.

Late October (Present Day)

Tuesday

"Race you to the sea, Ames."

"Dad, you're too old to run," I reply, squinting towards the glistening water. "Maybe if I give you a ten-metre head start."

He flicks his hair out of his eyes and readies himself into the starting position. "Ames, you're going to be so sorry you said that."

"Mum, can you do the countdown? And get ready to grab a lifeguard in case Dad has a heart attack."

She offers a snigger, hands on hips and shaking her head. "Grab a lifeguard? Don't have to ask me twice."

"Mum!"

"Oi, I second that, Ruth," Dad says.

"Geoff, are you sure you should be doing this?" Mum says, her eyes sparkling through the chestnut hair splayed across her forehead. As the breeze drops, she fingers it behind her ears and offers me a wink. "And is your life insurance up to date, dear?"

"Don't you start, Ruth; I'm in my bloody prime. Did I not tell you girls that I was cross country champion at school?"

"Once or twice, Dad," I reply, "but wasn't that over a hundred years ago?"

"Oh, you just—" Dad scrapes his foot across the sand like a bull about to charge. "Don't cry if you lose, darling."

"Same to you." Ahead, seagulls fight for chips that are being tossed to the sand by a chubby kid with a sunburnt face. An old woman slumped in a chair with what looks like a handkerchief on her head offers him a dirty scowl, but he pays no heed, bringing out another handful from the paper bag, his fingers glistening with oil.

"Three," Mum says.

Heart pounding, skin prickling with heat and excitement, I aim for the centre of the squawking mass of feathers and beaks.

"Are you racing?" the chubby genius hollers, adding to my nerves.

"Two."

A warm breeze brings the scent of sun lotion, seaweed, and fast food. Laughter plays like a backing track, along with the relentless crashing of the waves. I'm happy. So very happy.

"One."

And I'm off, feet sinking into warm sand, feeling the fat kid's eyes burning into me. "You're fast," he says.

"Oi," Dad shouts from behind to the sound of Mum's laughter. "You bloody cheat."

Arms pumping, I turn my attention to the line of foam, the gulls parting, letting me know how they feel about being disturbed by offering cacophonous squawks and violently flapping their wings. As we hit the heavier and denser sand, I hear Dad behind, but he doesn't appear to be catching up. Encouraged by my lead, I grit my teeth and pump my arms even faster, my feet slapping as they come down against ever-dampening sand.

"Doesn't count," Dad shouts from behind, his breathing laboured.

"Just a bad loser," I yell into the wind, subsequently sucking in a mouthful of hot air. "It's the end times, Dad."

The water takes my breath away, much cooler than expected, but it isn't long before I'm waist deep, a strange combination of hot and warm. Running my hands across the softness, I hear a dog barking, likely the one I saw chasing the stray seagull before.

I take a deep breath.

And I'm under, scanning the ocean floor, running my eyes across shells and coral reefs, watching the fish as they dart in and out of small aquatic jungles. Using my hands, I push against the water to turn myself around.

But there's no sign of Dad, and suddenly, the water feels impossibly cold.

I break the surface, taking in a mouthful of—staleness? The sun is nowhere to be seen, hidden behind a thick blanket of dark clouds. "Dad?" But there's nobody else here, in or out of the water. "Dad!"

Shivering violently, I begin making my way back to shore, but the water feels impossibly heavy, my body cramping, limbs protesting against the iciness. Seaweed becomes more abundant, wrapping around my ankles and calves, creating even further resistance.

"Mum!"

But I'm alone.

The wind ramps up, the water instantly responding, dark and choppy waves breaking against my back. Thickness fills my lungs as I inhale, staleness turning to pungency and leaving a bitter aftertaste.

Not a seagull to be seen. No vehicles in the car park.

As light dwindles further, I keep my stare on the foam, driving harder and harder. The water gets no shallower, though, only colder, harder even. What I wouldn't give to hear the bark of a dog.

But all is quiet apart from the breaking waves that slap against me with ever-increasing intensity. Breathless, unable to get enough air in, I grit my teeth, but I'm losing the fight, the water now pulling at me, making it a struggle just to stay on my feet.

"Help!"

I spread my arms out, trying to make myself as large as possible, but I'm no match for nature. Steadily, the foam gets further away, my feet skimming the sand until I'm drifting, the ocean bed well out of reach.

Only five minutes ago, we were talking about getting pizza on the way home from the beach. Dad said he wanted to try the new one on Newland Terrace, but Mum said he should consider getting salad or Sushi.

It all seems like a lifetime ago.

"Help!" I scream, thrashing away with my legs and arms, the dark water paying me no heed and sucking me further away from shore. Some splashes into my mouth, tasting even worse than it smells, and I feel its thickness sliding down my throat. Before I know what's happening, I'm spinning underwater, searching for light, but finding none.

Disoriented, feeling as though my lungs might explode, I hold onto my breath for as long as possible, but unable to fight back to the surface, I finally yield, taking in a mouthful of dark treacle-like substance.

Sinking fast, I offer one last kick and stretch my arms, noting blackness working through my veins, spreading through my body like mould. I feel it, filling my limbs with poison and further heaviness. And as I continue my descent, more darkness fills me.

The fight is over.

Silence.

Oblivion.

Bolting upright, I gasp for breath, the sight of my bedroom bringing only partial relief. Blood pulsates in my ears, and I feel fingernails cutting into my skin.

"Let me be!"

The dreams feel so real these days, especially the ones triggered by happy memories. But it's as though the house is trying to tarnish even them, not affording me an ounce of relief, even when unconscious.

Sheets are damp, sticking to me as I fight out of bed and make my way to the rotten window. Floorboards creak, the house groans, the trespassing draught lighting up every droplet of sweat. I hear the windchimes hanging from the back porch, their sounds, once melodic and harmonious, now clamorous and haunting.

I hate this place. I hate this place.

It's just after five in the afternoon, and I've slept restlessly for most of the day. This place weighs on me, sucking my energy and leaving nothing but a *faded memory* of the girl I once was. And besides, there's nothing else to do in the godawful place but hide and sleep.

Looking down at the puddle-drenched yard through the grimy and rotten window, I feel lonelier than ever. It carries a pain, a tightening in my chest that is beginning to spill over. "I hate this place."

A few *friends* used to text, but I figure I'm even more of an outsider now, one that is just hanging on for dear life. 'Gifted,' my English teacher once called me. Said I had a 'tremendous vocabulary and turn of language for someone my age.' Could one call that irony for someone experiencing so much isolation? The accolade alienated me frequently, but at least a few could see past it. Now I have nobody.

I wipe at the window, knowing the dirt is on the outside, more of a nervous reflex than anything else. Or perhaps a test of bravery. I'm already feeling uncomfortable, but although the sensation is becoming stronger each day, I resist the urge to pull away.

Besides my so-called parents, I can't even recall the last time I spoke to someone—Father not being keen on me venturing too far away from the place, having it in his head, for some strange reason, that everyone is out to get us. It got so unbearable that I ran away once, only getting as far as the village. Still, I heard about it for days afterwards. 'You can't put your mother under that kind of stress, not in her condition.'

Even the internet has gone from being patchy to almost non-existent. Father insists that it's a good thing, 'something we're better off without,' but I don't feel better off at all.

It's this place; I know it is. There's something wrong, and it's only getting worse.

As I finger my name across the pane, tracing the already present initials, prickles bristle across my right side. No draught caresses me, but something else takes hold—that charged and heavy feeling one gets just before a storm breaks.

My bravery dwindles almost immediately.

This spot. This spot right here is where I feel it the most.

It's as if the house is trying to tell me something. So strong of late, too, and even though I tell myself I'm being silly, and all of this is just because I miss our old house, my old friends, I'm never fully convinced. Unable to bear it any longer, I back away and lower myself to the bed, biting my lip and drawing the softness of the patchwork blanket against my skin. Even the crack in the ceiling looks longer today, deeper, as though a projection of my pain.

Middle of nowhere, nothing but sky and trees. *Hate it.* A smell I once put down to as just mouldt and dust has developed into something else in recent days, something hiding behind the façade of smoke and rotting leaves, a thickness laying at the back of my throat. And even underneath the fleecy blankets, I feel myself shivering.

"Dinner, Amy!" Father calls from downstairs.

It wasn't always like this. There was optimism in the first few weeks, Mum and Dad embracing the remoteness and distance from others. Dad said we were lucky to get the place and still have change. 'Bargains like this don't come around often.'

But I don't feel so lucky.

The first few days we spent playing hide and seek and climbing trees, warming ourselves in front of the open fire afterwards, one made from wood Dad chopped from the acres of surrounding trees. I even enjoyed the novelty of being home-schooled by mum, not that we got a whole amount of work done—lots of giggling and cake. 'I think we've found our place, Amy,' she once said.

Dad's initial plan was to do up the place and sell it for a tidy profit, him being sick of working for other people and figuring the money would be better off going straight into his own pocket. A carpenter by trade, he's good with his hands and can fix almost anything. Between the renovations, he would find local work: painting, fixing fences, 'even mowing lawns if that's what it came down to.' But passion has taken a standstill, him preferring to be out of the house or in front of the open fire nursing his whisky and new-found paranoia. It's this place; I'm sure of it, spreading through our minds like rot.

And Mum, once a high school teacher, left her job to help out with the renovations. So enthusiastic to begin with, spending hours with her knitting and embroidery, creating furnishings for the house, even this patchwork blanket clenched between my fingers.

God, I miss her so much; it makes my heart ache just thinking about it.

She offered her services to the community for a while, listing her number at the local hardware and food store. Whether it be hemming dresses or taking up curtains, she wasn't proud; she just seemed to adapt to the rural lifestyle. Silly, I know, but sometimes I imagine if I squeeze down hard enough on the fabric, it will somehow help to return her, release the energy and passion expended back into the air for *Mother* to inhale.

There were so many plans, and all seemed to be going well until Mother fell pregnant. Since that day, I can't recall her breaking a smile, not a good one anyway.

"Amy!" Father bellows from downstairs.

"Coming."

There's a now-familiar sharpness to Father's voice that was never there before. 'He's got the patience of a saint when it comes to you,' Mum said once. But that was before, in a previous life, before the bump in *Mother's* belly appeared.

Letting go of the blanket but coiling my fingers into fists again, I push myself from the bed, hating the sound of every creak as I make my way to the door. It's as if the house is hurting, too, perhaps initially experiencing a brief glimmer of hope, of possible restoration to former glory, only to succumb to misery, joining in our despair.

Hearing only the sound of a knife hitting the chopping board, I pause at the top of the stairs, coiling my fingers tightly around the banister. Thoughts of laughter are overly optimistic, but I pray for words not loaded with resentment. Worse still, aside from the harshness of steel hitting wood, silence continues to reign. Slowly, I began my descent, the shadows of flames dancing across the dusty boards below but not providing an ounce of warmth. Nostalgic melancholy and anxiety twist at my stomach as I draw closer to the kitchen, and each time the knife comes down, I can't help but wince.

"Amy!"

"I'm here, Father. I'm here." Inhale. Exhale. Inhale. I say a little prayer to whoever might be listening, pinching at the skin on my right thigh as I take the final three steps.

The storm is almost upon us. I can sense it and have been able to for some time.

As I stand at the bottom of the stairs, watching Mother behind the counter, Father sheepishly hovering close by, nothing but a nervous shadow, I know the first strike isn't too far away.

I expect he feels Mother's indifference, even her hatred too, but he's blinded by duty, doing what must be done. "Do you need a hand with anything, love?" he says weakly, nursing his empty beer bottle.

Mother shakes her head, bringing the knife down with even more venom.

Each time the blade finds the chopping board, it feels like another part of me dies. Another home-cooked meal, but I doubt an ounce of love is finding its way into that pan.

I hate myself for it, but I've wished her dead of late.

Offering another half-assed smile, Father takes his place at the far side of the table, his sallow and lifeless eyes giving him away. I used to feel sorry for him, but I'm all out of everything.

"How's the schoolwork coming?" he asks.

Offering a glare towards Mother, I shrug. Father nods, bringing the empty beer bottle to his lips.

"Can I come with you tomorrow?" I say hopefully. "On the truck."

Father offers a flat smile again. "Sounds great, Amy, but you should stay and help your mother with the chores. And then there's your schooling."

He's hardly at the house anymore. Said with another child on the way, he needs to work all the hours he can, but even I know there was only so much work to go around, especially out in the sticks. And I've seen his work boots standing beside the woodpile even when the truck isn't there.

"Mother, would you mind if I went tomorrow?"

The house creaks and moans as the cold wraps around it, but it's Mother's eyes that chill me to the bone as she lifts her stare, continuing to bring the knife down.

I miss Mum; this isn't her. I can't bring myself to use the word anymore, but even calling this person 'Mother' doesn't sound right. Still kidding myself that it could happen if I squeeze down hard enough on that blanket and wish enough times, I hang onto the hope that Mum might one day return.

"Mother?"

I don't even realise what's happening until Father sends his chair sliding behind him. In the blink of an eye, he's at Mother's shoulders, holding her hand under the tap, a pinkish waterfall gushing into the sink. Not so much as a flicker on Mother's face as she continues her menacing stare towards me.

"Get the first aid kit, Amy," Father shouts. "It's on the bottom shelf in the pantry."

Mother continues eyeing me across the kitchen floor, her expression unchanged. It comes as some relief to open the door between us.

"Hurry, Amy."

But I can still feel *her* eyes burning through the wood.

"Amy!"

Unable to milk it any longer, I grab the box, close the door, and begin fumbling through the various compartments.

"Probably best you stay with your mother tomorrow," Father says.

"Why can't you stay with her?"

We used to be so close. 'Peas in a pod,' Mum used to say, but how he sometimes looks at me these days makes me feel lonelier still.

"Because someone needs to bring the money in," he says through gritted teeth.

I guess everyone has a limit.

"Yes, Father."

Devout Catholics, church every Sunday until a few weeks ago, this baby wasn't planned, and everything seems to be turning sour because of it. Mother told me they tried for a while after me, but 'it just didn't happen.' I feel awful, but I wish that had remained the case.

Awoken by another nightmare, I heard them arguing one night, Father accusing Mother of sleeping around, saying things didn't add up after what the doctor told him. I didn't understand much of that conversation, only that I hated every second of it, the way they spoke to each other. Father had been at the whisky, that much was obvious, his speech all slurred, but what left Mother's mouth left me shocked, phrases that will stay with me until my dying breath, disgusting words running into each other, loading the air with further heaviness. It's still so vivid as I remember how the house screamed along with them, its moans and cries elevating with each round of venom. It felt like the roof might come down on my head at one point and certainly made the crack in my ceiling bigger.

Things are a little different now, the fight all but leaving Father and his paranoia directed away from Mother. Anyone's a target now.

"Here we go, love. Take it easy," he says, helping Mother to her preferred chair, the one in front of the lounge window, the one she spends hours looking out of, pretending to work on her knitting. Humming the familiar tune that grates on my bones, Mother eases into the leather.

"Sandwich okay?" Father says to me on the way back into the kitchen.

"I'm not hungry. Can I go out?"

He turns, looking like he's on the verge of tears. I feel an urge to hug him, hold him tight, and not let go, but the truth is, I resent him for letting things get so bad. He chews at his lip for what feels like an eternity, his gaze fixed on the chequered tiles between us.

"Can I then?"

"Just to the boundary, no further," he says, breaking from his trance.

I don't know where this paranoia came from or what he thinks might happen. Back at our old place, we used to hike the mountains, leaving the trail to freely explore, pretending to look for hidden treasure or those who had died trying to find it. 'Don't tell Mum,' he'd say, reminding me of the same just before we got back in the car to pick up donuts and milkshakes on the way home.

I've given up trying to argue, knowing Dad is too far buried within this stranger. Even his words of concern are uttered without meaning of late as if they're something habitual he needs to get out of his head.

A shudder runs down my spine as I open the door. The air is crisp, wisps of mist forming before me as I run towards the line of trees. But as though this entire area is somehow tainted, the heaviness remains even as I enter the small, wooded area, gasping for air.

Not an animal in sight, not even a bird. How is that possible, I wonder.

We spent hours in these woods, chasing, hiding, our laughter scaring the birds from the branches. Dad was a better climber than me, but he didn't have a belly when we moved in. Making chimp sounds, he'd swing from the strongest branch, beating at his chest and pretending to throw poo. Beneath us, Mum would be sighing, telling us to come down, but I know she really thrived on our happiness. I'd often look down to see her collecting pinecones, sometimes even humming, not the awful tune Mother does in front of the window, but one that always somehow made me feel safe.

"Hey!"

I turn, heart pounding, searching between the trees for the source of the voice. Laughter floats on the breeze, seeming to come from all directions. A child. A boy, I think. But as wood moans against the escalating gust, I only find bark and swaying shadows.

"Up here, silly."

It takes me a while, searching the autumnal palate of the trees before I see his pale skinny legs dangling from a branch near the top. The boy looks no heavier than a feather.

"Who are you?" I yell.

He moves quickly from branch to branch until he finds the trunk and begins to shimmy down, showing no caution. "I'm a ghost," he says upon reaching the bottom. The boy's young face is as pale as his legs, lending substance to his claim, so I can't deny the twinge of relief as his feet begin squelching into softness.

"Tom," he says, kicking at a pile of leaves.

"I'm Amy." It's a strange encounter, this being on the border of our property and having not seen another person for days. "How old are you, Tom?"

"Thirteen, nearly fourteen. You live in that house, don't you?"

"What are you doing here, Tom?"

The wind wraps around us with a howl, forcing a groan from the trees, the perfect soundtrack to this odd exchange. A shudder escapes me as the boy looks beyond me to our *beloved* house behind.

"I knew her," he says, "the girl who lived there before you."

My instinct is to tell him that he shouldn't be here, knowing Dad would disapprove, especially in his current paranoia-fuelled state. But this is my first proper interaction with someone close to my own age for months.

"Iris," he continues. "Attended the school until her dad pulled her out. She was quiet with most but not with me. Nice as pie. Crazy, too, but in a good way, and only I knew how much. Her hair smelled like apples, and she was my best friend."

I smile at this, thinking about them weaving between these very trees, almost able to hear their laughter floating on the breeze. Hard to imagine this place as a source of joy, but I recall how quickly Mum became Mother.

"We used to scare the crap out of each other," he continues, "jumping out and screaming 'boo' trying to get the best reaction. We'd giggle for ages, setting each other off, until we collapsed to the floor, eyes wet and gasping for air." He shrugs, turning his stare to the ground. "Kids' stuff really, but I miss it."

"Where is she now?"

"Heaven. At least, I hope."

My stomach twists, and I feel the skin tightening around my skull. "She died?"

There's unmistakable sadness in his eyes, his thoughts likely still on times spent playing at the house. Instantly, I know he's a nice kid, unlike most of the pigs at my last school. Finally, he nods, kicking at the remaining leaves. "Used to come here a lot, somehow hoping it was all a bad joke. Or that there was some other explanation. Don't really like it here, to tell you the truth. The air's too thick and doesn't smell right to me."

"I know what you mean."

"Anyhow, I had a dream last night—sounds stupid, I know. We were playing hide and seek, and it was my turn to seek, but just as I started looking, I heard her crying. When I found her, she wasn't hidden at all, just standing at the tree line looking towards the house. She was shaking, too. When I asked what was wrong, she turned to me and said, 'something bad is going to happen.' He kicks the base of a nearby tree. "Why did I have to dream that?"

"What happened to her? To Iris."

He shrugs again. "News started saying things, people, too. Mostly about the dad, Frank. Said he lost his mind when Iris's mum died of cancer, that he couldn't cope. Rumours are that he got nasty, took it out on—" the boy breaks off, moving his stare away to the patch of ground where the leaves used to be. "I mean, he gave me an odd look every now and again, but never that kind of heebie-jeebie look, you know?"

"I'm sorry," is all I can think to say, joining in his stare towards the ground as the wind whistles around us. We stay like that for a while, Tom grieving for his friend and me for my old parents.

"Aren't you cold?" He finally asks.

I shrug. "Aren't you?"

"Freezing."

"Where do you live, Tom?"

"A mile or so down the road. Parents wouldn't like me being here, but I feel guilty if I leave it too long between visits. And after last night—" he breaks off and shakes his head. "How come you don't attend the school anyways?"

"My mother home-schools me. Thinks I'm too smart to be around other kids. Reckons she can do a better job than the 'underpaid teachers at the makeshift barn they call the local school.' Her words, not mine."

"She's probably right," the boy says. He smiles, and I instinctively offer one in return. "Do you like living around here?" he asks.

"I miss my friends." *And Mum and Dad.* "I miss being able to walk to the store." *I miss not waking up in the middle of the night covered in sweat. I miss the sounds of the birds outside my bedroom window. I miss wondering what the day will bring.*

I miss myself.

The boy nods. "I'll take that as a no."

"It's just different. Everything's different."

"Living out here isn't for everyone. You get used to it, though."

As a tear threatens to break, I turn my glance to the canopy. "I really hope not, Tom."

"I best be getting back," he says, eyes on the dull sky.

"Will you come again?"

"Do you want me to?"

"I do."

"Then I will." He opens his mouth to say something else but enters a trance-like state as he looks beyond my shoulder again towards the house.

"Tom?"

"The house looks different than it used to."

"My dad started doing some work on it when we first—"

"No, I don't mean that. I thought it before, too. It looks sadder. Smaller, even."

I join his stare, my heart sinking at the sight of the place. Exposed further by the lack of leaves on the surrounding trees and the absence of sunlight, the house looks as lonely and sorrowful as I feel. If anything, such barrenness should lend size to the building. Yet, it appears withdrawn, shrivelled paintwork emphasised by dullness, windows like dead eyes, and walls appearing to lean inwards as though the house is trying to disappear.

"Do you—do you ever sense her?"

My skin tightens further as I turn my attention back to the boy. Even the thought makes me feel funny inside and more wary about having to make the walk back. I wonder what he wants me to say, what would appease him most. "No," I finally reply, the answer as much for me as it is for him, the thought of such lingering sadness too much to bear. The heaviness, though, the charge in the air, more than just foreboding, making me wonder if places can hold onto grief as much as people.

"Thought I saw her in the bedroom window once," he says. "But I guess if you look hard and long enough."

I nod, offering a shudder at the thought.

"I'll see you soon, okay?" he says.

"Sure. Tomorrow?"

He shrugs, beginning to back away. "Maybe. Mum wouldn't be so keen on me being here, though."

"Wait."

He smiles. "Ghost69. I'm everywhere, like a—"

"Rude ghost? Our internet is crap, though."

"Yeah, it can be flaky out here, to say the least." He reaches into his pocket, sliding his phone out. "Here."

I type in my number and hand it back, feeling inexplicably happy as he punches in a message and hits send. "I've got yours, and you've got mine," he says. "Guess that makes us friends."

I smile just as he turns and launches into a run, his dirt-smeared skinny legs moving remarkably quickly. And just like that, I'm alone once more.

Boo, the message says.

The house looks smaller still as I finally turn and make my way back, Tom's words still swimming in my mind. *Do you ever sense her?*

Mother's expressionless face staring through the lounge room window only adds to the chill as I approach the house. Sometimes I want to hit her, just to try and evoke a reaction, something other than the cold way she eyes me.

As for Father, as soon as I see him, I intend to ask him about the family who lived here before. I want to know if he knew, how much he knew. *Bargains like this don't come around very often.*

The front door opens with the usual moan, the log fire taking the chill from my bones but not my soul. With no sign of movement from Mother, I carefully peek my head around the doorframe to see Father slumped on his chair, his head aimed at the ceiling and his mouth wide open, an empty tumbler loosely gripped in his left hand.

God, I miss them.

There's little comfort upstairs, just layers of dust and misery. My room, once a sanctuary, moans the same way the rest of the house does, as though not a single corner of the place is untainted by *her* mood. Into what feels like a bath of cold water, I slide between my sheets and stare at the ever-lengthening crack in my ceiling, biting my lip to stem the tears. Even the smell of old smoke is wrong; usually sweet and musky, it now fills the house with an oppressively stale heaviness that feels harder to swallow.

It's my birthday tomorrow, but I'm not expecting anything. There'll be no candles, but I'll make a wish regardless and squeeze down on my blanket harder than ever.

As the house offers another series of moans, blades of cold air cutting across my face, I bring the covers to my chin and slide my phone out.

Boo.

The short time spent with Tom is something I will hold onto for a while, at least until his next visit. That skinny little boy with wide eyes and dirty knees offered a glimpse of life beyond this house, an innocence I yearn for. And the fact he continues to visit—*Don't really like it here, to tell you the truth*—as if his presence might be enough to conjure her back from the dead fills me with sadness, for him, but also myself, that nobody would care in such a way if I were to vanish from the face of the earth.

Please tell me you will come back tomorrow.

I hit send, feeling a prickle of excitement.

That poor girl, Iris. I hate to think of what she went through. First losing her mother to cancer, and then—

Message not delivered.

I hit send again, clenching my teeth as if it might help.

Message not delivered.

No service, but I've still been able to send messages before.

Message not delivered.

Message not delivered.

Message not delivered.

Message not delivered.

"Come on, please." This isn't fair. One bit of happiness, one glimmer of light in the darkness. "Please!"

Message not delivered.

As tears come raw and unfiltered, quickly absorbed into the blanket Mum made, the house moans with me, its creaks and rattles almost drowning me out. These wails, feeling at once sympathetic and mocking, offer no comfort.

Message not delivered.

Message not delivered.

In desperation, I drag the sash window up and lean out, aiming the phone at the sky. *Please. Please. Please.* But as expected, the same message coldly emphasises that I'm all alone again. Defeated, I begin drawing myself back in, only for my sweater to catch on a splinter of wood.

"Not fair," I say, trying to work it free. "Not fucking—"

At first, I freeze, trying to process what I'm seeing, the young girl staring up at me from the concrete, body all contorted and twisted, grey concrete darkening further around her head. Only as she reaches towards me with a deformed arm does adrenaline kick in and have me yanking at the sweater until I'm staggering backwards, finally plunging into softness again as my legs hit the bed.

Oh, God. Oh, God.

I can still see the pale legs twitching, red hair splayed across the grey, eyes so wide, and her mouth forming a scream.

Thought I saw her in the bedroom window once.

As I slowly draw myself to my elbows, the house maintains its haunting soundtrack. Icy cold continues to envelop me, rattling the window in its frame but unable to shift the heaviness of the air. Stronger than ever, the feeling has returned that something bad will happen soon. I swallow hard, trying to dislodge the lump, but it only seems to grow as though nourishing on my fear.

Can't move. Can't breathe.

It's all in your head, Amy. Just your mind playing games. But what Tom said about them finding the child's body on the concrete path. *It can't be. It just can't be.*

Not a drop of saliva in my mouth, her name comes out only as a wispy croak. "Iris?"

Eyes screwed shut, I listen. For what, I don't know. A reply? A moan. A scream.

But all is quiet apart from the wailing walls and the whistling wind. Holding my breath, I slowly shuffle across, perching on the end of the bed, eyes on the dullness of the sky and the distant canopy that gives a contrasting ever-so-gentle sway.

I swallow hard, once again trying to dislodge the lump. "Iris."

Feeling almost certain the wind will carry a whisper in return, I remain seated, sure my legs would fail me anyway. My senses heightened by the cold and skin continuing to contract, I wait.

More creaks and more whistles lend to the dread.

Finally, I work the courage to push myself from the bed and slowly make my way towards the window. With each step, I imagine my legs buckling beneath me, becoming as useless as the red-haired girl's contorted limbs that twitched against the concrete.

In your head. In your head. In your head.

But the energy is undeniable as I draw close to the window again

—an odd sensation that takes me back to a camping trip. I can't recall the name of the place, but there was a bridge running across a fast-flowing stream full of sharp rocks. I remember standing next to my dad, watching the lolly sticks fighting their way through, shuddering at the thought of falling onto the rocks below, but also feeling a strange compulsion to jump, something more than gravity pulling me towards the edge.

Yes, like that, but so much stronger.

Gripping the ledge unnecessarily tight, I gently lean over, screwing my eyes half-shut, preparing for the sight below. Only a brown leaf awaits before finally losing the fight against the breeze, carried onto its next stage of the afterlife.

In your head. Just all in your—.

Pressure on my shoulder snaps my head around. I offer another croak, feeling little comfort at the sight of the off-colour walls on the other side of the room. "Who—who's there?"

Only the wind replies.

Message not delivered.

I feel my nails digging into my skin. My heart thumps. I can still feel where pressure was applied.

Message not delivered.

More wind. More creaks.

There's no escape, not a spot in the house that prevents fear from leaking into my bones. Even outside of late, I've felt that same claustrophobic feeling, as though someone is stealing the breathable air, replacing it with the staleness that resides in the house.

"I'm not scared!"

Still trying to convince myself that all of this is in my head, I shut the window and throw myself to my bed. The blanket is already dry, as if such softness, once providing comfort, has developed an appetite for my grief. Still, I clutch at it, hoping it will make the ghosts, or whatever this is, slink back into the woodwork. Still, the trespassing wind continues to torment even with the window closed. "Let me be! Why won't you let me be?"

I used to read to escape, consuming words until the letters

jumped from the page, but the relentless cries of the house became too distracting, snatching me from whatever magic world I tried to lose myself in.

Hands translucently pale and shaky, I grab the earbuds from my bedside table and plug them into my phone, frantically pressing the buttons, desperate to drown out the ever-increasing shrill. With the unreliability of the internet, especially in recent weeks, I took my chances when I could, downloading my favourite podcasts and music. Again, I suspect such patchy accessibility is more than just being remote, that this house and land are somehow stifling outside influence, choking any potential happiness from our existence. It's as if the place has claimed us rather than us claiming it, dragging us into its bowels of misery.

Come on. Come on.

The first chance I get, I'm going to confront Father again. Talk to him about leaving. Beg if I have to. This place has brought nothing but sadness, and I fear the worst is yet to come.

Come on!

My playlist has changed; once made up of pop and happy stuff, that kind of music has no place here. It's usually ASMR now, a combination of tapping and whispering that induces relaxation and dopamine. For me, it's more about hyper-focussing on something other than the groans from this restless house; a means to keep the bad thoughts out, which is easier said than done of late. My friend —*old friend*—Stacey told me about it. She said it helped her sleep if she was worried about something.

Tap. Tap. Tap.

The first time I tried it, it took me back to laying across my grandma's lap, feeling the gentle tickle of her fingers along my spine and head. Ever since, it has provided an escape, a sanctuary, a fortress even, protecting memories and hope.

Tap. Tap. Tap.

Closing my eyes, I let my head sink into the pillow, but even that feels harder than it used to, as though the place allows no respite from harshness. Occasionally snapping my eyes open to ensure I'm alone, I eventually feel the stiffness leaving my neck.

Tap. Tap. Tap.

I begin cycling through some of my favourite memories, all belonging to a time before we moved here—baking in the old kitchen with Mum and the flour fight we had. On our backs, giggling and making snow angels on the floor. It took ages to wash it all from my hair and even longer to tidy up.

Tap. Tap. Tap.

The time my kite snapped from its string at the beach. How my tears turned to laughter as Dad and I ran after it, feet splashing through the warmth of the water. We never did get the kite back, yet it's a memory that fills me with immeasurable joy.

Tap. Tap. Tap.

I remember Mum picking me up from school at the end of term and taking me for pancakes and ice cream to celebrate my report card. 'I'm so proud of you,' she said. Her words I recall so clearly. 'You are the best of Dad and me; you truly are. Smart in all the ways.'

Tap. Tap. Tap.

It's working, my heart rate coming down and my body sinking further into softness. The soundtrack of the house is barely audible, disguised by soft incoherent whispers and gentle tapping. Prickles of fear give way to tingles, and memories mix with hopes and dreams.

I feel myself going deep.

Tap. Tap. Tap.

I'm in a living room full of balloons and friends from the past, a song from my old playlist floating across the room. It's a mix of the old and the new house, decorated with modern furniture and large paintings hanging from discoloured and cracked walls. Mum comes in wearing the biggest smile, carrying a cake topped with candles and fizzing sparklers. "Happy Birthday, my angel."

Almost forgetting this is all in my head, I momentarily feel so happy I could burst. Half-expecting the scene to disappear with the awareness, I focus intensely on the tapping and soft utterances, desperate to hold onto such imagery. I'm sitting down, the cake on the table in front of me, my friends gathering at my shoulders.

Mum taps me on the shoulder. "Make a wish, darling."

And I do, releasing my grip on the blanket as my fingers begin to ache.

Tap. Tap. Tap.

I blow out the candles and watch the smoke trails disappear.

We sing, we dance, but as if sensing my joy, the moans from the house get louder. Lights in the room flicker and the walls begin to crumble, deep cracks working their way through.

No, you're not taking this!

Squeezing down hard on the blanket again, I begin rebuilding the room. Some friends dance, and some remain seated on the couch, eating cake and talking about their boyfriends, girlfriends, crushes. Mother smiles at me from the corner of the room, even offering a playful jiggle of her hips.

"Where's Dad?" I ask.

She winks. "Bringing your big present through."

But the goddamn moans from the house are still finding their way in.

"Can you turn the music up, Mum?"

She nods and dances her way across the room.

Tap. Tap. Tap.

As the music blares, the floor begins vibrating. Stacey and I play keepy-uppy with some of the balloons, laughing and giggling.

The house gets louder.

Someone yells my name, and I snap my head to the left, only to see a crack in the wall deepen again.

Tap. Tap. Tap.

As my friends form a conga line, laughing and screaming, I make my way to the stereo to turn the music up again, determined not to let the house steal this from me. Eyes wide, gummy smiles stretching across their faces, I watch my friends disappear through to the kitchen. Giddy with anticipation, following the sound of their footsteps looping around, I ready myself to tag onto the end of the line. But as stomping turns to a strange shuffling sound, my heart sinks.

Tap. Tap. Tap.

I see the leg first, dark green in parts, bone sticking out, foot turned the wrong way. The flash of red follows, wild and unbrushed but matted down with blood at the back. It's her, the girl I saw from my window. Hand clasping a grey teddy, *she* leads the conga into the room, the group following, imitating her jerky and uncoordinated movements, left legs dragging behind. Even from here, I see bits of her skull between the muted red strands of hair.

The conga breaks up with an explosion of giggles, the red-haired girl collapsing to the floor, limbs twisted just as they appeared from my bedroom window. No silent scream, but it's her for sure. "Anyone for Twister?" someone shouts to another eruption of guffaws.

"Present time," Mum shouts. "Geoff. Geoff!"

As the house continues screaming its violent protest as if upset at being ignored, I scrunch my eyes tighter still, turning the volume on the stereo up to max.

Why am I seeing her? How am I seeing her? Is it somehow connected to Tom's Dream?

Something bad is going to happen.

Focussing on the party, I try and conjure the broken girl away by imagining what my present could be.

Tap. Tap. Tap.

I've wanted a new laptop for what feels like forever. And Mum said if my grades kept being—

Underneath the glittery birthday banner, I notice a man standing in the corner of the room, features shadowy and unclear beneath the large hat. What do they call that type again? I remember dad almost buying one once, but Mum managed to talk him out of it, much to my relief.

Tap. Tap. T—

The man tilts his hat towards me. A trilby, that's it. One of the parents, perhaps? No, I don't think so. Behind him, on the wall, blackness spreads like mould.

Tap. Tap. Tap.

I don't like this anymore; I want out.

But no matter how hard I try, the scene won't leave me be.

Can't break out of it. Can't open my eyes—too heavy. Can't—

"No, Daddy, don't. Please," the red-haired girl cries as the music slows to a distorted mess.

Tap. Tap. Tap.

How is this happening? Get out of my head! Stop this!

But the groans of the house wrap around my brain and begin to squeeze.

"Leave me alone!"

The man in the trilby is no longer there, nor is the girl with the red hair. Still, blackness spreads across the art, furniture, and even the floor.

This was my haven, sanctuary, fortress, the only place so far untouched.

"STOP THIS!"

As Dad enters the room, Mum takes something from him and whispers into his ear. She turns towards me, hands behind her back. "Close your eyes, Amy; it's present time." *Mother's* in her place, wearing a snarl and the all too familiar look on her face.

Tap. Tap. Tap.

"Dad, please," I croak.

But he raises his glass and drains the dregs. "Happy Birthday from both of us, darling."

To resounding cheer, Mother brings the axe down, bursting a red balloon as the blade lodges into the floor. Teeth gritted, spittle spraying from her tight lips, Mother sways her hips violently left to right, finally managing to wrestle it free. Offering a roar, she swings at a yellow balloon, nudging it upwards and bringing the axe's blade into the skull of a dancing child. "Happy fucking birthday!" She's frenzied, foaming at the mouth.

It's like a nightmare I can't wake from. There's an awareness this is just in my head, yet my body feels impossibly heavy and my limbs redundant as though the burden of this place keeps me under. "Mother, please stop."

"Hip hip, hooray!" she cries, sinking the blade into Anthony's neck, a delayed flow of crimson spilling as he drops to his knees.

"Mother!"

"Was it everything you'd hoped for?" she yells, embedding the axe into Alisha's back.

Over the sound of the house's moans and the tapping in my ear, I hear the cries of my friends as they try to escape. But the network of black has spread all over, working across the doors, holding them in place. Blood-filled screams surround me as the permanence of flesh-tearing, limb-snapping sounds bore their way forever into my mind.

And one by one, they all fall down, bringing a bloody red curtain down on the party.

Tap. Tap. Tap.

As though *this place* has finally seen fit to release me, I snap my eyes open and unclench my fists. Vision still dotted with red streaks, I push myself up and rip the headphones from my ears.

I hate this place. I hate this place.

So many nightmares before, but never like this, not on my terms, not in my secret world. Still trembling, I bring the blankets around me, thoughts on the red-haired girl and the man in the trilby, who I assume to be her father.

What did Tom Say? Something about them finding him swaying from the ceiling of the barn.

It stays relatively quiet, as if, for now at least, the house has coughed up enough bile. I keep my eyes wide open, running them across the crack in the ceiling, occasionally hitting send on my phone, my stomach dropping each time the text fails to deliver.

Something bad is going to happen. Something bad is going to happen. Something bad is going to happen.

For the first time in my life, I pray. I pray to anyone who's listening that my new friend will turn up tomorrow. And I pray for enough strength to convince Father to take us away from this place, start afresh somewhere not touched by such sadness. "Amen."

In relative silence, the dark tide finally creeps towards me, and I have little fight left to give.

Tomorrow might be—

TAP. TAP. TAP.

It takes a while to adjust, grey floaters folding into shades of darkness. Groggy and disoriented, I reach for my phone but see the earbuds on the blanket next to me, lit by a sliver of white.

Tap. Tap. Tap.

Offering a sharp intake of breath, I push myself to my elbows to see Mother at the window, a finger pressed against one of the panes —*tap, tap, tap*—while her other hand strokes at her enlarged belly. When did her hair go completely grey? And her skin, once pristine, now hardened and duller.

"Mother?"

She walks around to the end of the bed, continuing to stroke her belly, whispering under her breath. With her head bowed, she clasps her fingers around the wooden frame, slowly lifting her gaze and offering a smile, but not a warm one. And the way the moon only catches one side of her face sends a shudder down my spine.

"Mother, what is it?"

Nostrils flaring, knuckles white, she continues staring, that hateful smile wrapped around her face. I swallow hard, but before I can offer more words to break the ominous deadlock, I'm sure I catch movement behind her, shadows flickering like a flame, settling on what looks like the silhouette of a man.

"Father?"

But just as I trace back to what looks like the outline of a hat, Mother nods, whispers something else under her breath, and turns away, humming that God-awful tune and leaving only greyness in her wake. Footsteps creaking into the distance, my stare remains fixed on the corner of the room, waiting for the shadows to move again. I stay like that for some time, rigid with fear, praying for Mother not to come back, nor the guy with the ribbon around his hat.

Finally, I turn away, resting my head on the pillow as I follow the clouds, and as I used to with Dad, I begin finding shapes: a dinosaur, a hamburger, a face. Such innocence lends thoughts to Tom, his little legs dangling from near the top of the tree, his cheeky smile filling my heart.

Iris was a red-haired girl, wasn't she, Tom?

I imagine the boy's eyes widening as he asked how I knew. *Have you seen her? Did you sense her?* Should I even tell him what I've seen with my eyes and inside my head? Or should I leave him be, let him go on believing death is death, and that's a wrap?

Then again, what have I seen? Shadows within shadows? Nightmares in dreams? But I felt that hand on my shoulder and saw that girl's bloodied hair across the pavement beneath my window.

What if he gets upset with me? What if he runs off into the woods, never to return?

Guess that makes us friends.

The only person I can talk to for miles, I can't bear the thought of losing that glimmer of normality, that attachment to a world beyond these four walls and the adults who pose as my mum and dad.

Message not delivered.

With my sanctuary tainted, I'm left listening to the rattle and creaking of the house, doing my best to keep the poison from getting inside me again. Eventually, I fall into a trance-like state, staring at the window and the clouds beyond but not really watching. I'm awake but numb, and that's just fine with me.

WEDNESDAY

. . .

MY ROOM LIGHTS UP A LITTLE AFTER FOUR, NO SLEEP HAVING YET found me. I listen to Father's truck skidding on gravel as though he can't get away fast enough. The earliest to date, I envy his escape and can't help feeling more than a little anger at the feeling of abandonment.

Just me and *her* now.

With thoughts of Mother's recent visit still fresh in my head, it's well over an hour before my eyelids finally begin losing the fight.

THE ALARM WAKES ME UP JUST AFTER EIGHT.

I can't bear the thought of class today, Mother rocking in the chair, occasionally looking up from her belly to offer me one of her hurtful looks. Words are few and far between, usually mumbling for me to get on with the day's tasks with no intention of looking over my work.

"Happy Birthday to me."

As morning light continues to break through, I reach over to my bedside table and open the top drawer. Four cards await, the number fifteen written across the top of each in various fonts. And as I've done many times of late, I read through the verses and the hand-written words, saving the card with last year's declaration of love from my parents until last.

Amy,
You are the sun, the moon, the grass, the sky
You are everything to us and more
Happy Birthday, sweetheart
Love Mum and Dad
xxx

I recall thinking how cheesy it was then, but now I cherish every word, imagining it all to be true. It was only last year, yet it feels like a lifetime ago. Placing the card next to the others, I habitually chew at the inside of my cheek, wondering if I'll ever feel happiness again. Or love.

Even on tiptoes, the landing creaks, seemingly out of time with my steps.

Hate this place.

Pausing briefly at the top of the stairs, I listen for Mother but hear nothing apart from the continued wails of the house.

Hate it!

As I close the bathroom door behind me, the face reflected in the mirror doesn't even look like me anymore—sallow eyes sunken from lack of sleep and pale skin emphasising the darkness underneath. My hair is dishevelled and dry; something Mum would never let me get away with.

"I'd kill to have hair like yours," she used to say. "You need to look after it better."

There's an emptiness, a hole where she once was, darkness where there was once light. No opportunity to say goodbye, no chance to grieve, and in her place, an evil twin whose sole intention is to make my life miserable.

"I miss you, Mum."

In front of the fireplace in our old house, she'd brush my hair for ages while we ate candy and put the world to rights. She was my best friend, too, my confidante, nothing off limits. "Please come back to me, Mum."

I feel myself beginning to shake, a charge running through me. Unable to bottle it any longer, I grit my teeth and offer a stifled scream, beating the bottom of my fists against the mirror until they're sore. "I don't deserve this! I don't deserve this!" As my breathing becomes heavy and erratic, I let my forehead fall against the glass's coolness and begin to sob. "I don't deserve this."

Rusty pipes groan, and the walls thrum as I duck my head under the water. Momentarily, I manage to clear my head, simply enjoying its warm embrace, but as relentless as the house's screams, the bad thoughts begin pouring into my head. Thinking about Father, his insistence that I stay back and assist Mother, knowing all well and good that she helps herself to what she wants, caring for the bump in her belly and nothing but.

How could he leave me with her? On my birthday.

"How could you?"

But the thought crosses my mind that he isn't even aware that it's my birthday.

As more tears wash away with the water, I begin to wonder if the further away he gets from here, the more his smile returns. The thought fills me with jealousy, rage, an intense hatred for someone I once loved. Perhaps he thinks my presence would spoil what little freedom he has, his tiny vacations from Hell. Or maybe he blames me somehow for all of this. Another thought crosses my mind that one day he might not return, that it might just be me and *her* and the thing in her belly that turned her mean.

I hate it. I hate the fucking thing, and I hate this fucking place.

Imagining it cleansing me from all the badness, I wait until the shower runs cold before stepping out. It's freezing, clouds of my breath forming rapidly, goosebumps running across my skin. Wrapping myself in the relative warmth of a towel, I approach the mirror and run a finger across the condensation, managing to muster half a smile.

Boo.

I'm going to make the best of today, put on a brave face in the hope I might even convince myself. I might even bake a cake if Mother's out of the way and in her chair. She won't be getting any, but I'll give Tom a slice if he turns up. Dressed in my best jeans, I choose the nicest sweater I have from my cupboard.

"Please visit, Tom. Please come."

After pacing up and down the landing a few times, I summon the courage to head downstairs, clinging to the railing and hoping that today might be different. Mother's neither in her chair by the lounge window nor in the kitchen. There's no relief, thoughts of her rocking gently back and forth next to the blackboard in the barn twisting at my stomach.

Not today. Not on my birthday.

But she likely doesn't even know, probably doesn't even care.

I help myself to dregs of cereal, but after three mouthfuls, my appetite wanes.

It's my fucking birthday.

Adamant that I'm going to confront her and demand she become Mum again, if only for one day, I push myself from the table and all but throw my dish into the sink.

Mother hasn't been keeping to her own time recently. She turned up late yesterday, and when she got there, she hardly spoke a word, just gestured for me to read my textbook. Still, the thought of making her angry doesn't sit well—flashbacks to her standing at the end of my bed, the dark somehow winning against the moonlight.

Tap. Tap. Tap.

Mother took so much pride in setting it up initially, spending a small fortune: blackboard, filing cabinets, maps, books, even plants. She made it into such a lovely space, but without the prospect of laughter, the structure ahead now looks stark, mean almost.

I hate that bump. Hate this place.

Even Father suggested leaving once, before this place took hold and started choking him. But the way Mother eyed him as soon as the words left his lips made me feel all funny inside. After that day, he's not broached the subject, but when he returns, I'll drop to my hands and knees, hoping there's an ounce of love left in his heart.

My stomach drops. Invisible ants march across my skin.

As the gentle breeze wraps around me, I spy her bleary silhouette through the dust-covered window at the front of the building. I can imagine her face screwed up, thin lips mumbling hate under her breath, stunted by occasional contrasting declarations of love for the baby growing within.

Hate it. Hate it. Hate it.

With Mother's horrible tune escaping through the broken pane next to my head, I wrap my fingers around the impossibly cold handle and take a deep breath.

Three. Two. One.

And after a further pause, I finally push the door open and step into a place once full of laughter and the smell of freshly baked cookies.

"Mother."

Wrapped in a blanket and staring at the back wall of the makeshift classroom, she rocks back and forth in her usual way. Seemingly oblivious to my presence, her humming occasionally gives way to a sniffle or more ominous muttering. With my breath held, I take a few small steps forward, eyes on the scratchy writing on the blackboard next to her.

There's no place like home.
There's no place like home.
There's no place like

"Mother."

Without a flicker of acknowledgment, the humming and rocking continue. The chair squeaks, the barn moans, and dust swirls are sent towards the ceiling as the wind kicks up to a squall.

"Mother."

My skin prickles another warning, trying to shrink around my bones. I count to three and edge forwards.

Just more gentle humming. More creaking.

"Mother, please."

As I take another tentative step forward, I hear her whisper something under her breath. "What was that, Mother?"

Just more inaudible muttering, broken by the occasional whimper.

"Mother, it's my birthday today."

It's all I can do to hold back the tears, thinking back to last year's party, all my friends springing out from behind the furniture as soon as I stepped foot into the lounge. The trouble Mum and Dad went to, making it so special. I wonder if this might be my punishment for taking things for granted, for taking them for granted. Pinching at the flesh on my left arm, I take a couple more cautious steps forward. "I was thinking instead of class, we could—"

Mother snaps her head around, face all twisted and eyes full of hate. "LEAVE ME ALONE, YOU NEEDY LITTLE CUNT!"

I doubted anything could be worse than the silent treatment, but as I back away towards the door, tears filling my eyes, it's myself I wish dead.

"NEEDY LITTLE CUNT! NEEDY LITTLE CUNT!"

Emerging from the barn, I feel even more defeated. I begin to bawl like a *child*. Nowhere to hide, not even in dreams. "I hate this place!"

Not a breath of wind outside, but the house still groans as I push open the door and make my way up the stairs. My pillow, still damp, offers little comfort as I lay down, staring at the crack in my ceiling and wishing it to swallow me whole.

For the rest of the day, I mostly stay in my room, venturing downstairs only for food and when my bladder feels like it may burst. At one point, I summon the bravery to peek around the front door, only to see Mother's silhouette still rocking in the grimy barn window. I know Mum is lost somewhere deep within, but I worry more than ever she'll not find her way out.

As evening draws close, I try picking up my book again, but as though the place cares to deny me even the most minor of pleasures, the creaks and groans expectantly ramp up until they fill my head, leaving room for nothing else. Momentarily, I consider wearing my headphones to block it all out, but after last time, I'm far too afraid I'll be blocking it in instead.

Message not delivered.

I'm more determined than ever to throw everything at Father to convince him we must leave, that there's something bad here, revelling in our sadness. I don't care what he does; there's no punishment worse than what we live through. Heart in my mouth, I listen all day for his truck, but the gravel outside remains undisturbed even as the sun begins its descent.

Clinging onto thoughts of Tom's return, I grab my backpack and sneak downstairs, snatching the last of the snacks on the way out. No sign of Mother in her favourite lounge chair, and dullness prevents a good look through the barn window.

Backpack swinging around my shoulders, I sprint towards the

trees, already searching the distant canopy for those skinny little legs. Just the thought of seeing another face not wearing despair fills me with giddiness. I've forgotten what it's like to feel normal, like a child, but even the brief conversation with that little boy yesterday made me realise what I'm missing. Ducking under branches and kicking at the leaves, I call for him, imagining him sitting on one of the top branches holding onto his giggle.

"Tom!"

Glancing over my shoulder to ensure he's not sneaking up on me, I spy the house looking greyer than ever and somehow smaller. A shudder runs down my spine, and I resume my search, spinning in circles, moving my eyes from one branch to the next. "Tom, I have candy." I unzip the pack and bring out a handful of chocolate bars, waving them towards the sky. "But I've got one hell of a sweet tooth." Using my teeth, I rip at the first of them. "And if you don't hurry down, there'll be none left, and I'll be as fat as a pig. Oink! Oink!"

Holding my breath, I listen intently for movement, but only the trees oblige, offering loud creaks in the slightest breeze. Still, I dance across the woody carpet for some time, chomping on the candy bar, convincing myself he's up there somewhere, biding his time.

"Come on, Tom."

Halfway through the second bar, I slump against a tree and let myself slide down, the backpack scratching against the bark and riding up my shoulders. Knees tightly pulled against my chest, I finish the rest of the chocolate and toss the wrapper at the sky, watching as it floats impossibly slowly towards the ground.

The air's too thick and doesn't smell right to me.

Helped on its course to my right by the gentle breeze, I watch the wrapper land next to a pile of leaves, continuing to unfurl. Earthiness fills my nostrils, mostly the scent of rotting leaves, but something else floats on the air's heaviness, something I can only describe as the smell of decay, the breaking down of everything one has known.

I'm unsure what compels me to slide myself up against the tree and walk across to the wrapper. Halfway to bending down, I spot the two small lolly sticks a couple of feet behind it, tied together with string to fashion a cross. Instinctively, I snap it up and begin clawing at the damp ground, each icy breath visible and unpleasant vibrations riding through my fingers. An inch down, my fingers start to sing, but I see something poking through the mud.

Soil works away quickly as urgency has me digging my fingers in deeper until they latch around my found treasure. After glancing back towards the house and running my eyes across the trees, I lift out my find, shaking some of the dirt from the small, discoloured teddy. There's a ribbon around its neck, blue as far as I can tell. The fur is matted with little patches of grey poking from the dirt.

An image forms of the poor girl ripping at the ground, fingernails full of dirt, the hem of her dress spread out beneath her. What must have been going through her mind to do this? Was she somehow trying to save part of her innocence, not letting her father take it from her? Or did she know that death was coming, that she perhaps wanted teddy with her on the other side?

"I'm so sorry, Iris."

As the thought sets tears free, sending them spilling to the same patch of ground I imagine Iris's to have fallen, a long shadow sweeps across, prompting me to snap my head around.

Just the trees. Just the trees.

But it's impossible to deny the charge in the air, even stronger than the feeling at my bedroom window.

"Iris?"

In reply, floating on the breeze, I get the faintest waft of—*apples?*

Holding my breath, I stand, clutching onto the small teddy, half expecting to see a flash of red hair and that buckled foot. Only a croak emerges as I finally try to speak her name again.

But just as quickly, the scent is gone, something else carrying on the breeze, something bad, and as a harsher wind wraps around me, I feel icy fingers riding up my spine and clamping around my skull. My chest feels heavy, the air becoming less breathable. The trees offer their moans as they give, but somehow all towards me, like bony digits folding to a fist.

It's him.

It's Frank; I know it.

Beginning my retreat towards the distant treeline, I open my mouth to call for help, but a sharper gust steals my breath, prompting another involuntary shudder and my hair into a frenzy.

Hate this place.

Knowing nobody's around to come to my aid, I increase my pace, noting the surrounding leaves as they kick up in a chaotic and directionless spiral.

Hate it. Hate it. "Hate it!"

Futilely, I finger the hair from my face, but the gust refuses to die, instead gathering pace and sending leaves even higher, back towards their old branches. And as though someone has just clicked their fingers, the rest of the evening bleeds out impossibly quickly, the strength of darkness in its place.

I don't deserve this. I don't!

Eyes on the house in the distance, which suddenly feels the lesser of two evils, I turn and quicken my pace, but so does the wind that now gives off an audible howl. It's changing directions, pushing and pulling, strands of my hair stretching in all directions like taut kite strings, damp leaves laying against my clothes, slapping against my cheeks.

With the tree line less than a hundred feet away, I'm running almost blind, arms alternating between swiping at my face and blindly reaching ahead, my clothes catching on branches that suddenly seem reluctant to let me through. Just like I squeeze on the blanket Mum made for me, I find myself squeezing down on the teddy, a silly attempt to try and conjure goodness into this place, a time before the decay, a time I took for granted.

I'm close, the tree line less than fifty feet away, but I see the lumpy limb emerging from the ground far too late, and I'm suddenly flying, a surge of fire running up my right leg as I brace for impact. Landing fast and heavy, the world becomes a montage of blurred greens and browns.

Fuuuuuuck!

Pain swells at the back of my head as I eye the rolling clouds, unable to get enough air as though the wind is forcing my breath back inside. Woody limbs lean in towards me as though mocking, all part of this nightmare I cannot wake from. Waiting for the worst of the throbbing to subside, I finally push myself onto my back, grimacing as my ankle offers a surge of pain.

Hate this place.

The gust fools me by momentarily easing but returning with renewed strength, sending the skeletal trees into a haunting series of cracks and moans, an at once weary and excitable audience for what may come. Waiting for another wave of pain to dampen, I helplessly watch some of the leaves to my right dancing in the air, one moment appearing to move independently, the next impossibly spiralling around each other in indistinct formation as though trying to come together.

Clenching the teddy until my fingers ache, I glance over my shoulder, taking no comfort from the lifeless building that seems no closer.

It looks sadder. Smaller, even.

Eyes back on the leaves, I try to rationalise what I'm seeing, convincing myself it might be a mini-tornado or some other natural phenomenon. But as bright as my old parents claimed me to be, I don't have an answer. I imagine telling Mum about it, subsequently studying it in class, reading some books, and then writing a summary. But Mum isn't here, only the mean old-looking bitch back in the sad-looking house.

Warily, I begin pushing myself, pausing as I get to my elbows, as I hear what sounds like a slow-motion gunshot echoing through the woods.

And another.

Another.

A branch falls to the ground with a soft thud. And a second, only feet to my right.

Tears in my eyes, I claw at the ground, ignoring the searing pain and managing to edge back a couple of inches before a sharper, cleaner *snapping* sound carries across the woods. And as my eyes turn to the canopy, catching sight of the thick bough beginning to give directly above me, a thought flicks through my head that Mother and Father might be happier without me.

Before I can form a scream, a gust of wind steals my breath and forces my eyes shut, lighting up the tears and sending my hair whipping around me. Above my head, I hear leaves rattling and slapping against each other. I hear the screech of the gale. And —*screaming?*

Only at the belated soft thud do I unclench my jaw and open my eyes, noting the large branch impossibly a good three feet to my left. The wind, too, has dropped to nothing but a whisper, but what keeps my breath held and my heart thumping is the formation of leaves less than ten feet ahead, the hazy silhouette of a young girl now impossible to deny.

I dig my heels into the ground, a garbled cry leaving my lips as the shape takes a step forward, leaves gently rustling.

"I'm so sorry," I croak, pushing against the ground until my back hits a tree. Without taking my stare from the shape ahead, I use the coarseness of the bark to leverage myself to my feet.

Do you ever sense her?

A gentle breeze blows across, carrying the faint but unmistakable smell of apples and the sound of tears. "Thank you for saving me, Iris. I'm sorry nobody was there to save you."

The shape moves forward again, raising a leafy right arm towards me. A much softer breeze gently caresses my cheek, carrying a child's croaky but gentle voice. *Say hi to Tommy for me.*

Breathing no longer feels automatic. Skin prickles and contracts as if trying to crush my bones to dust. Before I can open my mouth to respond, the formation takes another step forwards, the breeze again blowing through, carrying immeasurable sorrow. *I thought if I could stop the man from taking the sign*—she breaks off into a series of sniffles. *This place is no good. Leave!*

Trying to stay brave, I swallow hard, but my heart won't let up. Pinching at the flesh of my elbow, I leave the support of the tree, managing a small step forward. "I've tried, Iris. They won't—"

Without warning, again, as though someone has just flicked a switch, the wind ramps up, setting off an orchestra of creaks and groans. The formation of leaves shrinks back into the woods, some already breaking off, erratically dancing on the gust again.

He's coming back! Run!

And at the sound of her warning, I clench my teeth and begin to sprint, averting my view to the canopy as more cracking and snapping surrounds me. Branches bend, twist, and break, some already raining down around me. The wind howls, carrying more screaming and doing its best to blind me from my path.

Fighting against the pain, I continue making ground, a heavy thud to my left drawing my eyes to a fallen branch twice the size as the one that nearly hit me. Head down, I alternate my attention from the ground, searching for more devious limbs, to the timid-looking house in the distance. Compulsion overwhelms me as I draw close to the end of the tree line, and a glance over my shoulder shows the wind sweeping the last of the leaves away.

As I finally make it out, the wind drops, and the creaking dampens. This place might be done with me for now, but I take little comfort as I drop my run to a walk, studying the bleakness of the house ahead. It feels relentless, fear riding through my bones and in my head, revving towards an unstoppable crescendo.

This place is no good. Leave!

If only it were that easy.

Even the sight of Father's truck can't perk my mood, the inevitability of the conversation weighing heavily on my mind. He'll not believe what I tell him; I'm just a kid. The window, the leaves, the groans and creeks, the falling branch and bad dreams, all things he'll put down to my imagination and the age of this place. But I'll not give up without a fight.

On the sight of Mother's stern face circled by a contrasting soft orange glow, I increase my pace, shoving the teddy down the back of my jeans. She eyes me all the way to the door, her thin lips uttering something I imagine far from pleasant. Fuck you too, Mother.

I open the door to see Father leaning over the stove, one hand wrapped around a glass containing a generous measure of gold and another around a spatula. He turns and offers a nod before moving his attention back to the pan and taking another swig. "Where have you been?"

"Just for a walk. In the woods."

He nods, prodding at the meat. "What have I told you about leaving your mother? You need to be here, looking after her."

The phone vibrates in my pocket. "I was only gone a few minutes."

"I've been back twenty, and I count that as more than a few." He drops his shoulders and lets out a sigh. "I don't know how many times we need to have this conversation, Amy."

Sorry, got loads of chores. I'll try and get down tomorrow, though.

I begin typing a reply, my fingers not moving quickly enough. *Yes. Please come. I hop yiu get this text as—*

"Amy!"

I snap my head up only to see Father looking his angriest to date, teeth clenched, fingers white around the spatula that appears to be shaking. "Yes. Sorry, Father."

"Give me the phone."

"I just need to finish the—"

"Give me the fucking phone!"

It's the first time he's sworn at me, catching me off guard. Never really got angry with me before, not properly, even in recent weeks while under Mother's cloud. But the veins in his neck bulge, and there's a fleeting look behind his eyes that Mother carries. As I warily make my way towards him, though, holding the phone out, his face begins to soften, offering a version of my old dad. A tear escapes down his cheek, and I feel renewed hope that this is the moment, the turning point when we can start heading back to the way things used to be.

Leave!

He holds his arms out towards me, and I take the chance, jogging the last few steps into his arms. "I'm so sorry, Ames. I'm just tired, stressed." And as though he's been doing nothing but holding on, he finally breaks, trembling in my arms, offering a series of muted cries. "It's okay, Dad. But we need to leave this place. It's—bad."

"What do you mean?"

"Can't you feel it, Dad? Can't you see it in her?" I'm getting through; I can feel it, weakening whatever hold this place has. As I squeeze even tighter, the house's moans seemingly dampen, and it's all I can do not to cry myself. "When was the last time we laughed like we used to? When was the last time we made a campfire and searched the sky? Did you even know it was my birthday today?"

"Oh God, Ames. Christ. I'm so sorry. I'm just—just so goddamn tired all the time."

"It's taking pieces of us, Dad, replacing them with rot. It's in our heads; it's everywhere. There's no escape, especially for me. At least you get to go to *work*, the store, and wherever else you go. Why won't you ever let me come? You used to let me ride everywhere with you."

"I know, Ames; I know." He brings his lips towards my ear and gently grabs my arm. "But it's the people around here, though, see. They're not like city folk." It's the stranger talking again, not my dad. I can see the *rot* behind his eyes. He's losing the fight. "They have a look," he continues, "a wildness that puts me on edge. Don't trust anyone of them, especially not with a pretty girl like you."

"Can you hear yourself?" I say, shaking him off. "This isn't the bloody wild west, just a quiet little country town with a nice church. Nobody is out to get us. It's all in your head, and this house put it there. Take me with you tomorrow, please? We can get away from here for a bit. I'll even let you put that horrible music on. You can give me a driving lesson. We can get pie."

"Ames, I—"

"Don't say no. Don't say no."

"I just don't think it's such a good idea, not with your mother—"

"But this isn't fair. You have to be fair!" I'm doing my best to keep calm but slipping fast. "I can't do this for much longer. I'm locked away with her all day."

"Geoff," Mother's voice cries from the other room as if sensing the dormancy of the house. "Geoff!"

"Ignore her," I whisper, locking my arms around him again, willing Dad to return. "She's bad too; you must see it."

"That's your mother you're talking about, Amy. Pregnancy affects people in different ways; we have to be understanding." He sighs deeply, breaking our embrace and reaching for a tea towel. As he dabs his tears away, I feel Father taking control. "Your mother's just feeling it. We're all feeling it. But we have to look after her. I promise it won't be like this—"

"Geoff!"

"Coming, dear."

I watch him walk away with his head down, slumped over as though carrying the weight of this place on his shoulders. There was weakness, though; I could see it behind his eyes. The *dad* in him wants to leave this place as much as I do, but while there's a baby in Mother's belly, I know he'll only appease. Once again, as though mocking my failure, the groans return along with the feeling of the walls shrinking towards me, and even before Father's voice beckons me, I sense Mother's retaliation.

"Amy, come through to the lounge." The softness from his tone has gone, his puppet master taking charge. Letting out a sigh but refusing to appear as weak, I hold my shoulders straight and make my way to our little *family meeting.*

Mother's chair is turned to face me, Father by her side, crouched over, listening, nodding as the poison enters her ear. I watch Mother's lips moving, trying to prepare myself for what might be coming, knowing it will not be good. And at the sight of my phone between her fingers, I feel the darkness growing inside me.

Father straightens, the regretful Dad from the kitchen nothing more but another memory to cling to. "Who's Tom?"

My mind goes blank, panic taking over, an overwhelming need to protect the little slice of normality. "Just a friend from my old school."

"If there's one thing I hate, it's liars," Father says. "There are enough liars on the outside."

Mother taps him on the arm—*tap, tap, tap*—prompting him to lean in again. As she finishes uttering more bile into his ear, I swear I see the flicker of a smile across her lips.

"He was here?" Father asks, eyes growing wide.

She's fuelling his ever-present paranoia, working at his strings. This place is eating us alive, feeding on our fears, squeezing the hope out of us with its claustrophobic nature.

"Amy, was he here?"

Reluctantly I nod, not wanting to prolong the lecture. "Lives down the road. He's nice. He's coming—"

"No. No, he isn't." Father places a hand on Mother's shoulders, further emphasising where his loyalty sits. "Your mother texted him back. It's trespassing is what it is, Amy. And besides, your mother needs you around in case—"

"She doesn't need me; she hates me."

"How dare you say that. Your mother loves you."

"She called me a needy little cunt."

"Amy!"

"And it's not trespassing if he's invited."

The blood leaves Father's face, accentuating the dark patches under his eyes. He shudders, his nostrils flaring as though his body doesn't know what to do with the excess energy. This is unfamiliar territory for him, unchartered ground. "Amy, that—"

Tap. Tap. Tap.

He leans over, nodding as Mother offers more mutterings into his ear. Finally, he comes up for air, squeezing Mother's shoulder again. "You'll see him no more. Mother doesn't need this kind of stress."

But I stand my ground and lift my chin, hands clasped behind my back to conceal the teddy and channel the rage. "He knew the girl that lived here—Iris. They used to play together. He's nice."

"Enough!" Father says through gritted teeth.

One of my fingers cracks, reminding me how the branches fell in the woods. "Did you know that the family here died? That the father went crazy and—"

"Amy!" Father yells. "Stop this!"

As Mother's fingers coil around the arms of her chair, the wood beneath offers a pitiful contribution to the elevating soundtrack of the house.

"You'll not see him again, Amy," Father repeats. "Filling your head with such nonsense. Now go to your room."

I feel myself shaking, feel the adrenaline looking for a way out. Sixteen! Sixteen years old and a prisoner in this godforsaken place. Words bounce around my head, but I can't find the right ones. So much to say, yet I can't speak a damned thing.

"I said go to your room!" Father yells. He slinks behind Mother's chair and begins working on both her shoulders, Mother's smile lingering long enough for it not to be my imagination this time.

"No," I say, straightening up again. "That's not all."

Wood creaks beneath Mother's fingers again as Father stops rubbing, his stare lifting back to me, mouth falling open.

"I'm sixteen years old today. You can't keep me here, locked away from the outside world. I'm allowed a friend; God knows I've prayed for one long enough."

Mother releases her grip, coiling her fingers around Father's wrists and bringing him down towards her. The lips start again, but I refuse to wait my turn.

"I hate it here. Hate it!" Keeping my stare on them, I go for broke. "Everything about it. The smell, the feel. I saw her too, the dead girl, beneath my bedroom window. Tom said he saw her in the window once. And in the woods, there was—"

"Stop this!" Father yells.

"It's killing us. I don't even know who you are anymore. You're not my parents; you're just a couple of strangers, nothing but—"

"Amy, God help me!"

"It's my fucking birthday today!"

"Amy, I swear I'll—"

"What? Hit me? That's what it wants. It's what she wants."

Mother leans forward away from the window, eyes darker as they leave the last of the evening light. Father pushes from the chair, teeth gritted as he marches towards me. Still, I hold my ground, keeping my eyes on him, wincing as my fingers offer further feedback.

"It's this place. We have to move. We have to get—" Father grabs my arm, but I refuse to budge. "We need to get away!"

He clamps down harder as he tries to drag me away, his eyes pleading for me to relent.

"Don't you understand? We have to get out of here!" I continue wrestling, turning my stare towards the stranger in the chair and reflecting her look of disdain. "I mean, look at her. Look at her! That's not my mum; that's not her!"

Finally pulling me off balance, Father drags me towards the kitchen.

"That's not her," I cry, still trying to fight him off. "That's not my mum!" Just before Father yanks me through the doorway, I see her offer another cold smile. "That's not my mum! That's not my mum!"

He swings me towards the stairs, veins in his neck now standing out like the tree limbs in the woods. Momentarily, I think he's going to strike me; I can see it in his eyes that he wants to and can almost feel the rage and frustration leaking from his pores. "Amy, you have to stop this," he finally says, loosening his grip and sweeping the hair from his forehead. "I know things are tough at the moment, but you have to hang in there, just for a little bit longer. Once the baby's here, I'll discuss it with your mother again, but she doesn't need the extra stress right now. It isn't good for her, and it isn't good for the baby."

"It will be too late then."

"Amy, please."

I open my mouth to protest but can see it would be futile. This place continues to drain him, leaving just enough for her.

"I promise, you," he says, trying his best to sound convincing. "Things will be back to normal again soon. Hang in there, okay?"

"Geoff!" Mother cries.

"Probably best you steer clear for a while." He says, straightening up and offering me a gentle pat on the shoulder.

"Can I at least have my phone back?"

"Sorry, love. Your mother said you've broken our trust. In a couple of days when things have settled, perhaps."

I want to scream. I want to punch and kick the banister, yet I nod and begin making my way upstairs, knowing Mother has all the power.

"And stay away from that boy, and anyone else around here for that matter," Father shouts after me, probably more for Mother's benefit. "No such a thing as ghosts, but rumours are aplenty in a small town like this, nothing else for folk to do."

Halfway up, I stop and turn, seeing another tear working down his cheek. "Did you know, though?" I whisper. "That those people died?"

He opens his mouth, but his eyes give him away.

"Geoff!"

"Coming, love."

This place is beating him; anyone can see that. And *she* will finish what's left. Making my way up the rest of the stairs, I consider how desperately we're both hoping things will return to normal once the baby is out. Father keeps insisting we have to try and be understanding and stay patient, yet I see in his eyes how close to the edge he is.

Hope is all we have, but according to Father, the baby is still a fair way from coming, and I'm not sure it's enough to get us through.

Back in my room, I throw the teddy on my bed and take down the birthday cards, ripping through each of them. Whatever memories they once presented have become another victim of this place, another little part of me plunged into darkness, the candle flames choked of air.

"Happy Birthday. Sweet sixteen."

I pick up my book again, but my mind won't let me leave this world, nor will the noises, loud and urgent moans emerging from the walls, the floor, the ceiling. This house is hurting, too, losing what fight it has, just like Father.

I'm not sure how much more we can take.

It occurs to me how long it's been since I last ate, but I can't face going back downstairs; instead, I open my bottom drawer and work through the remaining chocolate while perched on the end of my bed. Light fades quickly, ending my game with the clouds and conjuring ominous thoughts of another impromptu visit from Mother. The way she looked at me today, not like a mother at a child, or even how someone might scrutinise a stranger. No, there was evil in her eyes and malice in her smile.

Mother dearest.

What do I do? What can I do?

I turn my attention to the matted fur of the teddy, shaking off the excess dirt and running a finger over the marble-like eyes. Again, thoughts turn to what might have been going through the little girl's head as she shovelled the earth back over it. Perhaps if she went to the effort of burying it, she might have even said a few words. Maybe she was in too much of a hurry, knowing a storm was coming.

"You need a shower," I say, carrying the teddy to the bathroom.

Brown water flows down the plughole as I urgently work the old toothbrush through the fur, careful not to rip at the stitching. I even give it a squirt of lavender shampoo, lathering its makeshift hair as Mum used to for me sometimes. Alternating between scrubbing and holding the hairdryer over it, the teddy soon resembles something that was once cared for, not store quality by any means, but perhaps akin to something one might find in a charity store. I finish by giving it a squirt of the perfume Mum used to wear, its scent taking me back to happier times before this place buried her alive under layers of dust and misery.

"Come back to me, Mum."

Mother even smells like the place now, giving off a faint underlying dankness, like washing that has dried too quickly indoors. As the thought rushes through my head that I might smell the same, I urgently strip off, fumbling at the shower taps. The notion of the place claiming me in such a way has me scrubbing at my skin until it's red and raw, the water finally running too cold to bear.

"Boo," I whisper, noting the faint letters on the mirror as I wrap the towel around me. "That's what I'm going to call you," I mutter, picking up the teddy. Would that be okay, Iris?"

I wait for a while as if expecting an answer.

It's freezing on the landing, prompting a quick march towards my room, the towel wrapped tightly around Boo and me. I got rid of all my stuffed toys shortly before my fifteenth birthday and regretted it ever since, especially of late when such innocence might have helped shield me a little.

"Cold, isn't it, Boo?" I reach down to the storage space and grab a couple of the thickest blankets I can find. "We'll put extra layers on tonight and wrap up warm, yeah?"

Feels silly enough even holding a teddy at sixteen years of age, never mind talking to it, but there's nobody here to mock me or tell me I'm too old. Besides, my words help cut through the heaviness, temporarily dampening the relentless wails of the house, and Boo's replies, although in my head, carry some comfort.

Laid across the bed, we talk for some time, chew the fat, and shoot the shit, as Dad would say. Mainly about the old days, the good times, before this place stole the people we loved. Boo tells me all about Iris, how she used to love playing hide and sneak, jumping out on her friend Tom. They talk of her long red hair, how it smelt like apples and resembled a flame flickering in the wind. She and her friend Tom would laugh so hard they could hardly breathe or see through the tears.

In turn, I talk about my once best friend, Stacey, and how we'd save our school dinner money for the candy shop on our walk home. And how we'd always forget our sneakers so we could get out of playing netball. The crushes, the problems we spent hours discussing, all seem so minuscule today, but it temporarily lightens the air with childhood innocence. The conversation turns to my dad, a gushing monologue of praise and how I wished I never took him for granted at the time. We also talk about Mum. I tell Boo how she used to catch Dad winking at me when he was supposed to be scolding me and how mad it made her at the time, but how she chastised us about it later. I tell Boo about how we used to cuddle up for movie night and eat candy until we felt sick. I tell them how proud Mum used to be of my report card and how she drove me everywhere I wanted to go, even letting me listen to my playlist. And how she comforted me when our dog died. And how she'd spend hours on my hair and helping with my makeup.

Wrapped under several layers, we talk until my eyelids get heavy. "Goodnight, Boo." *Goodnight, Amy.* Such a silly thing, a pretend conversation with a teddy bear that was underground only hours ago. Yet, it has brought a wave of calm, temporarily starving my mind of badness and inducing exhaustion, even optimism that I might finally get a decent night's sleep.

But just as my eyes begin to close, my room lights up, thunder quickly following, the house offering a gentle rumble and disproportionate cry. Heaviness wraps around us, and the palpable charge grows stronger than ever.

Oh no.

The cries of the house are becoming more urgent, longer too, as if it's—dying.

"Oh, God, please, no."

It's here. The storm is here.

One hand gripping the blanket, the other gripping the teddy, I wince at each thunderclap, my back driving against the headboard. "Please go away. Please go away." But the sound of my own voice no longer offers comfort.

Another extended boom shakes the walls, subsequent lightning basking the canopy of trees in white. I see the clouds rolling towards us and hear the windows rattling, but there's not a single branch that moves.

Something bad is going to happen.

The storm is imminent, but I was praying the baby would come before it broke.

"I'm scared, Boo."

Eyes on the complete darkness beyond the window, the moon hidden tonight behind layers of cloud, I pull the blanket to my neck, wincing at each flash of light, folding my toes at the subsequent thunder crashes. Energy in the room continues to build until I can almost hear it fizz. It runs across my arms, legs, and chest until no part of me is untouched, my body a hypersensitive composition of nerve endings.

Please make it stop. Please.

Dad and I used to sit on the patio with a bowl of popcorn when a storm threatened. We'd cheer with each bolt of lightning, and if a particularly loud crack of thunder followed, we'd turn to each other, eyes wide and wearing half a smile. "It's just God farting," he'd say, even when I was too old to appreciate such cheesiness.

I'd give anything to hear him utter those words now.

As the window rattles more violently than ever, I bring Boo closer, inhaling the concoction of Mum's perfume and the lavender shampoo. Comfort is short-lived as lightning flickers, prompting an instant explosion that sends the floors trembling, the walls shaking, and even a sprinkling of dust across the blanket. Snapping my head up, I note the crack is at least an inch longer as more of the white powder rains down.

There's no place like home. There's no place like home.

I suddenly can't get it out of my head; the writing scrawled across the blackboard and Mother's face as she turned as mean as a yard dog. *Needy little cunt.*

Eyes shut, I try and conjure more happy memories to discuss with Boo, but the storm easily wins, accentuating the screams of the house and shutting down my thoughts. Instead, I pray again, pleading for mercy and release from this hell.

Tap. Tap. Tap.

Even beyond the symphony of creaks and rattles, it's unmistakable.

Tap. Tap. Tap.

I dare not open my eyes. *Oh, God. Oh, Christ.*

What if it's Mother? What if she's here to discipline me in a way Father couldn't?

Tap. Tap. Tap.

With the blanket to my nose, heart pounding, it's all I can do not to cry out. But I already know Father will be asleep, clutching his tumbler, and Mother would likely revel in such a declaration of suffering.

Tap. Tap. Tap.

Half expecting to see her at the window wearing her scowl, I slowly unscrew my eyes, still gripping the blanket so hard my fingers ache. Only darkness greets me initially until a series of flashes illuminate the three letters scratched across the window.

B-o-o.

My first thought is that I might have written it, just like in the bathroom, using the word like a shield to protect me. A silly name for a pretend furry guardian, but also an utterance of fun between Tom and the girl who used to live here.

The theory collapses as lightning flashes again, bringing an instant explosion of thunder. The letters are backwards. No, not backwards, mirrored as if—

No. That can't be, can't be real. But you've seen leaves in the shape of a girl, heard her voice carry on the wind.

My brain has stopped protecting me, another series of flickers basking the house in white and highlighting the writing on the *outside* of the glass as plain as day.

"Iris?"

Waiting for the next series of taps, I hold my breath, my stomach groaning along with the house. I'm unsure what I expect as I squeeze down on Boo, feeling the iciness through the rattling window.

But no more tapping comes.

Do you ever sense her? Thought I saw her in the bedroom window once.

What does she want with me? Aren't I suffering enough?

Thoughts turn to the wooded area and how she saved me from the falling branch. Maybe she's a friend? Tom said she was 'as nice as pie,' and God knows I need someone I can trust. '*Crazy, too.*' But I was talking to a teddy a few minutes ago, so what does that make me?

A combination of nerves and to force down the air's thickness, I swallow hard. "Iris?"

In reply, nothing but incessant thunder and lightning and the now more high-pitched, human-like screams of the house. Waiting for further tapping at the glass or the draught to carry her words, I screw my eyes half-shut and squeeze down harder on Boo.

Still nothing.

What happened to you, Iris?

And my heart sinks at the thought of the sad little makeshift grave for the teddy marked by the two lolly sticks. The only thing she had left to care for, and I even had to deny her that by digging it up. Still, she helped me, saving me from the falling branch.

This place is no good. Leave!

My brain abandoning all logical thought, I shuffle to the edge of the bed, goosebumps lighting up my arms, legs feeling as heavy as logs as I force myself to my feet.

Am I really going to do this?

Eyes on the distant canopy, I see a lightning bolt strike within the cluster of trees, feeling the almost instantaneous rumble in the floorboards beneath my feet. I'm unsure if I can; I don't know if my legs have the strength.

She saved your life, Amy, and you desecrated her teddy's grave. You owe her this, at least.

Inhaling deeply, I slowly make my way towards the window, flinching at each lightning bolt, the energy intensifying with each small step. I feel fear crawling across me, swarming my skin, arousing every hair on my body. A mixture of petrichor and rot fill my nostrils.

Please let it end. Please!

Just a couple of feet from the window, I reach over and slide it up, ready at any second to run back to the bed and bring the blankets over my head. Like a wave of cold water, the wind wraps around me, accelerating the fear that relentlessly explores my skin and guts.

Oh, God. Oh, God.

And with my teeth biting into my lip, I raise the teddy towards the darkness. "I'm sorry, Iris, I shouldn't have—"

A muted cry leaves my lips as a flash of lightning momentarily exposes the pale hand that wraps around Boo's arm. Freckles, so many freckles. And such a strong smell of apples, too. Every part of me wants to run, but I hold my ground, feeling the tension on the end of my arm as it once again extends only into darkness.

"Iris?"

Lightning strikes, this time giving me a snapshot of her face, red hair spread over her shoulders, green eyes bright but sad, and I've seen that type of half-smile before. But how can she muster sympathy after everything she's been through? And what does she know?

Into the darkness again, I issue my plea, "Iris, what do I do?"

Staring past teddy, I wait for the next flicker, hoping she might somehow be the key to ending all this misery. God knows I've tried, but this place has a tight hold and won't let go. "Iris, please, I—"

Coldness snaps around my wrist as more flashes of stark white light accentuate the paleness of her fingers against my skin. Her touch sends shivers down my spine, but worst of all are the scenes that flood my mind. At her mother's side, fingers locked around each other's as the shadow of a woman took her last breaths. I feel her pain deep within, feel her loneliness. Pleading to a father for help, only for him to turn to the bottle for therapy. A rare type of cancer affecting cells left behind from pregnancy finally won its war, but even when the woman died, cancer continued to spread, kept alive by grief and resentment. And then it was the husband's turn—paranoia, hate, blame, growing inside him like a tumour, turning a good man sour. Innocence was her shield, but not for long.

THUNDER CRASHES, FOLLOWED BY MORE LIGHTNING. I SEE HER HIDING in the storage space. I see her crying at the end of her bed. I see her running through the woods, away from a man wearing a snarl and carrying an almost empty bottle in his right hand. "It's your fault she's dead," he cries. "You killed her!" The sickly-sweet waft of rotten apples carries on the breeze as the girl with red hair launches herself from my bedroom window.

Darkness falls, tension still at the end of my arm, my heart pounding. The breeze wraps around me, carrying the sound of tears. Sadness twists ay my stomach. I feel for myself, but mostly for her, what she must have endured, how desperate she must have been. "Iris, I'm so sorry you had to go through—"

Lightning flickers again, exposing wide green eyes looking over my shoulder and a mouth forming a scream. Before the house offers its accompanying cry, I feel a hand clasp around my shoulder, and I'm only just able to whip my arm away before the window comes crashing down, teddy no longer in my grip.

Blood whooshing in my ears, I let out a garbled cry, launching myself back on the bed and bringing the blankets over my head. To a now eerie silence, I curl myself as small as possible, sure as hell at any moment I will feel Frank's touch again.

Seconds pass.

Not even a hint of wind or the slightest rumble of thunder.

Has the storm passed? Perhaps it's cleared the air. Maybe it —*clutching at straws, Amy, clutching at straws.*

Three.

Two.

One.

As I finally poke my head over the top of the blanket, it's the shadowy brim of the hat I see. Ducking my head straight under again and curling up like a fetus, I wish the bed would swallow me.

Go away. Go away!

Bringing my knees even tighter into my chest, I clench my fists, suddenly feeling silly for thinking it over.

Please go away. Please leave us.

But the stench of whisky and cheap aftershave is seeping through the covers. And as the gruff voice emerges, I feel Frank's hot breath against my cheek. "There's no place like home."

Unable to hold onto a scream, I bury my head into softness and bring my hands to my ears. Without even the luxury of being able to put things down to a bad dream or my mind playing tricks, I feel certain things will never be normal again. Limbs singing in agony, I listen, for something, anything, and I'm not sure how much time goes by before I finally emerge from the blankets again, no sign of the hat or the storm that had shaken the house's walls only moments ago.

Still, I take shallow breaths and continue to listen. For footsteps outside the door, for the familiar cries of the house. I continue looking, too, searching the shadows of my room and beyond the word scratched into my window. Drowsiness comes in waves, and I let my eyelids shut for only seconds at a time until they become too heavy to lift.

THURSDAY

AFTER MANY MORE HOURS AWAKE THAN ASLEEP, AND AT ONE TIME, sure I see the shadow-man in the corner of my room; I finally push myself from the bed. It's just before seven, the red sky outside painting my room with softness but offering little comfort at this stage. And I don't know how to feel at the sight of Father's truck in the driveway.

The house is as still as can be, not a murmur from its walls.

"Mother?"

Between patches of dirt on the glass, I follow her as she walks across the gravel, pausing to smell one of the yellow roses before continuing along the driveway.

Hope.

She's out of that chair, and—wait, her belly—it's gone! Early, but still.

And is she—yes, she's smiling.

Could it be over, the storm simply clearing the air?

Slipping a dress over my shoulders, a wave of giddiness sweeps across me as I imagine Father downstairs cradling the baby in his arms. A little brother or sister. Things can return to normal, and we can be a proper family again!

Bringing my nose to the glass, just above the scratched letters, I bite down hard on the inside of my lip, unable to prevent a tear. I feel awful, but I hated *it* when it was inside her. Now the baby's out, and I can't wait to—

I watch Mother reaching for the large axe leaning against the woodpile.

My chest tightens.

She turns, her squinting eyes finding my bedroom window, a dark stain running the full length of her dress. Her smile widens, but it isn't really a smile. Trailing the axe behind her, cutting a narrow path through the gravel, Mother begins a slow walk back to the house, eyes remaining fixed on my window.

Oh no. No. No. No.

"Dad!"

Legs leaden, blood pulsating in my ears, I freeze. I can't think, can't breathe. As the room begins to spin, I reach for the bed, just managing to save myself from going down. "Dad!"

I hear the front door.

Now I hear the axe scraping across the wooden floor.

"Dad, where are you?"

Now the clunk of each step as she ascends the stairs.

"Amy, dear," Mother sings, the first time she's used my name for weeks. And the humming begins, and the walls around resume their cries. "You have a sister."

Panicking, I rush to the window and prise it open, but I already know it's too far down, my mind conjuring more images of Iris's twisted limbs.

Clunk. Clunk.

What do I do? What do I do?

Tap-tap-tap on my door.

I drop to the ground and crawl towards the storage space in the far wall, yanking open the door and quietly shutting it behind me. With my neck bent to avoid the ceiling, I scramble over textbooks and board games we used to play, sliding myself as far into the dark recess as possible, finally nestling into the hiding place Iris showed me before.

Tap. Tap. Tap. Just to make me suffer.

As I continue pushing back, trying to disappear into the darkness, my hand brushes against something hard. Fingers searching the floor, I wrap my hand around smoothness and bring the object towards my face. A doll. Wooden. Not mine. And to my right, I can just make out the word *Iris* scribbled into the wall.

"Ready or not." My bedroom door opens.

I can feel Iris beside me, shaking, biting her lip to stop her tears. What must he have done to make her jump? How terrified she must have been.

Whispering beyond the cupboard door has me holding my breath, trying to listen in, the smell of whisky telling me she isn't talking to herself.

"I think I know where you are, Amy."

I hold my breath and pray some more.

"Amy, come on out, and we can be a family again. We can bake muffins, and after that, I can brush your hair." The laughter that follows chills my soul. "And you can meet your new daddy, too."

I hear the axe clatter to the ground and the click of the door.

Every part of me wants to scream as her hand begins searching the darkness. Still, somehow, I remain quiet, imagining myself locking fingers with Iris for solidarity, Boo nestled somewhere between us. Shivering and cowering, I dare not move, dare not breathe, but as Mother's fingers finally wrap around my ankle, I finally attempt a scream but only find a croak.

MY HEAD HITS THE FLOOR AS SHE DRAGS ME OUT, HER HUMMING occasionally interrupted with more whispering.

"No, Mother. Please," is all I can manage, clawing at the ground and kicking out.

As one of the blows catches her arm, she releases her grip, and I take my chance, scrambling to my feet and making my run across the landing.

"Darling, where are you going?"

The haunting screams of the house surround me, made worse by the sound of the axe once again dragging across the floor.

"Mother knows best."

All the curtains and shutters are closed, yet still, from the top of the staircase, I see Father's legs sticking out of the fireplace and the knife embedded in his lower back. "Dad!" Grabbing the handrail, I swing myself down the first few steps, but my legs can't keep up, finally caving beneath me, momentum sending me tumbling down into an explosion of pain and white light.

Can't see, can't move.

Clunk.

The ringing in my ears begins to subside, but the axe continues scraping across my brain. I turn to Father—Dad—to see his flesh smouldering, the black and red chequered shirt I bought for his birthday last year melding to his skin. The smell is overbearing, churning my stomach, but I force myself to my feet and stagger to his side.

Clunk. Clunk. Clunk.

Trying not to gag, the taste of blood and charred flesh at the back of my mouth, I wrestle the knife from his back and heave him away from the tiny flames.

Unrecognisable.

Unforgettable.

Dad.

Clunk. Clunk.

Four steps to go, Mother's stare burns into me, her eyebrows furrowed, her lips curled. Deep groans from the walls feed through to my bones as I back away towards the kitchen archway, praying for my legs to keep working this time.

Clunk. Clunk.

Finally, I turn, ready to make my run towards the back door, but adjacent to the kitchen table, I see the baby sitting in a yellowing highchair, head lolloped to one side, food smeared across its deep purple lips and grey chest. *You have a sister.*

Clunk.

The kitchen begins to spin.

"I don't know what's wrong with her," Mother says from behind. "She won't eat."

Clunk.

My legs finally freeze, and worse than ever, the house's groans begin riding up and down my spine, exploding in my head with ever-increasing ferocity.

"Been like that since she came out," Mother says from the archway. "Iris, that's her name. Frank chose it, but I rather like it, don't you?"

"Momma, please." *Momma?* Certainly not Mum, but I have to believe there's someone else in there other than Mother.

"You and your father did this; I know it. Frank told me so."

As Mother approaches, hauling the axe behind her, my mind continues to fog. She killed him. She killed my dad.

"Conspiring. Up to no good. Always as thick as thieves, you two were."

"Momma, no. I—"

But the vacancy in her eyes lets me know I would be wasting my words. Snapping my head towards the door, I see the shadow-man, Frank, standing guard and running his fingers across the brim of his hat, blackness spreading across the walls on either side just like it did at my made-up birthday party.

"Thick as thieves," Mother mutters as she begins her approach.

With no choice, I run towards the door and yank down on the handle, but it doesn't budge. Offering a high-pitched cry, I try again and again until my fingers sing with pain. "Momma, stop!"

But there's a wildness in her narrowed eyes beyond that of sheer contempt. "There's no place like home. There's no place like home."

Feeling like my head might explode, I leave the door and reach for the knife block on the counter, pulling out the one with the biggest handle. The blade trembles as I hold it towards her, the house now approaching an orchestral crescendo.

Nodding her head and offering more whisperings, Mother continues her approach, teeth gritted, axe exaggerating the uneven-ness of the floor. "Frank says we can try again, but we need to get rid of the poison first."

"Momma, it's this place, it's—"

"Shut up. Just shut up!" She kicks a chair out of the way and begins lifting the axe. "You'll be with daddy soon. Peas in a pod."

As tears fill my eyes, I make my run, but she shoves the table across, blocking my path. "Momma!" A stand-off ensues, her wielding the axe and me weakly waving the blade in front. She snarls and lurches forward, and I retreat towards the blackening wall, finally finding a scream.

"Frank says you haven't got it in you," Mother says. "Nothing but a whiney little bitch. Daddy's girl."

"Momma, stop!" But the axe is already at her shoulders. "Momma, pl—"

She swings it towards me with a roar. I squeal, throwing myself to the right, just managing to avoid the blade as it sinks into the plasterboard with an undramatic thud. Mother growls, pulling at the axe, and I take my chance, but she snatches at my dress before I can mount the table.

"Come here, you whiny little bitch!"

Eyes frenzied, nostrils flaring, the veins in her neck pop as she continues wrestling with the axe. This woman stopped behaving like Mum long ago, but at least there was a resemblance. Now, I see an unrecognisable face contorted with hate and rage, made worse by the blood running down her lip. "Peas in a pod," she says again through gritted pink teeth.

The house screams, walls shake, and dust particles rain down from the ceiling.

I desperately try and drag myself free, but her bony fingers remain clamped around the fabric while the other hand begins working the blade free.

"Let go, Momma, please."

"Peas in a pod. Peas in a pod. PEAS IN A MOTHER-FUCKING POD!"

As the steel head of the axe drops to the wooden floor among a flurry of white powder, Mother turns to me and smiles, nothing in her eyes but evil as she begins lifting it again.

My grip on the knife tightens as the house offers another bellyache.

I suddenly feel weak. Worthless. *I can't do this. I can't do this.* Nobody would miss me anyway. No friends, no parents, nothing to—

"Amy!"

Tom? Snapping my head towards the loud thump, I see his dirty face pressed against the shadowy glass. "Do it, Amy. Do it," he yells, struggling against the handle.

With my eyes screwed half-shut, I turn to Mother and thrust the knife in front. But skin is tougher than I ever expected, and the blade only grazes her chest.

Mother's smile widens, breaking her reddened face in two. Her arms tremble as they hold the axe high. "I never loved you. Always were a spineless little fuck."

More thumping from behind. "Do it for Iris, Amy!"

And thinking of Dad, poor Iris, and the thing in front of me that stole my mum, I snatch the handle back and let out a scream, bringing the blade into Mother's neck with as much force as I can muster. Her eyes grow wide, and the axe drops behind her with an impossibly loud clatter.

Dropping to my knees, I watch as she staggers back, hands to her throat, blood spilling through her fingers. She slides to the floor as her back hits the kitchen counter, offering a series of desperate watery gurgles.

"The door," Tom cries from behind as I feel the slightest draught against my neck. "Help me with the door!"

But my eyes are still on the woman I once called Mum, watching the blood pooling around her and her twitching legs. A hand still to her throat, she tries to say something, but the words never make it out, only a final drawn-out and laboured breath as her eyes offer a flicker of the woman I once knew.

I'm sorry, Momma.

Behind, I hear the door finally give, a blanket of cool air wrapping around my back.

"Thank God, Amy," Tom says, wrapping his cold fingers around my wrist. "I tried to get here as fast as I could."

And over the familiar but shriller screams of the house and Tom's relentless apologies, a guttural and blood-curdling howl surrounds us, raising the hairs on my arms and neck. I follow the blackness on the walls as it recedes towards *Frank*, who slowly but surely fades to nothing, but not before removing his hat and holding it to his chest.

"Amy, let's go."

I turn to face the boy, the guilt in his glistening eyes enough to make me collapse into his skinny arms and begin to sob. We stay like that for a while, Tom awkwardly patting me on the back as he tells me without any conviction that everything will be okay. "Please. Let's get out of here," he finally whispers.

As we enter brightness, I take a deep breath, inhaling nothing but freshness and feeling it already displacing the poison. Even the taste at the back of my throat is no longer as potent. Perhaps one day, it might fade altogether, but I doubt it.

I can see in his eyes Tom has so many questions, but for now, he lets us walk in silence towards the trees. It's too soon to process grief, but I do know a part of me has died and that I'll forever be mourning. Still, having lived under the shadow of this place for far too long, all I can think about right now is getting as far away as possible.

"My parents will know what to do," Tom finally says. "Ah shit, I'm sorry. I didn't mean—"

"It's okay, Tom. It's okay. How did you know? To come, I mean."

"Strangest thing," he replies. "Opened the door this morning and heard her voice on the breeze. So faint, but she sounded scared, and I knew she wanted me to come looking."

As I walk past Father's—*Dad's*—truck, eyeing the blackened rose petals on the ground, my stomach knots. It tightens further as I turn my stare towards the barn, almost expecting to see Mother still rocking in that chair. It's Frank's silhouette I see, though, hanging from the roof, gently swaying like a silent wind chime.

"Tom," I say, reaching for the boy's hand.

"Yeah?"

"Thank you."

"No problem. But I got here late," he says, offering a shrug. "Didn't really do anything."

"You did, Tom. More than you'll ever know."

After walking in silence some more, curiosity finally gets the better of my new friend. "Did you see her?" he asks, the guilt evident in his voice. "Iris?"

I nod. "She said to say hi."

Somehow the cancer that took Iris's Mum lived on in that house, surviving on Frank and Iris's misery, spreading like mould, living in the walls, the floors, the trees, and the air they breathed. And then it got inside our heads, especially Momma's. Even her belly, too.

Frank says we can try again, but we need to get rid of the poison first.

With every step, grief starts to hit, but there's also a guilty pang of undeniable relief. Finally, I'm getting away from the claustro-phobic dankness and the threat of danger.

My future? Only one thing's for sure—*that place will live inside me* for the rest of my life.

"Are you going to be okay?" Tom asks.

"I don't think so."

Nearing the wooded area, I lift my gaze to see the shape of the little girl next to the tree where she buried Boo. Before I can alert Tom, the breeze displaces the leaves, carrying them to rest on the ground.

Thank you, Iris. I hope one day you can find some peace.

It takes a while to summon the courage to look back over my shoulder. "Goodbye, Momma. Goodbye, Poppa," is all I can think to say before I finally crumple to the ground.

MUSIC MAN

EVEN I KNOW he isn't quite in tune, but the old man with the discoloured beard sings as though his life depends on it. Eyes screwed tightly shut, head bopping up and down, he taps his worn-out shoes against the pavement ahead.

"He's not going to do it," Harry blurts. "Nothing but fresh air between those legs."

"I am! I'm just waiting for the right time, okay?" The last word comes out as a croak.

"Or perhaps a vagina," Harry mumbles.

Dad always says never give in to peer pressure, but I'm not sure he ever experienced what it's like to be the new kid in school, sitting in a crowded and noisy dining hall, but feeling like the loneliest person in the world.

"The man's blind, Tom," Sam says. "Look at the white cane leaning against the store window. You could stand in front of him butt naked and gyrating, meat stick slapping against your thighs, and he'd never know."

I turn my attention back to yellow beard, his matching fingers strumming at the old guitar. "What's the point then?"

"Because we're bored, and it's your turn!" Harry spits impatiently. "But if you're too fucking chicken!"

My dad doesn't like Harry, and neither do I, but "Beggars can't be choosers," as Mum would say. Sam took me under his wing, which made his tag-along, Harry, all kinds of bitter.

"It doesn't feel right, though," I utter as the man launches into a new tune.

Too many times, I've walked this ashen plaaaaace

"For fuck's sake, Tom, it's just a coin!" Sam spits. "We're not asking you to kneel down and choke his rooster."

Dreaming of sand, the sun on my faaaaace

"He won't do it," Harry says.

But death hangs in the barren air

My skin prickles a warning as I snap my head from left to right. Some adults are wrapped up in awkward chit chat, others are stuffing their car with the week's groceries, but it suddenly seems much busier than before. This is pure wrong, and I know it.

Carried on waves that haunt this lair

My heart pounds against my chest, building tension and importance. *Shit.* I watch the huddle of people through the entrance as the doors slowly close behind them to the sound of the screaming guitar.

"Now!" Sam commands.

Unclenching my hands, I make my move towards the open case.

But I carry on down this rooooaaaaaad

The slap of my sneakers against the ground seems impossibly loud, but the guy is lost in his song and pays me no attention. I'm just another shopper, no change to spare, increasing their urgency on the way past.

Singing my worthless songs of madness

Glancing urgently over my shoulder, praying for a reason not to do it, I only see Sam and Harry looking my way, teeth gritted together and nodding in accidental synchronisation to the current guitar riff. Everyone else appears oblivious to the man's wailings.

Oh yeah, I'll carry on. I'll carry ooooon

I swoop down, my eyes drawn to the shiniest coin in the guitar case. But I can't get hold of it. Chewed nails down to the skin offer no leverage, and all I'm doing is chasing it around the stiff purple velvet. The smell of stale tobacco permeates the air so strongly that it almost forces a cough.

Cuz hope is my melody, my way out of darkness

Someone else pulls into the car park. It has to be now. Finally, I pinch the coin a few inches above the case, fingers trembling, half-expecting it to fall or for a bony hand to clamp across my shoulder. But he's lost in a different world, putting on the performance of his life.

The slam of a car door prompts me into action, and I snap my hand away and slide the coin into my pocket, screwing my face up as I make a run towards my new friends. I'm convinced someone saw the whole thing, expecting at any second to hear calls of "Thief!" but I'm almost home and dry. Ahead, Sam offers a thumbs up, and Harry a scowl of disappointment.

Made it!

Although I can't contain the smile of relief, I hear my father's warnings of following the crowd. There's an accompanying twist in my gut, and a sharp sting in my pocket adds further weight to his words.

"You're one of us now, Tom," Sam says, but his voice is distant, wrapped in layers of guilt and notes from that guitar that are suddenly so loud in my head.

"You okay, mate? You look a little shaky," Harry says, lips curled into his familiar sneer.

I offer a quick nod, but I don't feel okay. Not at all. The tarmac below no longer feels solid, and the world is beginning to spin. Fast.

This is why I sing the bluuuuues

The man's voice carries a gravelly coarseness that reverberates painfully up and down my spine. An accompanying searing pain in my thigh continues to remind me of the coin's presence, but it's the least of my worries now.

"Tom!" Sam's tinny voice floats across over the impossibly loud guitar.

To see her face, I'll pay my duuuuues

Words rattle in my head until each one brands itself painfully into my brain. Chords screech, building towards an ear-bleeding crescendo.

Sam mouths my name, but I hear nothing above the man's gravelly and desolate voice.

The chances are slim; I can't denyyyyy

All I can hear and all I can think about are the words that fill my head. It's too much.

Still, there's nothing left to do but tryyyyy

Like a lonely groupie, I begin swaying back and forth.

Going to—

Eyes screwed tightly shut-in anticipation; I feel only slight discomfort on my back. I remain perfectly still, wary that perhaps I'm in shock, and at any moment, nerve endings will begin to scream.

The music stops. Something else in the background, now. What is that? The ocean? Am I unconscious, dreaming perhaps? It would explain the lack of pain.

As I open my eyes to no looming faces of concerns, something crunching beneath my palm. Dread consumes me.

This place is—ashen.

Tears come without warning, my head swamped with flashbacks of breakfast this morning—Mum ribbing Dad about putting empty cereal boxes back in the cupboard and not putting the lid back on the margarine.

This isn't a dream; it's because I took that goddamned coin!

Like a child, I drag my knees towards my chin, curling into a ball and wishing nothing more than to be back at the breakfast table. I take in my surroundings, rocking back and forth, feeling even lonelier than the kid in the dinner hall picking at his lunch. Above me, the sky is a montage of swirling grey, and on either side of me, waves of red curl on top of one another and crash back into the bubbling crimson sea with enormous ferocity. Ahead and behind is an endless landscape of black rock and ash.

And that smell.

"Hello," I croak.

Nothing.

I push myself up, dusting the blackness from my pants. "Hello."

One foot in front of the other, I tentatively head in the direction I'm facing, every so often glancing around at my blackened footprints, trying to ignore the lump in my throat and the now-familiar pressure behind my eyes.

So bleak.

"But I carry on down this road." My voice croaks with grief, but the distraction helps stem further tears. "Singing my worthless songs of madness."

I should have listened, shouldn't have caved to peer pressure.

"Oh, yeah, I'll carry on." *Dad.* "I'll carry on."

A solitary tear rolls down my right cheek.

"Cuz *hope is my melody, my way out of this darkness.*"

Heavy with hopelessness, my legs buckle in resignation, but I force myself onwards.

"This is why I sing the blues."

I didn't even say goodbye to Mum when I left the house this morning.

"To see her face, I'll pay my dues."

In the distance, I hear a guitar playing me into the next line.

"The chances are slim; I can't deny."

It's him, the music man! Each chord played exactly as I remember it, as though I could ever forget.

"Still, there's nothing left to do but try."

With each footstep, each word, the music draws closer until it abruptly stops, and only the sounds of crashing waves remain. The man steps out from behind a black rock, one arm wrapped around the guitar, the other waving me towards him, as though he can—

"We see down here," he shouts. "Not that there's much to see; that's the cruelty of it."

"Am I dead?" I utter, not really wanting an answer.

"Not quite," he replies, "but as good as, I suppose. Your heart still pumps, but he owns your soul now—bought it with that silver coin you plucked from my case."

"I want to go home." I won't cry again. I won't. "I didn't mean to take the coin; it was just a stupid bet."

The man nods. "I know, son, I know, but it's not as easy as that."

"Tell me what's happening," I croak. "Please!"

Music man rests his guitar against the rock and lets out a sigh. "He loves his music; loves the blues. Been playing for him for nigh on five years, and he still won't let me back, figures I've still got my best performance in me."

"I—I don't understand."

"Do you play guitar, kid? Sing?"

"No."

"Neither did I, but you will. If you're lucky, that is. He's looking for that one performance, you see—the perfect combination of lyrics and emotion—the one that brings him to his knees, makes him feel what it's like to be—human. If only for a moment. Do that, and he'll send you back home. No catch."

"But you look like you're really trying, singing your heart out? And you say that you've been here—"

"Almost five years, yeah. I don't know what he's looking for, to tell you the truth, but he saw potential in me, and I'll never stop trying. I want it for myself now, a slave to the music as much as to him."

"What if I won't? What if I can't?" My heart is racing, legs heavy with fear.

"The moment he suspects you stop playing for your life is when it all ends. Up there, your heart will stop, and down here, your soul will be tossed into the dead sea, and you'll burn for eternity and feel every minute of it." He tucks a finger into his threadbare scarf as though it's suddenly too tight. "Any more questions?"

My mind races, skin prickling with anxiety and fear. "How do we get up there?"

MUSIC MAN | 111

"He opens the door when it's time, but don't get too excited, kid. We don't get to play on home soil, and he only lets us up there to remind us of what we're missing, giving us hope and the will to become better. Sometimes to recruit." The man takes a few steps towards the furious sea, tapping his fingers against his thigh. "As I said, we're blind up there, but it's better than nothing. The smell of a hot dog, the feel of the breeze on your face. Besides, he figures it makes us play better—forced to draw from memories and fewer distractions."

"But I told you; I can't play the guitar, can't sing."

"I can teach you all that down here. You just gotta hope he sees a spark in you."

The smell of death gets undoubtedly stronger. Waves begin to crash with further ferocity, small globs of fizzing violence landing only a few feet away from us. "He's coming," the man whispers, shifting from one foot to the next. "Just adrenaline, kid. You'll learn how to use the fear."

"What now?"

"Your first audition."

"But I don't know the words to any songs!"

"Yes, you do."

Cuz hope is my melody, my way out of this darkness. "I can't do this," I croak. "I can't."

"You don't have a choice unless you fancy an afternoon swim in the heated pool. I'll play you in after four, okay?" He picks up the guitar and starts tapping his shabby shoes on the crusty blackened surface.

Not a drop of saliva in my throat. I can't get any air in.

A tail emerges out of the raging sea, whipping over our heads by inches and snapping back just as quickly into the impetuous redness.

Heart pounding, skin tightening, I look to the man for help, but he's already lost, swaying his head from side to side, skin a mass of emotive wrinkles as his fingers pluck at the strings.

"Sing as though your life depends on it, kid," he whispers. "One —two—three—"

Only a garbled rasp emerges as I open my mouth. Blood pounds relentlessly in my ears, and I can no longer hear the notes of the guitar. Music man turns to me and nods, eyes wide and full of urgency. He mouths something, but I hear nothing above the thumping bass of my own blood.

My legs buckle. I feel sick.

The tail emerges from the sea once more, twitching above the froth.

Music man's eyes grow wider still, but I have nothing. I can't breathe. I want to go home! With tears streaming down my cheeks, warmth spilling down my thigh, I watch the tail begin to whip back.

I look to the man with the guitar one last time, noting the solitary tear that rolls down his right cheek. He offers me a smile and—

BUCKET OF CHICKEN

He FEELS the next wave of burning discomfort making its way, the heavy patter of rain on the roof providing little distraction.

It had started to rain that night, too.

12.04 am—one hell of a shift. Just over fourteen hours and the last few made more arduous with light-trapping saturated roads causing all sorts of trickery on tired eyes. He grabs the eyedrops from the glove box and squeezes the solution into the corner of his left eye, using the rear-view mirror for guidance. Some of it splashes across the bridge of his nose as a thud on the metal of the car startles him. "Caw!"

The bird is enormous. "Caw!" it screams again.

"Feathery fuck! Scared the living daylights out of me!" he yells back, slamming his fist against the windshield. "Piss off."

The crow scratches its claws against the bonnet, finally merging into the blackness with a defiant cry.

"Fucking bird," he mumbles. "Fucking day." So many impolite customers and not one goddamn tip.

Blinking away the residual moisture, he falls back into the head-rest with a groan.

Can't even enjoy his fried chicken, chest all knotted up, bubbles of acid erupting at the back of his throat. He winds down the window halfway and swallows some comforting night air, but the lingering burn prompts him to pop another antacid in his mouth and angrily crunch down.

Fucking reflux!

This place is his sanctuary, his escape, but its relentless onslaught won't let him enjoy it tonight. It's getting worse, no doubt. Fourteen hours in the same seat is taking its toll on the rest of his aching body, too. He stretches his tingling fingers against the rim of the steering wheel as a series of harsh crackles interrupt the song on the radio. Another gust wraps around the car, increasing the tempo of the swing that moans on rusty hinges in the centre of the nearby park. He lets out a shudder, quickly winding up the window, maintaining his gaze on the playground until another trail of lava begins working its way along his oesophagus. Taking a deep breath, he closes his eyes and rides it out. He tries to reimagine the sounds and the smells of that pre-rain summer evening, but the show's off today—no let-up from the goddamn acid party in his stomach. *Fuck!*

Crunching down on another tablet, he dips his chubby hand into the bucket again and lifts the last colourless piece to his mouth. *Fuck's sake!* There isn't even any chicken in this one, just air surrounded by fat. He swallows it anyway, wiping his greasy fingers across a mound of fabric-covered gut and popping in another two antacids.

As thoughts turn to a beer and the comfort of soft sheets, he collects the substantial wrappers and soda cans from the passenger seat, almost half-filling the bucket. Bracing himself for the blast of cold, he swings open the car door, grimacing against the ever-increasing tightness in his chest as he hobbles across to the wheelie bin to dump the rubbish. He takes another look at the moaning swing. "Storm's brewing, kid," he mutters. An icy wind cuts through him, creating urgency to get back to the relative warmth of the car.

The fuck?

Another shudder rattles down his spine as he eyes the silhouette of the hat through the car window, acid fizzing at the back of his slightly ajar mouth. Cold rain running down his back, he arches his neck to try and get a better view of the asshole in the back seat that's just stepped into his off-duty taxi. As if the night couldn't get any worse.

"I'm off duty," he mutters into darkness.

More than a little peeved, Tony opens the rear door and leans in to observe the smartly dressed man, blue pin-striped suit, impossibly white teeth exposed in the broadest smile. He also notices the perfectly manicured fingers holding the cane and the notes crudely stuffed into the suit jacket pocket. His first thought is pimp, but the ones he's been used to running around are a million miles away from the well-dressed man sitting in the back of his cab.

"I'm sorry, mate; I've finished. I'm going home."

"Yes, you are. But this won't take long." The man reaches towards his pocket and brings out a handful of hundred-dollar bills. "More when you get there."

Tony studies the man's clear blue eyes, and even though some of the notes are stained with what he guesses to be blood, he already knows he's going to give the guy his ride. Countless drug runs, contract work for the shadiest people in town, and here sits the cleanest cut person he's seen all night offering him a stack of cash. It won't be the first time he's accepted tainted notes and likely not the last.

"Where are you heading?"

"Drive for now. I'll tell you when we get there."

"Tell me when we get there," Tony grumbles quietly under his breath as he steps back into the driver's seat. "Direction, at least?"

"South, away from the city."

Tony starts the engine, alternating his glance between the mirror and the glistening road. They drive in silence for a while.

"I knew I'd find you here," the man eventually mutters matter-of-factly.

"What do you mean?"

"I've seen you here before. Day, night, in between."

Tony nervously shuffles in his seat. "You been out on the town? I mean, all dressed up and that."

"You have to make an effort. I mean, one can't just drive around town eating fried chicken all night, can one?"

Tony eyes him in the mirror but refuses to bite. "Not carried you before, have I?"

"No. Never more than once."

Tony exhales slowly, another wave of acid terminating in his throat, bringing a feeling of constriction with it. The prickling in his fingers is getting worse, too, and once again, he presses them against the wheel until they're almost white.

"What's your business in town?" Tony asks, keen to break the silence inexplicably making his skin crawl. He's had all sorts in the back of his cab, but there's something about this one.

"I'm here for pleasure," the man replies.

That smell?

Tony eyes the passenger bringing a lit cigar to his lips, but he swears he never heard the ignition of a lighter or the strike of a match. He thinks about saying something, but the man's paying good money, so he lets it pass. And something tells him he might need to stay on the right side of this one.

"When did you quit, Tony?"

"What? Oh, how did you—"

"Fingers."

"Yeah, okay. Just under two years ago."

"Why?"

"Health reasons."

"That's a lot of chickens."

"Rough night out there," Tony says, switching to autopilot as he deals with the fire rushing through his body.

The man lifts his arm, tilting his gold watch but paying it no heed. "I don't think we have enough time for small talk, Tony."

Tony grabs the half-empty packet of antacids and fingers three urgently into his mouth. Hairs standing on the back of his neck, he senses an oppressive heaviness in the air, just like before a big storm hits, but instead of filling him with excitement like it did *that* day, his body begins to cramp with ominous dread.

Goddamn creatures of the night.

Glancing at the rear-view mirror, he finds the man's smile again, now appearing more sinister than warm. It strikes him too; the guy's suit and hat are as dry as a bone. His heart issues a warning, increasing in pace, accompanied by a sharp tightening.

"May I ask what that is for," the man says, poking his cane between the headrests. "I'm referring to the cross that hangs so crudely from the mirror next to the action figure."

"It was my mother's. She gave it to me when she died."

"Helps with tips, I guess—if people think you are a man of God."

"I am a man of God. I've not missed Sunday church for months. Made a promise to Mum."

Worse than the last, another wave of burning pain rushes through him but unaccompanied by sourness this time. He grips the edge of the seat, pushing his fingers deep into the fabric and biting down hard on his lip. Finally, it passes, leaving a residual ache spanning his entire body.

"Take another tablet if you like, but it won't help, Tony. What made you look for him?"

"How far is it?"

"Not far now. What made you look? For God." The man's hand comes to rest on his shoulder, sending a searing heat down his left side. Crystal blue eyes in the mirror pierce through the otherwise darkness like a set of hypnotic headlights. He doesn't know the man from Adam, but there's a strange compulsion to—

"Forgiveness," he utters, tearing his gaze back to the blur, a bead of sweat rolling down his right cheek, something squeezing at his insides.

"Ah, yes—the get out of jail free card. And what may I ask, has he supposedly forgiven you for?"

"Many things, I guess." It's getting harder to get air. "But I'm a—changed man now." His heart thumps hard against his tender chest.

"Made a promise to my mother"—Bright lights blur into one—"on her death bed."

"The one you drove her to?"

The explosion of pain in his chest prevents any form of rebuttal as Tony leans into the wheel, letting out a cry of agony. It's in his arms and legs now, even his neck, no longer a dull throb but intense, heading towards a violent crescendo as though poison works its way through every part of him.

"I can't—"

"You're having a heart attack, Tony. Your arteries are a mess."

"I—"

"Don't try and talk, Tony. We're nearly there now."

"Wh—where?" he croaks, steering blindly into the sea of bright lights.

The burning sensation intensifies as his passenger leans in, bony fingers tightening around his shoulder. Once again, he finds himself hypnotised by the impossibly blue eyes, oblivious to the impending collision. Metal scrapes and twists, glass splintering as his head propels into the airbag. He hears his nose snap, but there's no accompanying pain; all he can feel is the intense heat of his passenger's hand still impossibly coiled around his shoulder.

And blackness.

Mum?

He's whipped out of the vehicle, a confused spectator to the carnage on the road and his lifeless body sitting awkwardly behind the steering wheel. Now resting on the crunched bonnet, the crow gives out a final cry.

"Been waiting five years to collect, Tony. I had you down for six, but they made the buckets even bigger."

As he's dragged through dark puddles that go undisturbed, Tony claws desperately at the ground, but he's no longer of this world, and he knows it. "I'm a man of God, though," he mutters at the now distant lights.

The hand on his shoulder is now a claw, thick black nails curling into his flesh.

"If you truly did seek repentance, why did you continue to visit the park? Why did you have that little boy's toy dangling from the mirror? And why, when watching the swing moving in the breeze, did you play the scene in your head over and over again?"

"I'm a man of God."

"Those poor parents. No closure."

"—man of God."

"If you truly did repent, you would have gone to the police."

"Blessed is the one whose—"

"Just like your mother told you when she found out."

"—if you do not forgive—"

"Sent her to an early grave, didn't it? No longer able to live with the guilt of covering for you."

"—of God."

"Boosted my numbers, though."

Tony's skin begins to prickle, the heat returning but no longer internal.

"Forgive me, Father—"

"Too late, Tony."

"Where are we going?"

"Home. The fire's on."

COSY STREET

So much crap in the mailbox! I need to have a chat with Fiona about getting one of those 'No Junkmail' stickers.

"Morning, Mavis."

"Good morning," she replies, little poodle in tow.

I do love this place. Usually, I struggle to settle, getting itchy feet, but this place is starting to feel like home: number six, Cosy Street. Everyone carries a smile and has time for a chat, apart from the grumpy old lady, Marge, at number sixteen. She just needs to hurry up and die.

My back gives out a twinge as I bend down and begin ripping weeds from between the cracks of the path. I'll have to get some spray from the shop tomorrow. The bloody things grow back too damn quickly.

"Goddamn it." Pain flares up my spine as I stand.

A few things need doing, really. The weatherboard down the side of the house is looking a bit worse for wear, and as for the windows, they're so filthy you can hardly even see the faded neighbourhood watch sticker on the inside.

I move the kid's bikes from the side of the house to the back; no point leaving them on show. It's almost as if they want someone to steal them. Fi gets sick of telling them the same thing. Fortunately, we don't have much trouble here, but you can't be too careful.

Geoff from two doors down is home from work early. He's watering the plants and gracing the neighbourhood with an awful Dean Martin rendition. He should pay as much attention to his marriage, and then perhaps his wife, Judith, wouldn't be knocking at number thirty-two every time he leaves for work. Nice guy, though. Sometimes we chat for ages, but I couldn't tell you what about.

The patio door reflects my sallow face, and I instinctively feel even more tired than before. My back is getting worse, but the tablets only seem to make me drowsy. I took twice the dose a couple of hours ago, but I can still feel the niggle, getting ready to explode again soon.

Carnage confronts me as I slide the door open. Clothes and toys everywhere, breakfast dishes from this morning overturned in front of the television, and the faint but rancid odour of cat piss. I hate cats, especially ours. It's me that changes the cat litter most days, so I guess that might explain it.

I can't blame Fi for any of it. She needs to drop Jack and Anna at before-school care, then negotiate her way through heavy peak traffic. She's always complaining about how bad it is, the number of arseholes on the road. I feel bad that she's the one left to do it. God knows what time it was when she woke me this morning, but it was well before the sun started to do its bit.

I reach for the milk carton and pour some into a glass on the benchtop that still has Fi's lipstick on the side. There's only a dreg of powder left in the chocolate malt tin, so I pour it in and stir, making a mental note to add it to the shopping list.

As I climb the stairs, the nasty smell gives to the scent of one of Fi's perfumes. Even though I'm exhausted, it still arouses me—not so much in a sexual way, but just in the way perfume is cleverly formulated to induce mystery and appeal. It's not my favourite by any means; that one's in the pyramid-shaped bottle and reserved for special occasions—tonight, for instance.

Christ, I look like shit.

I throw some water on my face and pat myself down with the brown hand towel, grimacing as my back issues a threat. A couple of minutes with the electric toothbrush removes the mysterious coating on my teeth and tongue, and I finish with a swig of mouthwash.

Wrestling with my sweater as I step back into the bedroom, I try not to make any sudden movements, keeping my eyes shut tightly in preparation for pain. Thankfully, only a mild ache makes itself known. I unbuckle my belt and turn back the sheets, gently lowering myself into the unmade bed, face screwed up with anticipation. Relief kicks in as I let the mattress take my weight, sinking into the still-warm sheets—the familiar cocktail of perfume and fabric conditioner providing further comfort.

A glance at my watch tells me it's 10.30 am.

I'll just rest my eyes for a couple of hours, and then I'll get around to my jobs.

I'm sure that crack in the ceiling is getting bigger—can't be a hundred percent, though. Since taking the extra dose of painkillers, my vision has been hazy, to say the least. And as I lie here, motionless, I feel quite lightheaded all of a sudden, the room starting to wash over me in a series of waves.

Mustn't let myself fall asleep.

So tired, though, and that crack—it's coming for me—getting—

WHAT THE—

The front door. That was the front door!

Shit. What time is it? I throw my legs out of bed and grab my clothes from the floor. 5.15 pm. Fuck! She's home. Fi's home! I didn't even get the chance to tidy up.

Heart thumping, and with a lurching feeling in my stomach, I make the bed, frantically patting the sheets down. I catch sight of myself in the mirrored doors of the wardrobe and suddenly feel pathetic. But no relationship is without its ups and downs.

Fumbling with my pants, I hear the kids chasing each other through the house, no doubt on the way to the snack cupboard and then to fire up the games console.

"Slow down!" Fi shouts.

It's the same every night. She sounds so tired, though—and she'll have seen the mess downstairs.

Damn, she's coming up. She usually pours herself a glass of wine.

"The babysitter is coming at six. I want you ready for bed by then; bedtime is seven-thirty."

I want to offer my help, but instead, I quickly slide the door open and crouch behind the veil of dresses. What kind of man am I?

I hold my breath, skin prickling as I hear the hallway floor creak. Did she hear me? This will ruin everything. But there are no signs of distress or fleeing footsteps, and I afford myself a big sigh of relief. The feel of her soft nightgown against my cheek calms me further.

Together again.

"Hey. Yeah, I'm fine... Just tired... No, of course, I can't wait... Seven, yep... Ah, you're so sweet... See you soon. Bye."

Tom. The prick.

Fi's voice usually makes me feel special, but it makes my spine shudder when she's talking to him. We were fine before he came along. But he won't stick around; they never do—can't handle it—the children. I'm different, though. Loyal. I love the kids just like they were my own. Sometimes, we play *rock, paper, scissors*—if I catch them before or after school, that is, which I usually do as I know the pattern. Often, in the afternoon or early morning, I hide behind the row of trees in the back garden and watch my family play together.

It gives me such a warm feeling.

I have stayed with others but never really felt the same sense of belonging as I do here with Fi and her children.

The soft sound of her grey skirt landing on the carpet makes me feel uneasy and awkward, yet I can't help but crane my neck to peek through the gap. She unbuttons her shirt, throwing it on the bed, and I nervously watch as she reaches behind to unclip her bra.

I love her.

Mother says I fall in love too easily and am too trusting with people. She also says that if I can't even keep my room tidy at thirty-five years of age, there is little hope of being able to look after anyone else.

I think Fiona loves me, though. Sometimes, I'm sure I can see it in her face when I pass her in the street, the nervous glimmer in her eyes, the slightly flushed cheeks. Hopefully, if I put the effort in and stick around, she'll begin to appreciate me and see me for what I am.

When I hear the shower turn on, I shift position; my bloody back beginning its orchestra of pain. Biting at my lip, I peer through the gap to make sure she's gone and carefully raise myself, sliding open the door. She's singing now. She sounds happy.

But Tom isn't the one.

I tiptoe across the carpet, reach towards her skirt, and snap up the underwear, placing it in the pocket of my joggers. I know what you're thinking—just the typical pervert—but it's genuinely not like that. You must understand that I love this woman. For me, this is a relationship, so nothing is sacred. Besides, she won't miss them; she's always too busy to notice, just as she never notices the clean cat litter, the tidy garden, or the items in her kitchen that I often replenish.

They never do.

But as I said, this is different. I knew that I loved her as soon as I saw her. And watching them all together from behind the line of conifers only made the feelings stronger.

She really should lock that patio door; too much complacency in a neighbourhood that's never actually around to watch. Ironically, the first leaflet I delivered here was advertising security systems. You know, video surveillance, burglar alarms, etc. I remember it well as it was the first time I met the kids. I knew it was the place for me immediately. It became my regular round, and the rest is history.

There are other day creatures like me—watching, waiting, interacting—and some are not as nice. Some of us deliver pamphlets or newspapers, and others operate under the guise of door-to-door sales or collecting for made-up charities. But when you close that door behind you, shaking your head or cussing and throwing the crumpled leaflet in the bin, don't always assume the relationship is over.

I am jealous of Tom. But it will be me that will climb in bed with her tonight, nestling into her warmth, the softness of her hair against my cheek. One day, perhaps I will be able to stay there, too, instead of silently slinking back into that tiny closet.

THE UNDERTONES

"WHAT THE HELL IS IT, FI?"

"John, I can't hear a thing; it's ALL in your head. Now please go to sleep," my wife replies dismissively.

"It's Tuesday night, for Christ's sake. After eleven."

She sighs before flipping dramatically to her side, a physical full stop to our exchange. Within minutes, she will be open-mouthed, and soon after, the resentment-inducing whistle through her nostrils will begin.

I lay my head on the pillow but feel the bed vibrating with the noise. Blood pulsates in my ear as if synchronising with the slow beat. Fuck's sake. How the hell can she not hear it? Not a hope in hell I'll sleep through this.

It's happening a lot of late, sometimes early in the morning, sometimes midday, through the night occasionally. Saturday night, for instance, it started just before six and carried on until well after one. Exasperated, I went for a walk around the block to try and find the source, but it was as if it was everywhere. Fi said I should get my hearing checked out; she said it's more than likely tinnitus, the internet never being wrong, of course. Next door, Harold and Joan also claim not to hear it, but they've been knocking on Heaven's door for a good while now.

I always just assumed that I had sensitive ears, picking up sounds that others couldn't. Even as a child, I recall looking out the window, trying to find the single illuminated house on the estate.

As I rifle through the drawer in the bedside table, my wife sighs again and turns over, taking most of the covers with her. How fucking nice it must be to be so oblivious to everything. I pick out a fresh pair of pink earbuds, urgently cramming them in as deep as they will go.

Fuck it.

The vein in my neck is joining in, strumming punishingly to the phantom beat. It's working across my temples, too, as though trying to find a way inside my head so I can set up camp forever.

This level of sensitivity is a curse, for sure.

Until a few weeks ago, there was another hum. It began like clockwork at 3 pm every day, lasting for precisely thirty minutes which I thought odd. It was monotone and subtle, but I couldn't focus on anything else for that brief period. Fi denies it all, says I have too much time on my hands, reiterating the advice from another *expert* on the internet to get checked out. This noise is different, random and untamed.

Today I can feel it as well as hear it.

There are others; I've looked them up on the internet and even joined the group. It's called 'The Undertones,' and membership grows continuously. And Christ, there's no shortage of theories: experiments by the government, aliens trying to communicate, some even believing it's the sound of the world slowly dying. We are scientists, doctors, astrologers, and nutcases—so many ideas, but there's one thing we all agree on, Earth is fucked—on fire, flooded, and poisoned.

Staring at the crack in the ceiling that I am all too familiar with, patches of my skin begin to thrum rhythmically in time with the distant tune. I turn over to my side, but this only offers temporary relief as the skin on my back begins to sing. Frustrated, I turn again, but the noise seems to be invading my body, slowly awakening each nerve ending.

"John, will you please lie still?"

Resignedly, I swing my legs from the bed. "I wish I fuckin' could." If she makes a response, I don't hear it.

Just want a good night's sleep, for Christ's sake!

I shuffle across to the window and move the curtains aside, squinting at the glow from the streetlights as I study the diluted darkness. The beat pounds in my head, but aside from the artificial patches of light, there's no sign of life. A fucking curse. But just as I'm about to turn, something catches my eye.

Gone.

I refocus, moving my stare from one streetlight to the next. And again, again. It's as though I'm just missing it each time I move my gaze, a series of opaque shadows appearing but just as quickly blending back into the stillness of the night. I move closer to the window to investigate, but my attention draws to the streetlights as they begin flickering in unison, in time with the dull beat. What the fuck? Finally, they return to their dirty yellow glow, leaving me with the promised serenity of night. I march out of the room like a petulant teenager and begin my descent down the landing stairs.

It's getting even louder, stronger. I can feel it on my bare feet, coming through the floor, vibrating through the wooden planks. I've never known it this bad before. En route to the kitchen, I press the power button on my laptop, immediately picking up the vibration coming from the machine. What the fuck is going on? Is this just me—my fingertips a collection of nerve endings in my exhausted and frenzied state? Are my senses all screwed up from sleep deprivation? I don't know anymore.

I place my hand on the surface of the kitchen bench and can feel its monotonous harmony. Running the back of my hands against the wall provides the same tremor-like feedback. I can feel it in my spine now, pulsating, an undulating vibration that feels like it's running up and down the bone. Another first. It stops at my neck, runs back to the base, and repeats.

Jesus fucking Christ!

The now relentless buzz in my ears has brought an unbearable headache. My skull feels like a pressure cooker, the redundant earbuds feeling like they could pop like corks at any moment. I rip them out and throw them against the back wall. "Get out of my fuckin' head!"

And it hits me. What if we're onto something? The Undertones. It's one thing to postulate such wild hypotheses, but what if there is substance to them. What if—

"Jesus fuckity-fuck!" Pressure in my head ramps up again. No undulation now, no troughs of relief, the noise settling into a single and haunting discordant drone that continues to get louder. My head sings along, approaching a brain-bleeding crescendo.

I grab a glass and run to the sink, turning on the tap and noting the feedback from the metal. The same resonant hum feeds from the drawer handle as I reach inside for the painkillers. I quickly wash a couple down and return to the living room.

The screen is where I left it, on the forum page.

I knew it. It's the government!

They're trying to control us. It's the noise—that's how they get into our heads!

They're outside. They've come for me. What do I—

Fuck. It's true. It's them!

We were right. All this time.

My phone line is dead. Having to use the hotspot.

They've been turning up the frequency—increasing their control. But they still can't get us, can they?

They're controlling people's brainwaves with this sound—manipulating emotions—brainwashing them.

All this time, they've been watching us. The ones they couldn't control —we must show up on fucking google maps or something.

I think there's someone in my fucking garden.

Now we've united, they want us under or gone—they know we are onto them.

They're turning it up; it's so fucking loud. They've sent hitmen in case it doesn't work. I think I see them outside.

I can't bear it.

If you have a gun, go and—

Help.

Help. That was the last message that someone typed—ten minutes ago. Noting the internet light on the modem is unlit, I grab my phone, that same vibration running up my arm. No signal. No fucking signal!

"Fuck!"

My skull feels as though it could cave in at any moment. The air feels heavy, claustrophobic, and it's as though the entire house is alive—floor, walls, surfaces—all vibrating with increasing intensity.

The outside light flickers on.

My heart stops.

Legs suddenly incapable of movement, I stare towards the lit-up patio, hearing nothing but the relentless drone. It's debilitating. Disorienting. I slowly back away, feeling my way across the furniture until I'm back to the bottom of the stairs. Shit, what the hell was that? Something moved—behind the pillar.

The group was only ever a distraction, an opportunity to share experiences and theories, but for this to be—

More movement, shadows within shadows.

"Fi!" I say, but I'd likely not even hear her response above the mercilessly loud hum in my ears. Finally, I run, stumbling up the stairs, staring at the dimly lit patio for as long as it remains in view, and clinging to the trembling handrail for support. What do I say to her? Thoughts rush through my head, but all I know is that we are in real danger.

This fucking noise!

I cover my ears with my palms, but it only makes things worse, as though I am trapping it inside my head. The sensation in my spine becomes more intense, as though someone is reaching in and applying pressure. The air feels even heavier, as though trying to pin me to the spot.

"Fi!" I scream from the doorway. She looks peaceful, offering no whistling, only a smile across her face. "Fi!"

Still no response.

It feels like a blanket of thick fog is wrapping around my brain. I can't think, can't get past the noise and pressure. "Fi!" I continue to fight but wonder how long I can carry on. My limbs feel leaden and scream at me to concede. Blood pounds violently around my body. I'm filled with a sudden urge to plead to the shadows to put me out of my fucking misery.

"Fi!"

Something isn't right. I give her a gentle shake, but her head lollops on the pillow like a rag doll. "Fi!" I try again with more vigour.

Still nothing.

As if making up for both of us, my heart races as I search for signs of life. But I can't find a pulse. "Fi, please." And only a glassy vacancy awaits as I prise open her eyelids.

I think she's—gone.

Before I can form my cry, an explosion of blinding light and an accompanying bolt of pain sends me slumping to the floor. I try to push myself up, but every bone in my body rattles with ferocious intensity, forcing me to grit my teeth and ride it out. It feels like my spine is about to snap and that my skull is only seconds away from cracking like an egg. As the floor shakes violently beneath me, I helplessly stare at the ceiling illuminated in impossibly bright light. White dust sprinkling down in its wake, I watch the crack slowly working its way across. I can't fucking breathe. As though this sonic undertone is trying to possess me, I feel crippling pressure on my ribcage.

I can't take this anymore; I'm ready to go. Fingers clawing at the carpet, I manage to turn over and begin dragging myself towards the stairs again. They can have me—just let it end.

"Kill me. Do it now!"

My teeth tear through my top lip as the already excruciating shrill elevates further, and I feel a stream of warm blood running from my right nostril. As they continue burying into the carpet, my fingers turn as white as the surrounding light, and if it weren't for the feel of the fabric beneath them, I'd think I was already dead.

The vibration stops.

I see a shadow approaching down the hallway.

I hold my breath.

White gives way to black—

EVEN BEFORE KNOWING MY FATE, RELIEF WASHES OVER ME, ONLY A feeling of slight cloudiness in my head. And that goddamn interminable buzz is finally gone.

Fi.

I open my eyes and try to get up, but the shiny silver restraints around my wrists and ankles give me limited movement. Instinctively, I let out a cry and begin squirming like an earthworm. But through the glass-fronted room, I see a pair of black eyes staring back at me, and my body freezes.

Its body is hairless, almost translucent, spiralling through a multitude of colours until it settles on a bland greyness. The elongated cranium is twice the size of a human's, a single large vein pounding rhythmically across the forehead.

It moves.

I hold my breath.

Legs look weak and spindly, but its movement is smooth, ethereal, as though it's floating across the ground rather than walking. It has no ears as far as I can tell. Its long thin silver arms remain by its side as it approaches the silver door.

A single vibration comes through the bed, echoing through the metallic restraints. The doors slide open, and, heart racing, I watch the alien step into the room.

A million thoughts rush through my head, but I offer no words; I don't think I have the courage. It nods, and I take that as a cordial acknowledgement of my questions and fears. As it moves to the side of my bed and reaches its hand towards me, I instinctively recoil, snapping my head away. Its spindly fingers change to a warm orange hue—one of my favourite colours. It waits as if needing my approval. Warily, I nod, and the hand settles against my forehead.

As soon as the vibrations begin, it all starts to make sense.

For years, the 3 pm broadcast was how they communicated between themselves, those here, and those back home. They were reporting back on our progress, but most recently, signalling dire warnings that we were killing Earth. They've been here for centuries, the original caretakers of the planet. No longer could they sit back and watch us destroy it, a race seemingly oblivious to the devastation they leave in their wake. Earth is dying quicker than we think. Some of them wanted to let us have another chance—to try and fix it—others thought it was too late. Arguments began, communications broke down, and factions formed—thus the random outbreaks of noise and tremors—prolonged debates of whether the human race should be wiped or not.

Finally, it came down to a vote. And they reached a last-minute compromise of sorts.

Only some would live, a handful of free thinkers—ones not already plugged into the machine—ones who had their eyes and ears wide open to everything around them, including the hum.

The alien places his other hand against my ear, and I immediately feel something responding inside my head. It's a cold and extremely unpleasant sensation as though something is working its way across my brain. My discomfort must be obvious as the alien nods once more. With a final icy surge, the sensation is gone, as is the remaining cloudiness. Only a garbled croak emerges as I watch the inch-long worm writhe across the alien's palm and as it begins burying into its skin.

When we were asleep, they got to us—The Undertones—put them there to protect us. The trail from the worms formed a protective barrier around our brains, pretty much making us immune. The rest of humanity is gone, wiped out by a sound they were oblivious to.

It's our final chance to put things right. Only when we save the planet can we grieve for those lost.

And all this time, I thought it was a curse.

A BAD HARVEST

JACK BOUGHT the farm with his mother's inheritance, thinking it would be a good investment.

Cursed bad luck.

The house has seen better days, not helped by the lack of maintenance and a stench of old take-out food and tobacco. Dirty yellow light pours through the threadbare orange curtains in the lounge, partially illuminating the mountain of empty beer cans that carpet the grubby floor. The television plays to itself in the corner, the snowy reception only for company these days.

His legs dangling over the edge of the grubby chair, Jack shifts in and out of an uncomfortable slumber. Sleep is spasmodic, kept at bay by anxiety and stress.

"Fucking farm! Who the hell would buy a fucking farm?" Jack mutters under his breath. "Cursed bad luck."

A fly circles his head, a fat blue bottle that buzzes through the air with impossible speed. He takes a half-hearted swat but only manages to clip the edge of his nose, bringing water to his eyes.

"Right, yer little fucker; that's it." His face all twisted, thin lips curling over his tobacco-stained teeth, Jack backs up his declaration of war by grabbing the newspaper from the discoloured coffee table and getting into position. *Come on. Come on.* Eventually, the fly comes to rest on the edge of the chair, seeming content with inspecting the newly discovered patch of crumbs.

Wait for it. Wait for it.

He lets out a loud and nonsensical war cry as he brings the paper down onto the chair with remarkable vigour. Almost immediately, he feels lightheaded, having to reach out for the arm of the chair with his other hand to steady his balance. "Fuck!"

Breathing slowly and deeply, he eventually regains composure and warily stands, hands positioned just slightly above his buttocks for the inevitable back pain. He lets out a little yelp as he straightens, followed by a sigh as he surveys the bombshell that is his lounge. Oh yes, the place has gone downhill, he thinks. The problem is he can't bring himself to do anything about it. Liz used to deal with all that stuff before she left—wouldn't even entertain the thought of letting his half-assed hands loose on any of the chores.

Tears surprise Jack. The foreclosure notice pinned to the front door when he came home last week made it far too real for him. Since then, he's been in and out of a drunken stupor, mumbling his troubles at the TV. But the beer money has run as dry as the soil outside.

They purchased the farm twelve months ago, just before Autumn kicked in. Liz fell in love with the place. "It will be great to get away from the bustle of the city. A bit of peace and solitude." They had no idea that the following summer would be the hottest and most dangerous for decades.

Cursed bad luck.

It started as a fun adventure, but neither realised just how much work it would be. The honeymoon period wore off quickly, and Liz soon got bored, leaving everything to Jack while she got dolled up, galivanting with God knows who and spending the last of his money at God knows where. Arguments became frequent—and loud—explosively so, and three months went by without any lovemaking or affection of any kind. The farm was destroying them, and the driest summer on record didn't help.

Just before the fires started, she told him it wasn't working. Something along the lines of it not being the life for her. She didn't love him anymore, etcetera, etcetera. Jack begged. He got down on all fours and implored her not to go. But then the truth came out, and she told him there was someone else. Jack kept pleading anyway, said they could get through it, work it out. He only stopped after her final bombshell that she was two months pregnant. That put him well out of the running.

The fly is back, and it's brought a friend.

"Fuck off!" Jack screams, wildly swinging as they spin in taunting formation inches from his face. The newspaper scrunches under his grip. *Game over, you little bastard.* He clenches his teeth, preparing for round two, and then—swing.

The buzz continues, albeit dampened.

Damn!

He steps over the beer cans, following the noise into the kitchen, wincing at the raucous din as both flies bounce frantically between the blinds and glass pane of the window.

"In the name of horseshit."

The flies provide only white noise now.

"You're pulling my plonker."

If he weren't sober, he would just put it down to the booze, but his last drink was two days ago, and his vision is as clear as day. He edges closer to the window, thinking if he creeps stealthily enough towards it, the image might not fade. Here he is, though, only a few feet away from the glass, and the view is no longer the anhydrous scene of devastation he's been used to but an impossibly bountiful mix of greens and browns.

Still afraid that if he gets too close, the scene will disappear, he arches his neck to take a better look. Row after row, there's hardly a patch of ground not taken up by lush leafy greens.

"Impossible. Goddamn miracle."

Some two hundred yards back, next to the poor excuse of a scarecrow that came with the farm, half a dozen crows are squabbling, viciously swooping down on each other with talons raised.

Jack opens the back door to their discordant cries, still half expecting to wake up, but the heat of the afternoon rushes him, and the birds continue their shrieks.

"Fuck off with yer!"

No rain for three months. Scorching temperatures, hottest on record according to the TV. None of it makes any sense.

Contemplating his run of bad luck might be coming to an end, Jack affords himself a brief smile, continuing to admire the crops that extend for as far as he can see, even the areas he doesn't remember planting out.

"Blasted crows." *Going to eat all my goddamn crops.*

He grabs the broom from the corner of the kitchen and marches towards the feathered pests, holding the end of the wooden handle out in front as though it was a bayonet. As soon as he reaches the field's border, his socks begin to squelch into the impossibly damp soil. "In the name of Mary!" He treads carefully, constantly wiping the sweat from the end of his nose and monitoring the ground to avoid the darker brown patches.

"Useless bastard," he shouts at the scarecrow on approach; nevertheless, his pace increases, a rush of adrenaline based on silly childhood fears. He's always been wary, the whole idea of adorning them with human clothes seeming so sinister. Old straw sprouts erratically through the holy fabric of the faded red and black check-ered shirt, and the legs, made from burlap sacks, dangle loosely on either side. But it's the painted face, red smile, and black eyes causing Jack to offer an involuntary shudder as he steps past it.

Not so far ahead, the crows continue their fighting. He wonders why they're so hyper; what has them so excited? One of them breaks free from the pack and flies upwards with something in its beak, but almost immediately, one of its competitors swoops in from above, driving the bird back to the dirt with a soft thud causing the crow to drop its catch. He watches as they thrash it out on the ground. "Oy!" he screams, increasing his pace, fearing for his new crops. Maniacally he waves the broom in front, clumsily stag-gering towards them until the soft ground eventually wins, bringing him to his knees. The crows offer some mocking caws and fly off.

"Stupid fucking birds!"

He scouts the ground ahead of him, looking for the object that appeared to be the root cause of the fracas. A few yards ahead, he spots something on the dirt. Wiping his knees down and craning his neck, he unfolds and squints into the glaring sun.

A wave of uneasiness washes over him.

Warily, he begins to edge closer to the object, moving past the row of cabbages, convincing himself his eyes are playing tricks. Each squelching step fills him with dread and drives his heart rate faster until he finally stands above it. He bends down and picks up the blackened object.

Jack studies the small charred human ear pinched between his fingers, warm from the sun and shaking in his grip. "This ain't funny." He looks around, feeling like he's being watched, and picking up the ear might have set off an unstoppable sequence of sinister events. In the reflection of the stationary cloud, he waits—for what—he's not sure, his entire body feeling heavy as if moving would require a mammoth effort. A craving for liquor consumes him.

A hot and powerful gust surprises him, sending his shirttail flapping and rattling the corn in the field only a few yards ahead. He watches in horror as more charred ears shake to the ground. "No, no, no, no." As the breeze dies, he remains frozen to the spot, blood pumping in his ear and stomach twisting. The smell of burning meat accompanying the carnage doesn't help, instinctively making him turn his head away from the corn and dry retch at the ground.

An eerie silence falls across the farm, but deep down in the pit of his stomach, Jack knows there is likely more to come.

He waits.

And waits.

A gentle crackling sound from behind finally grabs his attention. He turns, still holding the broom in his left hand and the human ear between his right hand's index finger and thumb.

Heads cocked and eyes on him, the crows sit in a line across the scarecrow's arms. The legs of the scarecrow are on fire, burlap sacks full of straw disintegrating, sending glowing floating embers drifting towards the damp ground. The hungry flames soon lick at the air beneath the crows, but the birds refuse to move.

"Shoo!" he screams.

But they continue to observe him, seemingly oblivious to the heat and their impending fate. The legs of the scarecrow burn quickly, and the fire spreads to the shirt, soon igniting the dry straw within. The first cries of pain begin, but still, the crows stubbornly do not take flight. Their beady black eyes continue to observe Jack, even as the flames start lapping at their bodies. He throws the broom towards them, and even though it strikes the underside of the arm, they remain unperturbed. The blood-curdling cries get gradually louder, and Jack finally turns his eyes away as the hungry fire begins to consume them. He clamps his hands tightly around his ears as the chorus of cries approaches a deafening level, but it feels as though their screams are inside his head.

As mud begins to cover his ankles, he panics and takes an urgent step forward, knocking one of the cabbages with his left foot. Half-screaming, half-retching, he observes the charred head at the centre of the lush green cabbage leaves, bits of blackened meat attached to the child-size skull.

"No way! No way!"

The ground continues taking him in. He tries to move, but his legs are leaden. Another hot blast wraps around him, stealing his breath. "No!" He watches helplessly as the leaves of the other cabbages begin to unfurl in front of him, revealing rows of burnt heads, child-sized faces gruesomely disfigured beyond recognition.

Finally, he drags himself free and begins to wade through the mud. But the house seems impossibly far away, and each sluggish movement only takes him further in. His feet and legs brush against unknown objects—some hard, some not—and he can only imagine the nastiness waiting for him down there. He's up to his knees but not even in line with the scarecrow yet. As sweat runs into his eyes and burns, he plants the ball of his hands into the sockets. They squelch like the ground beneath, the dirt within only making things worse.

His palm connects with something solid as he pushes against the ground for leverage, and from the sloppy soil, he brings out what appears to be a piece of blackened meat. This field of horrors is harvesting something unnatural, something vile. He screams for help once more as the mud continues to swallow him. And again—and again—until only a hoarse rasp emerges. Another laborious step forward—something harder—feels like bone. "Fuuuuuck!" He's up to his waist now, just about level with the scarecrow.

The hot breeze hits him from the other side. A change is coming.

Just like on that day, Jack thinks.

Cursed bad luck.

Breathing laboured, blood pounding in his ears, he arduously drags himself through the mud, but the back door still looks so far away.

He followed her one afternoon. Turned out she was shacking up with Tom, their closest neighbour—his vineyard half a mile south down the road. Jack guessed it to be the cars, iron gates, fairytale house that sucked her in. She always was a sucker for money—went through it quicker than a hot knife through butter. The drink took him to the house that afternoon, but when all's said and done, it was pure rage that made him leave the car and march into the woods with the matches and gasoline.

He counted six dry lightning strikes that afternoon. The perfect cover. Just another fire on the map that was already nearly half-yellow. Christ, it was quick, though. The whole place was ablaze in seconds. But then the damned wind came out of nowhere and took it out of control. *Cursed bad luck.* How was he to know that would happen.

Up to his chest, he tries to push forward, but his movement only makes things worse, and he sinks further in. He scrambles at the ground with his fingers but can't get traction. The dirt begins to run down his shirt collar.

"Help!"

As though the earth is constricting around him, he feels his chest tighten. Something's happening with the mud; it's solidifying. "Help!" He's stuck, unable to move from the neck down. And his eyes feel like they're on fire.

"I'm sorry!" he screams as the pressure increases. "I'm sorry," he croaks.

The wind change took the fire on a journey across three thousand acres of dry grass and vegetation, killing thirty-four children and two teachers at that Kindergarten. Jack watched the aftermath unfolding on the television with the other evacuees at the community centre in the safe zone. It even showed pictures of the victims, happy and smiling with their families.

He thought about killing himself for days afterwards, just couldn't find the courage. And the thought of confessing was too much—the hatred people would harbor against him; his life wouldn't be worth living. He still can't sleep, hardly eats, and the only way he can cope is through inebriation. The nightmares when he does manage to drift off are unbearable.

His farm was left untouched, but it would have been best if the fire took it as far as the insurance money was concerned.

Cursed bad luck.

As he futilely struggles against the ground that has now returned to its original arid state, he looks towards the scarecrow to see the charred and smouldering human body hanging from the cross's blackened wood. He watches it unhook itself and begin to walk towards him through crops that wither in front of his eyes, leaving a trail of human devastation: Skulls, blackened organs, internal and external, and unidentifiable strips of innards.

He didn't think he'd get away with it. You don't get away with things like that.

Not like this, though. I'll do it myself. This time I will. "Please!"

The charred body continues its approach, the sinewy and bony trespasser leaving footsteps of embers that set surrounding crops on fire. Jack can already feel the additional heat against his cheeks. His struggles are hopeless. Exhausted and trapped, he begins to sob.

A fly begins to circle his head.

"Cursed bad luck," the blackened figure says, partial lips curling into a menacing smile, revealing teeth that are so contrastingly white. The voice is raspy, and even though slightly otherworldly, he knows it's Liz. In the face, too, through all the gristle and bone, he still recognises her.

The ground around him is ablaze.

The crows are back, circling above in silence.

As she draws closer, she brings the fire with her. "This is your harvest, Jack. This is what you've done."

He screams as the first of the flames lick at his cheek.

LONG DISTANCE CALL

THE ROOM FEELS huge to Max, crammed full of emptiness.

Aside from the wine glass she frequently lifts to her lips, his mum's routine is the same, albeit a shortened, half-assed effort: dabbing at smudged makeup, an aggressive brush of dry hair, and a quick spray of perfume mist that mostly finds air.

But everything has changed.

Once powerful, like some weird explosion of chemicals and candy, the fragrance is faint these days, as though sadness feeds on it and everything else that was once familiar and safe about the room. There's a different scent now, and it's getting worse.

"Mum."

She hardly ever leaves the room anymore.

In the mirror's reflection, he can see her bottom lip trembling. She bites into it, slumps her elbows onto the dresser's wood, and buries her head into her hands. It's a battle she never wins.

"Mum."

It's hard to watch and gives him the feeling of being even less than a kid.

He misses *him*, too, though.

She pushes herself from the stool and flops onto the bed, curling into a ball, knees almost to her neck. When she cries like this, it makes him feel funny in his stomach and as empty as the room.

"Mum."

Never something he would ever admit to his friends, but they all used to pile on the bed sometimes to watch the smaller TV. His mum and dad would often argue about which movie to watch, but not how they did when Mum got one of her migraines; this was fun and always ended up with him being allowed to choose. Harder to recount those scenes now, the heaviness of the air not allowing anything else through.

He guesses there aren't any words that could make her feel better, but he wishes he could do something to make her see him, to see that he's hurting, too.

Her shoulders settle to an occasional twitch as Max climbs onto the bed. Continuing her sniffles into its damp cover, she wraps her arms tightly around the pillow.

"I love you, Max."

"I love you, Mum."

She's always the first to drift off, but that's fine with him. He closes his eyes, listening to her inhaling and exhaling, sometimes with a squeak that brings almost a smile to his lips. That used to be as close to sleep as he got, but the last few nights, he's been having dream-like visions, ones that stay with him long after he opens his eyes. They scare him, for sure, always roughly the same sequence, albeit slightly longer each time with the subtlest of differences. Last night, he thrust himself up so quickly that cloudy black floaters appeared in front of his eyes. He was shaking, a scream trapped in his throat and a burning sensation in his nostrils.

He knew he was close. But to what?

The crack in the ceiling gets more ominous, as if becoming deeper and longer. Even as his eyes begin to narrow, the jagged line seems to extend its path. Inhale. Exhale. Inhale. Exhale. Until finally, his breathing falls in line with hers, and he closes his eyes.

IT'S COLD, SO COLD.

His body lets out a predictable shudder as he waits in silence, surrounded by complete darkness. Smells seem stronger than before—petrichor mixed with the faint tang of his mum's perfume. Something else, too, an exaggerated version of the rancidness that lingers in his mum's room. Never failing to make his skin crawl, the first of the whispers emerges from behind, an incoherent mumble but irascible and threatening, just how Max would imagine the voice of darkness to sound.

Three.

More moans merge. Getting louder, too.

Two.

So many. Frenzied almost. Urgent.

One.

He can almost feel them on the back of his neck.

As the first streetlight flickers on and the ringing begins, distant but impossible to ignore, Max begins his march, glancing over his shoulder into the familiar black void that swallows light and wastes none. He's never lingered to find out what happens if he stays still. Never will. He increases his pace, wisps of breath adding to layers of the glowing mist ahead. Iciness creeps further and further up his legs as his feet splash through black puddles.

It's all familiar but no less ominous, the streetlight extinguishing as he draws level. The next one flickers on, his pace continuing to pick up. And like clockwork, the shrillness of the phone's ring vibrates down his bones, indicating he's close. As he begins a run, he glances over his shoulder again to see darkness predictably following and promising to swallow him whole. The whispers, too, from somewhere deep within, offering nothing but the usual dread.

He feels a ripple of relief as he snaps his head around. Even though the fog obscures, the red bleeds through, more magnificent than he can remember. He sprints the last few yards and coils his fingers around the cold metal handle, yanking at the heaviness and squeezing himself into the phone box. As the door shuts behind, the solitary streetlight flickers twice and cuts out, leaving him in total darkness once more.

He sucks in air, catching his breath, but the cacophonous ring gets louder still, overriding any reprieve from the icy mist and whispers. Unable to bear it any longer, he feels his way up the stiff and metallic alien-like tendril of cord and lifts the handset from the receiver, cold and clammy plastic greeting his skin as he wraps his fingers around it.

Inhale. Exhale. Inhale.

Without saying anything, he brings the phone to his ear, listening and waiting.

Hairs bristle on his neck as the first of the crackles come through. He brings the phone harder against his ear, hoping for something different this time, but the hiss gives way to another series of crackles and distant and familiar tinny music. Preparing himself, he wraps his other hand around the door handle. Another crackle fizzes down the line.

"Dad?"

But just like that, the signal drops, the flat tone sounding in his ear. It's all so linear, but no less terrifying for it. To his left, a street-light blinks, finally settling on dim. More distant ringing emerges from the mist.

He tried staying put once, resisting the urge to move, but the streetlight began to flicker, threatening nothingness, and through the grimy glass, he could hear the whispers becoming more excitable and louder still.

Once was enough.

He pushes against the door and slides himself out, marching into the ever-thickening fog towards the yellow blur of light. Behind him, the phone box has already given way to a dark that seems darker and whispers even more frenzied. It's colder, too, his skin translucently grey like the mist.

Things are the same but different somehow. He can feel it in the air, charged, like before a storm, his skin crawling with excited but nervous anticipation.

As the volume of the ringing increases, Max launches into a jog, wisps of his breath peppering the air with more frequency. There's an eagerness to escape the cold, along with undeniable fear and an urgency to find out what it all means.

If he stumbles now, falls to the cold and wet ground, or simply stops and turns—

The familiar thought sends him into a sprint. He can already see the corner of the next phone box poking out from the greyness, redder than anything in the real world, a beacon guiding him through the fog.

More hot air predictably caresses the back of his neck, more of that godawful whispering. It doesn't seem to matter how fast he runs; he can't outpace the darkness, can't avoid the voices that carry on it. He bites down hard on his lip, continuing to pump his arms and legs as fast as he can, only slowing to avoid smashing into the phone box. He gulps down some dampness and swings the door open, grimacing as he gets the onslaught of shrillness. Without taking a rest, he grabs the phone just before the streetlight flickers off.

He's been here plenty of times, standing in the dark, with nothing but the sound of his breathing as he waits for the crackles. He's tried to will himself out of the sequence when he got too scared. Back to the bedroom, back to his mum, but even that seems beyond his control.

The first crackle prompts another shudder.

He turns to face the blackness, the whispers abating.

Another crackle.

"Hello," he says, only for comfort.

The tune begins, distorted and undulating in volume, overlayed by a persistent hiss and occasional sharpness of that goddamned crackle.

"Hello?"

It's a tune that forever plays in his head—an oldie—he doesn't know its name or even the singer, but he could recite it back to front.

Hates it.

Hates it more than anything else in the world.

It was to give Mum a break; at her request, another of her big headaches. An impromptu trip, him and his dad to see the latest three-hour extravaganza of the movies. On the way home, the warmth of the car and the relentless patter of rain that still failed to displace stubborn midday mist made it a fight to keep his eyes open. He asked his dad to change the music to something a bit *younger*. But then he saw something in the road and—

Knowing what's coming, he screws his face up, but the high-pitched squeal still induces a shudder. He squeezes his eyes shut tighter still, bringing the phone away from his ear, but the piercing cry still churns his stomach. Before a tear can even escape, the monotonous tone sounds its drone, and the next streetlight flickers on.

He's back in the cold again, following the dull yellow light to the next pitstop, swatting at fog so thick he can taste it—a cloudy concoction of citrusy perfume, rancidness, and now the bitter taste of leather. Never so strong before.

In the distance, red bleeds through the mist.

Short bursts of warmth light up nerve endings on his neck as he brings his feet down hard onto the glistening tarmac, black water spraying either side. Part of him wants to give in, let the darkness consume him, but he knows, just like every other time, he'll see it through. He grabs the cold handle and shuts the door behind him to an impossibly loud ringing.

Inhale. Exhale. Inhale.

He snaps the phone from the receiver just as the streetlight fizzles out. "Hello!"

No hiss on the line. That's new.

"Hello," he croaks.

The single crackle is sharp and crystal clear, giving way to music that comes through with little distortion and sounds impossibly close.

His leg buckles, sending him slumping against the side of the booth, his breath misting up the already smoky glass. His grip on the handset tightens, the soft drone of an engine down the line unmistakable and the taste of leather stronger than ever.

It's as though he's—

Lights blur softly against the fog, and the wipers hypnotically thrum, doing their best against the softly pounding rain. He's warm now, toasty. He feels his eyes shutting but wills them to stay open as it wouldn't be fair on Dad. "Can we change the music, Dad? Something younger?"

To this day, he doesn't know what ran out into the middle of the road. Too large for a rabbit and too small for a deer.

"Dad!"

Inhale.

The tyres try, but it's a losing battle, traction already lost on a narrow country road that gets a handful of complaints every week. In eerie slow-motion, the world spins, a blur of darkness and light. He snaps his head towards his father to see his skin stretched across his skull, eyes wide, and stark white knuckles wrapped around the blackness of the wheel. His father turns towards him—no sign of the comedian from the breakfast table. He opens his mouth, and darkness spews.

Exhale.

Crackles from the handset.

But just as he's about to hang up, he realises there's no familiar flat drone. He lifts the phone back to his ear, heart pounding, skin tightening, trying his best to be brave.

"Run, son!" his father's voice screams down the line.

Max drops the phone, mouth gaping as he watches it crudely clang from side to side until the familiar flat tone finally brings things to an undramatic climax. The next streetlight flickers on, the one he was halfway to reaching last time before being jolted back into his mum's bedroom to her familiar gentle sobbing.

He hangs up the phone and thrusts the door open with his behind, bracing as the icy cold wraps around him once more. The whispers are louder, and blackness is already creeping towards him, consuming the road. It feels too real as he begins his run towards the light, as though each tiny droplet of fog is colliding with his skin. Blood pulsates violently in his ears as he pounds his feet against the drenched blackness, chasing whatever lies ahead.

Unable to see more than a yard in front, he follows the ringing into the lighter patches of fog. He tries to ignore the metallic taste at the back of his throat and the pain in his lungs, but he can't dismiss the darkness as it draws level with him, tiny tendrils of black mist polluting the grey of his peripheral vision. Gritting his teeth, he digs in, but his tank's nearly empty. Neck and neck with darkness, whispers in his ears, and warm and pungent breath prickling his skin, he catches sight of the first glimpse of red.

But something darts out from the grey—*too large for a rabbit, too small for a deer.*

It's too late.

Momentum does its best, but his legs are too fatigued; he can't move quickly enough. He tries to get his arms out, but blackness rushes him, his cheek scraping against the cold hard tarmac and the rest following in a clumsy heap. He lets out a pained moan, searching for the culprit, but just as quickly, it is gone. Strings of black begin weaving their way unnaturally through the fog, jerkily and aggressively as though racing towards him. He tries to push himself up, but every nerve ending sings, and with a wail of defeat, he drops his cheek back into the wetness.

The threads move quickly, the leader already halfway up his legs. "Stop!" A fizz from above brings blackness and more frenetic whispers as iciness approaches his waist. He wills himself back into the bedroom, but nothing.

"Please, stop."

Another fizz from the light, and he's back in the dimly lit grey, but for how long?

As he arches his neck towards the dampened ringing in the distance, he sees only the thinnest thread of red through the murkiness.

Run, son!

It was him; he knows it. *Dad.*

Letting out a garbled war cry, he thrusts himself up, teeth puncturing through his lip as he digs in for the home stretch, each step bringing surging pain down his side. He feels heavier, too, as though he's still dragging the blackness with him.

So damn tired.

But more red bleeds through the fog, offering hope. A different smell in the air, too; spicy, familiar, and getting stronger. The other putridness still lingers, but this is—

Cologne!

Tears begin rolling down both cheeks as he sprints through the grey and towards the comforting aroma and clangorous ringing. He's near the end; he can feel it.

Of what?

A flicker of the streetlight steals some of the hope.

God, please, no.

Fizz.

And blackness falls to the sound of whispers everywhere.

His heart thumps full throttle as leaden legs do their best to support him, but the only guide is the ringing, and it's discombobulating, nausea-inducing, his limbs feeling far from reliable.

Something splashes across the bridge of his nose. The back of his neck, too.

Rain.

Slowing his pace, he reaches an arm out into the blackness, twisting his face as iciness begins its ascent. So close. Or is the ringing just interminably in his head now? Up to his knees, and it feels like he's wading through a swamp. He stretches his fingers out, full of hope, hardly able to believe it when they find glass. Paintwork crumbles as he desperately claws for the handle. Another win. He yanks open the door, offering a high-pitched cry as he drags himself through.

Inhale. Exhale.

He lifts the phone off the hook and waits for the inevitable crackle.

But the music is crystal, as though he was back in—

"Do you think Mum's headache is gone?"

"Hope so, son."

The wipers whip back and forth across the glass, a mechanical orchestra that only adds to the hypnotic effect of the engine and the repetitive notes blaring from the radio.

His dad leans forward. "This mist is like something from a horror movie."

"Can we change the music, Dad? Something younger?"

His dad sniggers and leans in towards the glass, arms wrapping around the steering wheel. "I guess. What did you—"

"Dad!"

Max recoils at the sharpness of his own voice through the phone, but at the sound of squealing tyres, he's drawn back into the car; his father's face, pulled back in terror as the world spins around them, kaleidoscopic images of grey, black and dull yellow light. And a little flash of red.

The rest is a blur of light, pain, and sound. He recalls waking up shivering intensely to the sound of hard rain falling against what he thought to be the roof of the car but turned out to be the bottom. He remembers the feel of the cold biting at his cheek and the red phone box standing proud, no longer distorted by rain-flecked glass. Earthy petrichor breezed through the car, made slightly bitter by the metallic taste at the back of his throat. He remembers looking down to see the branch emerging from his side, looking like an extra limb of sorts, one that joined him and his father in a grisly bond.

No pain, just a leaking feeling inside.

The image fades. Warmth quickly begins to leave the booth, and the whispers start. Through the handset, he hears the music still playing—that awful, awful tune.

His own voice croaks down the line, "Dad?"

But there was never a response.

He reaches for the internal wall, biting at his lip, but the pressure behind his eyes is unbearable. "I miss you, Dad."

The handset crackles. He snaps it to his ear. "Hello?" Another series of crackles. "Dad?"

"Son?"

"Dad! Dad, where are you?"

"Son! My boy!" His father's voice is teary, croaky, but clear as day. "I've been trying to reach you, Max."

"Dad, is this really you?"

"Son, listen to me! You have to leave. You have to get out of this limbo."

"Dad, you're scaring me. What do you mean?"

"I haven't got much time. He's coming. You have to leave her behind!"

"Dad, where are you?"

"Max—"

Crackles explode down the line, but he squeezes the handset into his ear until it hurts. "Dad?"

"You've been there too long. He's close. He'll take you somewhere you don't want to go. Somewhere bad."

"I can't, Dad!"

"You don't belong in that world anymore, Max. There's a place for you here, but you have to let go."

"Dad!"

"He knows you're with her, in that bedroom. He's coming for you, son, and he'll find a way in. You must let go!"

The crack in the ceiling. The floaters.

"What about Mum?"

"She can sense you, Max, your aura. She'll never mend if you're still there."

"I'm scared."

"You'll see two doors, Max. You need to—"

"Dad!"

In the distance, another streetlight flickers on.

"Dad!"

The handset crackles, the music distorts, and the flat tone emerges.

Through the heavy rain that pounds against the glass, Max notes the blackness already beginning to bleed into the grey. He drops the phone and starts wrestling with the door, his muscles already cold and weak, fighting against whatever else holds the door in place. Finally, with a groan, he manages to pull himself from the confines of the box.

It's got a head start, though. Max feels like he's wading through puddles of treacle. He knows there'll be no easy escape this time, no waking up in his mother's bedroom to the sound of her gentle sniffles.

He's close, his dad warned. He'll take you somewhere you don't want to go.

He can picture it now, leaking through the ceiling, ready to wrap around him and take him *somewhere bad*. It's too much—grief, anger, fear—spilling over into a single wild roar as he slams his feet down into the black pools. All this time, it's—he's—been sniffing him out, getting ever closer as Max wallowed in limbo. He ducks his head to escape some of the rain, only to find he can no longer see below his kneecaps, blackness spiralling around him far too quickly. There's something else, too; stickiness on his hair and the back of his neck. He holds an arm out to find the rain falling black and syrupy, adding to the heaviness.

Up to his waist, he thrusts his arms out in front as if using invisible poles to drag himself through. It's slow going, each movement laboured and agonising, but finally, through the patches of thick mist, he sees a sliver of light falling against—*brick?* Letting out another cry, he buries his chin into his chest and lunges forward, nourished by something other than the greyness. *Come on!* As he draws closer still, he makes out two doors, both bleeding their redness into the fog.

The streetlight flickers, momentarily washing him in darkness.

No! No! No!

He can only see the top half of the doors, the black tide forever rising.

Another flicker.

Please, no!

Fizz.

He wades through darkness into darkness, no ringing to guide him, not even a whiff of hopefulness, only a malodorous cocktail of earth, rain, and death, tarnished further by the bitterness at the back of his throat.

As the downpour gets heavier still, he only manages a few more steps before it becomes almost impossible to walk. *Which one?* He thrusts from the ground, kicks his legs, and thrashes his arms against thick black soup, spitting out some of the darkness that leaks into his mouth. It's exhausting, bleeding him of any remaining strength, and the knowledge of the stickiness engulfing the remainder of the doors adds to the futility.

There's a place for you here.

He battles through the viscousness, some of it sliding down his throat and settling in his stomach like lead. *It has to be close.* And on the next stroke, his hand scrapes across brick. Depth unknown, he takes in a few short sharp breaths and one final mouthful of tainted air before plunging into oblivion.

Pressure wraps around his chest, immediately making him want to swim back up, but he knows he has one chance. He trails his hand across the coarseness as he kicks with his aching legs, submerging himself further into the sticky black void. Is he in the wrong place? Misjudged it completely? And hope begins to fade as fingers continue to claw against brick for far too long.

Finally, roughness turns to smoothness. Wood. And glass! He kicks his legs again, fumbling around the frames of the doors until he has hold of both handles.

Which one? *Which one?*

It feels like his chest is going to explode. He has to choose one, has to—

Which hand, Max?

Left.

One of these days, I'll call your bluff, son.

He grimaces as he turns the left handle, blurry brightness

filtering through as he rips himself from the murk into warmth. Closing the door behind him, he takes a breath, full of hope once more. But as he takes a few steps into the light, his heart sinks, that same godawful tune playing in the distance.

"Don't worry, son," his father's voice drifts across. "You can change it now."

"Am I safe, Dad?"

"Yes, son. You're home now."

RETAIL THERAPY

WE'VE FILLED the car with petrol at most a dozen times in the last four years. Everything's online these days; no need to leave home comforts to breathe in smog and fight with traffic and day walkers. "I can't believe you talked me into this, Maud."

"We can't hide forever, George."

"Nice mask, gimpy!" a greasy-haired kid shouts from a cluster of no-hopers.

Very original. What the hell are they doing up at this time anyway? "I don't see why not, Maud. I never liked humans before and don't like them now." Our pace synchronously increases, the neon-lit entrance to the local shopping plaza offering relative salvation from littered streets full of drunks, junkies, and the miscellaneous.

"We promised the kids we'd get out more," she says, nudging ahead. "Besides, they're right; it's not healthy, all day and night in front of the goggle box."

"We did a jigsaw last night."

"Whoop-de-bloody-doo."

"Look, I just don't see how shopping for cushion covers dramatically improves the quality of one's life, Maud."

She sighs. "I need a new hairdryer, too."

"Well, that's different. Buckle up."

She ups her pace, knowing damn well how bad my arthritis is this morning.

I launch into a hobble, just managing to avoid the already trodden-in pile of dog muck. "Wait up, Maud!" All I'm saying is we could get that stuff online, dear. All shapes, sizes, and colours."

"Yeah, just like the mask you're wearing, *gimpy.*"

"Maud!"

"Come on now, George, keep up."

I'm the first to admit the mask doesn't look like it did on the website, but safety before fashion every time. "I don't like this one bit, dragging us both out here, risking our lives. Besides, this mask is state of the art; nothing gets through. You can't get—"

She stops and turns, hands on her hips, teeth clenched.

Oh-oh.

"Sorry, love," I offer in advance. But the renowned lack of filter between my brain and mouth means this is one pile of doo-doo I'm already up to my arse in.

"You can't help yourself, can you?" She looks around, perhaps for witnesses. "Are people dying on the streets, George? Are we stepping over dead bodies en route to the shops? Is there a fetid smell of rotting flesh in the air?"

"More fishy than anything," I say meekly.

She takes in a deep breath, and I'm grateful for it. "Look, love, Covid will always be here in some form or other, but we can't hide ourselves away. I'm fed up with it, to tell you the truth—sick of cutting my hair, painting my own nails, doing laps around the bloody garden. And as for these monstrosities!"

My stomach drops. Invisible ants crawl across my skin. "You're not saying we take our masks off?"

She rolls her eyes. "No, George. But I think it's about time we stepped out of a zone that's become far too comfortable. We might as well be in bloody prison. Christ, if we spend one more day trapped in that house together, that might be where I end up."

Where are the witnesses now? "Yes, dear. Sorry, dear."

Her fibre-covered chin points to the sky. "Give me strength."

"Sorry, dear." *Sorry, sorry, sorry.* I'm bloody not, though.

"Now, come on, before it gets busy."

"Dear."

That was the play. We'll come in early, do a bit of shopping, let Maud get her nails done, and grab a coffee to mark the end of the ordeal. That's what people do. That's how they enjoy themselves, apparently. But anxiety twists at my stomach every second I'm here. Home is safe. Home is a haven, a comfortable vantage point to learn about all the advantages of staying right where you are. You only have to turn the telly on to learn about all the misery and hopelessness outside of the front door: Which celebrity is the latest to get a butt job, which bloody Covid variant is spreading now, the newest terrorist or splinter group fighting for this, that, or the other. So many of them; it's hard to keep track these days. I'll continue my silent protests from the armchair; thank you very much.

Warm air envelops my skin as we cross the threshold from outside to in. My palms are sweaty, and hairs bristle on the back of my neck.

"Will you please just relax, George? You look—odd."

Not a mask to be seen. "Even the staff aren't wearing them, Maud!" Shop by shop, I study the maskless faces, my chest tightening.

"Times have changed, George! We've got ours on; we're taking precautions."

Super Mart looms. Our destination. Our mission.

"Just in time," Maud says as the shutter opens and the line begins to disperse.

"That's a lot of people."

"You'll be right, George. Give me your hand."

"Mask wankers," a middle-aged fat guy yells from a doorway in front of his only slightly slimmer friend.

"Internet says they've got a sale on candles, too," Maud says, ignoring the attention.

"Well, we are running a bit low," I say. "Think we've dropped below a thousand." I keep my distance from other humans, holding my breath as someone's foot invades my invisible two-metre boundary.

Oh my God. Oh my God. We're actually doing this.

Here we go—free virus with every purchase.

I don't see him until he's on us, some masked idiot stepping out of nowhere, wielding a spray bottle.

"What the fuck?"

"The latest fragrance, sir, from Marceau Bleh-Bleh-Bleh."—at least that's what it sounds like to me.

"I don't care if there's a fucking genie in that bottle," I say, grimacing and holding my side. "Stay the fuck back!"

"George!"

"Maud, I could have stayed at home and sprayed scent into my eye!"

"Sorry," Maud says, her face reddening as she drags me away.

"Since when is that a thing?" I say, squelching the ball of my hand into my eye socket. "What else are they going to start doing? Shoving a cake in your gullet as soon as you walk in? Dousing you in fucking shampoo?" At least he was wearing a mask. I suppose the same one as mine at that.

Maud sighs and walks ahead.

I turn, intending to give the lone ranger an evil red eye, but he's back to spraying like a cat in heat.

"Smell this one, George. It's like walking through an orchard."

"If you say so, love." To my left, I hear shouting—some angry deadbeat at the *returns counter*, most likely.

"Smell it!"

Knowing she'll never give up, I go through the routine. "Not bad." I turn my attention back to the entrance to see spray-man no longer standing there. "Why are they pulling the shutters down?" Anxiety knots my stomach.

"What?" she says.

"The shutters. They're pulling them down."

Through her mask, Maud performs a series of short and sharp inhales. "Oh, Sunset Heaven. Smell this one, George."

"Smells like the last one, only a bit pissier." I turn again, eyes on the steel now blocking our exit. "Maud, I think something's wrong."

"Something's always wrong. It's probably just maintenance, love." She picks up a purple candle, inhales, furrows her eyebrows, and puts it back down again. "They'll have it open again soon. It'll be right."

But it doesn't feel right, not right at all. And while Phil Collins fills the store with the lyrics to 'In the Air Tonight,' my eyes draw to the electronics section, where an explosion of flames lights up every TV screen.

"Where are you going, George?"

"Just a minute, love."

A young mother trail-blazes in front of me, using the stroller like a battering ram. She glares at me, eyebrows furrowed as though I've just ripped her baby from the blankets and drop-kicked it into aisle seven.

"It didn't look like this on the internet," I say to her, but she continues walking, shaking her head.

Another old guy, mask-free, stands in front of one of the TVs, scratching the back of his neck. I position myself well away, watching the devastation unfold on one of the big screens.

"What's the world coming to," he says, proceeding to cough up a lung. "And what the fuck is that on your face?"

"It didn't look like—ah, mind your business." I edge that little bit further away, listening to the newscaster talking about a new spree of terrorist attacks occurring countrywide since early morning. Reports of buses detonating mid-route, litter bins exploding on busy streets, knife attacks, suicide bombers, shopping centres targeted—chaos everywhere, even accounts of people turning on each other.

Holy crap.

The man to my left continues hacking into a discoloured hand-kerchief. He turns to me again, eyes wide, face crumpled in discomfort. He drops to his knees, sucking in air and quickly retching it out.

Shit!

I want to help, but *virus, virus, virus.* I look around for someone's attention, but a young woman with red hair arrives at the scene and helps him to his feet. "Easy now." She digs out a water bottle from her handbag and holds it to the man's lips, allowing him to take a few generous mouthfuls. "Breathe," she says, holding his hand. "My name's Lucy. What's yours?" Slowly, the colour begins returning to his face, and the wheeziness eases slightly. He takes in a deep breath. "Gerald."

Thinking this mask was worth every penny, I watch as Lucy helps Gerald to a cushioned seat in front of 'Ladies Wear.'

"I was going to help," I say, "but—"

"Too busy thinking of yourself," she says.

Yes. "No, it's just—" I turn sharply, eyes on Maud, cursing her for it all.

"Yeah, walk away, mask-man, the I'm alright Jack-ass that you are," the woman hollers.

Exaggerating my limp for sympathy, I head back towards my wife, sure I hear a low growl emerging from behind.

"Do you need anything while we're here, love?" she says, still working her way through the candles.

"A portal to take me back to the seventies." Beyond her right shoulder, I see a kid jumping up and down, punching a mannequin in the boob. "Listen, Maud; I've a real bad feeling."

"Did you use your muscle spray this morning?"

"Not that. It's the terrorists; they're at it again." The kid's aiming between her legs now, really going for it, too.

"I blame the parents."

"Jesus Christ, Maud, I'm serious. Explosions, murders—it's all over the TV. I think we should go home."

"But we haven't got what we came for yet."

"Cushion covers and a hairdryer? You're pulling my plonker, aren't you?"

"No need for that tone, George."

I watch over her shoulder as the kid rugby tackles the mannequin to the ground and begins working on her arm. Where are his fucking parents? "Sorry, love, but this is serious. The news reporter said—"

He's got the bloody arm off. Why isn't anyone stopping him?

"Said what, George?"

Finally, the mother comes onto the scene. Thank God. Red-faced, letting out a raspy cough, she tries to prise the arm away, but the kid's not letting go.

"Said what, George?" Maud turns, following my stare towards the carnage. "My goodness."

Mother Dearest appears to be winning, dragging him across the store, both their faces wearing something well beyond rage as the kid's sneakers let out a squeal. But wait, he's biting at her arm, clawing at her face. And—holy shit—he just planted one of his Nikes into the very source from whence he came.

"My goodness," Maud repeats, dropping the Watermelon Fizz to the ground.

In a delayed reaction, the mother goes down with a squeal, hands to her groin.

"Maud, I told you. Things aren't right."

Unable to tear my stare away, I watch the kid bring the mannequin's arm behind his shoulders as though it was a baseball bat. Don't you do it, kid. Don't you—

With a roar, he lets it fly, the sound of the connection making me wince, but his mother's head moving an inch at best. First base, and that's generous. She gets to her feet and brushes herself down, offering a low guttural growl. Babe Ruth takes a step back, biting at the air, eyes narrowed in what looks like confused rage.

The first shoe hits him on the shoulder and the second glances off his right cheek.

"Mummy, stop. Mummy!"

The next one hits him square on the forehead, sending him stumbling backwards. Must have been a Doc Marten.

"Why isn't anyone helping, George?"

I turn, catching sight of two teenage girls as they rip at each other's hair. One of them reaches towards a sandwich maker; I'm not sure what brand, but I don't think toasties are on their mind.

Two people to my left are squabbling about which kettle to buy. The man likes the transparent one, but the woman insists the old-fashioned red one is more in keeping with their style. "Always so stubborn," the man says. The woman grabs the red kettle and drives it into his face. Dispute settled.

I feel fingers tighten around mine, and now I'm being whisked away down the lingerie aisle, an obstacle course of steel and super-sized panties. "Where are we going?"

"Fire exit, near the toy aisle."

"Good idea!"

Someone to our left coughs, creating a domino effect of raspy explosions.

I hold my mask to my face, overwhelmingly grateful we didn't go full hog.

"I'll fucking kill you," a voice screams from not too far away.

Shopping.

As I emerge from the *under-world*, something squeaks against my right cheek. Ow! The object lands a few feet ahead, letting out another squeak. A bone? I could be in my chair right now, sipping a cup of tea, halfway through a packet of custard creams, but no, I'm running through the middle of a superstore, having dog toys pelted towards me.

"This way," Maud says, yanking me to the right.

Above some Irish girl singing about zombies, another orchestra of coughs explodes around us—not the polite, understated barks usually reserved for public consumption; these are hernia-inducing, double-barrelled explosions of nastiness.

"I'm scared, George," she says, leading from the front, not noticing the tennis racket as it hurtles over her bird's nest hair.

"Just keep going, eyes forward." But the sound of a young child's cries snaps my head to the right and has me dragging on

Maud's wrist. "Wait." I follow the whimpering to see a little boy with frizzy hair standing under a sign marked *Homewares*. Beside him, a man and a woman are rolling on the floor smashing wooden plaques—one *Love*, one *Peace*—against the side of each other's heads. The woman's frothing at the mouth, eyes wide, lips curled back.

"Boy, come here."

He dragsa chubby arm across his face.

"I've got candy."

"George!"

"We've got puppies in the car, too, kid."

The boy begins his approach. Jesus, is it that easy? "That's it; come on now."

Hands in the cute little pockets of his sweatpants, he sniffles as he walks. "Mummy? Daddy?" But the savagery behind continues as *Mummy* smashes a vase into *Daddy's* face, sending splinters of glass towards our feet. Letting out a throaty yelp which turns into a hack, Daddy wraps his hands around Mummy's neck, but as the sharpness of the broken vase embeds into his eyeball, she pulls herself free.

"Don't look back, kid. Just a few more steps."

Mummy brings the weapon down again, creating a marshy sound and a fresh stream of magnificent red across Daddy's Van Halen T-shirt. "I'll fucking kill you," Daddy screams, trying to shake her off. But Mummy takes no heed. Veins popping in her neck, teeth bared, she brings the glass into his neck and begins working it across, tearing at Daddy's flesh.

Mummy Dearest is one mean motherfucker.

"Run, kid!"

And he does, straight towards me, letting out a cough just before he brings a steak knife from the pocket of his cute little sweatpants and sticks it into my left arm.

"George!"

There's no pain at first, and it's not particularly deep, but the intense tingling that follows, combined with the stream of blood running down my leathery skin, makes me feel more than a little woozy.

"Momma said not to talk to strangers," the boy says, reaching his chubby hand towards my mask.

Behind him, *Momma* guzzles at the blood on Daddy's neck, but I say nothing about her credentials as I thrust my fist into the little boy's face. "Not the mask, kid!"

"Daddy!" the boy screams, grabbing his nose.

But it's Mommy who looks up, her face smeared in Daddy's life source. She coughs a globule of blood onto the drab grey floor and offers a snarl as she pushes herself up. "Mask!"

"He tried to take it from me," I say, my arm beginning to throb. "I was just—"

"Mask," she repeats, her voice husky and devoid of human nuance. She growls and snaps her blood-smeared teeth at me. "Mask!" she says, louder this time, drawing the attention of some of the other *shoppers*.

Oh fuck.

"Run, Maud!" I cry, grabbing her wrist and whipping her along.

The hacking comes from all around, but undeniably the worst from directly ahead: Toy Section.

"Mask!"

"George! What do we do?"

I turn to see Mummy still lumbering after us, little-fucker in tow, a small army of other shoppers also tagging along. "Mask," Mummy says again, teeth gritted together. "Mask," her followers repeat.

Shit. Shit. Fuck. Fuck.

"George!"

"I don't fucking know, Maud." My left arm flaring, arthritis screaming at me, I try and take it all in, brushing away the countless pairs of stretchy pants to get a clear view. Ahead is a terrain of Lego pieces scattered across a blood-smeared floor. Worse still, directly in front of the fire exit, a hoard of parents play dodgeball with their children—as in using their kids as projectiles, launching them at each other with venom, savagery in their eyes. Bodies fly, young ones landing with a yelp and a soft thud among the bloody mine-field of Lego, some twisted form of karma. Some kids stay down; some get to their feet, biting and flailing at each other.

The fuck is this?

As we finally run out of stretch pants, staggering from cover into open ground, dodgeball is put on hold, and all eyes turn to us. Oh shit!

"Mask!" our new audience says, a sea of wild eyes and curled lips.

"Mask!" Mummy and gang chant as they continue their approach from behind.

I snap my head to the right only to see more of them coming, armed with plant pots, toothbrushes, and sandwich makers, the popular weapon of choice. Bringing up the rear, a big fella brandishes an outlandish feather duster. No thank you.

"Mask! Mask! Mask!"

Thoughts churn too quickly as I try and make sense of what is happening—terrorist attacks, shopping centres targeted. Above the Bee Gee's efforts to gee us up with the lyrics to Stayin' Alive, the store is a cacophony of coughing and growling. And my fucking arm is burning!

"What do we do, George?"

Pray.

Violence seems to be temporarily on pause as the *infected* focus on public enemy number one, the mask wearers.

"This way!" I yell, dragging her to the left.

"Mask! Mask! Mask!"

"George, I want to go home."

I hate to say I told you so, Maud. Words I so very much want to say, but I hold them in. Even I didn't expect this; it's worse than Black fucking Friday. "Come on!"

We run straight through the beauty aisle, feet crunching through glass, catching glimpses of our sallow skin and fucked up hair in the broken mirrors.

"Maud, watch out!"

But she doesn't see the woman in war paint step out from behind the eyeshadows until it's too late. Jennifer, the 'Here to help' staff member with cherry-coloured lips, thrusts a shard of glass into my wife's right leg, prompting a high-pitched scream and a look of disbelief across her face.

"George!"

"Enough's enough!" I scream, giving Jennifer a weak and arthritic kick in the crotch and dragging my wife towards the seemingly endless line of creams, all tauntingly promising to turn back time.

"Mask! Mask! Mask!"

They're everywhere, coming at us from all directions. Adults appear the most manic, as though they've less immunity to whatever's in their system, but the kids aren't far behind, following their *guardians* loyally, some limping, some bleeding. *Forgive and forget -* one of the unspoken rules of human dodgeball, it seems.

"Are you okay, love?"

"That's a stupid question, George."

Fair point.

As we reach the end of the beauty section, I release Maud's hand and wrap my fingers around one of the display hairdryers. "This way," I yell, ripping the appliance from the shelf and dragging us unwittingly towards the returns section. Seven of them, bloodied-up and puffy-faced turn their attention on us, dented boxes in hand —our fiercest audience to date. They snarl, howl, and cough—the grand slam. "Mask!" they say in unison.

"Come on, Maud!"

We continue staggering through the materialistic jungle to the sound of AC/DC and uninspired chants mocking our face wear.

"My leg really hurts, George," Maud cries, studying the stain of red that now runs to the hem of her dress.

"I know, love, but we have to keep moving." And as my eyes fall on the steel shutter ahead, a plan finally springs to mind: We'll draw them in, then make our run back to the fire exit.

"George!"

"I promise, Maud; it will be alright." But a couple of crusties against a hoard of angry virus-infected shoppers isn't a fair match on any day of the week, even pension day. "Now run!"

We move towards the edge of the store, beginning to loop around to where the nightmare started, to where the only other person wearing a mask sprayed us with—*wait.*

Holy shit, that's it! That's fucking it! It was in the spray.

"Mask! Mask! Mask!"

"What are we doing, George?"

"Get to the door!"

She offers a whimper but begins her shuffle, swatting my hand away as I extend it towards her. Charming. This was your fucking idea, love.

Exhausted, bloody, pain searing through every part of me, I make towards the shuttered entrance, the plug of the hairdryer bouncing behind. I see two staff members on the floor near the perfume counter, grounding and pounding, but they remain oblivious to us, a frenzied mess of blood, teeth, and atomisers.

Such a weak plan, but it's all I have.

"Nearly there, dear."

As I grit my teeth, trying my best to ignore the relentless throbbing in my arm, thoughts drift to the safety of our living room: Telly, biscuits, endless cups of tea, and as many bloody custard creams as one can eat! Paradise. I extend my arm towards the shutter, sucking in air through my mask and letting the cold steel take my weight.

"You okay, Maud?"

There's a sudden urge to move my mask aside, but the explosion of coughing and snarling from not too far away reminds me how stupid a decision that would be.

"Maud?"

No sign of her as I turn. "Maud!" If it weren't for the shutter door keeping me up, I'd be a crumpled mess on the floor. "Maud!"

Shit! Shit! Shit!

I imagine her writhing on the floor, nursing her leg, alone and terrified. But before I can even think of carrying out a search and rescue, I see the army approaching—hacking, growling, snarling, leering, biting, some even performing an angry little jig to Spandau Ballet.

"Mask! Mask! Mask!"

The sight of the Watermelon Fizz candle on the floor fills me with guilt, but there are too many of them; they'd rip me to shreds before getting back to her.

"Mask! Mask! Mask!"

Stand your ground, George.

Wait for it.

I plan my route, fingers clenched tightly around the hairdryer.

"Mask! Mask! Mask!"

Wait for it.

"Mask! Mask—"

Finally, I push myself from the shutter, swinging the hairdryer blindly in front, letting out a garbled war cry. "I'll come back for you, Maud!" Hunched over, I slip into cover behind the 'specials' rack, searching the shelves for anything that might make for a better weapon. A colander? No. Tea strainer? No. Cheese grater? They'd never stay still long enough. Resignedly, I maintain my grip on the hairdryer, staggering past the dog beds towards the homewares section.

A man with a ridiculous combover jumps out at me from behind the cat food. Instinctively, I swing the hairdryer hard into his face, pushing the candy cane I didn't see before even deeper into his eye socket. He lets out a whimper and staggers back.

"Sorry, not sorry," I say, pushing over a random mannequin adorned in a Hawaiian t-shirt and shorts. Momentarily, I contemplate turning back and ripping its leg off, but I stay loyal to the hairdryer.

Maud?

My pace slows as I see her rifling through cushion covers. She's singing along to Wham as though having one of her best mornings for ages.

"Maud, what the hell?"

"Mask Mask! Mask!"

I glance over my shoulder to see wide-eyed shoppers brandishing bizarre weapons like pitchforks as they close in on the masked monster.

"Run, Maud."

She turns and offers a smile, holding the bright yellow monstrosity towards me. "What about this one, Georgey?"

Panic perhaps? My mind trying to protect me? I didn't notice before, but—

"Mask! Mask! Mask!"

Helplessly, I watch my wife bring a hand to her maskless face and let out a bark. "My goodness," she says.

My Maud.

An image fills my mind of sitting at home in front of the fire, staring at the empty chair to my right, Maud's countless unfinished knitting projects sprawled across its arms and back. I imagine the single cup on the coffee table, long lonely nights staring at the telly, the cold space in the bed next to me. Forty years of marriage turned into nothing more than a broken heart and a poorly edited montage of memories.

My little Maudy-moo-moo.

"Mask! Mask! Mask!"

Returning my wife's smile, I continue towards her, thinking back to the day we first met. She was wearing a yellow summer dress with bright pink roses. Hardly a dash of makeup bar a little blusher, I thought her far too good for me. When she agreed to dance, I thought she was joking. "I like it, Maud," I say. "It will go nicely with the wallpaper." An arrangement of words I never thought would leave my lips.

She offers a growl as the zipper gets stuck halfway. "Fucking thing, George!"

It's the first time I've ever heard her use that cuss word. "It's okay, Maud." I place a hand on her shoulder and plant a soft kiss on her forehead. "It's okay."

"Mask! Mask! Mask!"

She looks up at me, her face crinkling like it does when she gets stuck on the cryptic crossword. "And will you take that stupid fucking mask off, you daft sod You look like a—"

"Okay, Maud. For you, I will."

But before I can even lift a hand to it, a tidal wave of pain explodes across the back of my head. I drop to my knees, disoriented, a high-pitched ringing in my ears drowning everything else out.

Cheers and coughs surround me.

Maud finally works the zipper free, her eyes and smile widening.

Too late to move, I catch sight of the sandwich maker coming towards me. White light fills my vision as my head bounces off the ground, delayed and overwhelming pain ripping through me.

As the world drifts in and out, feet fading to grey, back to feet, something trickles down my cheek. I'm not sure if it's blood or tears.

"I love you, Maud," I say, just able to hear my slurred words over the now incessant buzz.

She eyes me back as though I've just threatened to rip her insides out. "Mask!" she yells.

"I'm sorry I couldn't protect you, Maudy-moo-moo."

She kneels by my side and works my mask free, sliding a tiny hand under my head and bringing it into her lap. Around us, *chaos* resumes as it reverts to every person for themselves, no more witch-hunting of the lone mask wearer.

"I'll put the kettle on when we get there, Maud."

Pain swells, but the ringing abates, my wife's soft humming providing a modicum of relief.

My sweet Maud. My dearest sweet Maud.

She wraps the cushion cover around my head and prises the hairdryer from my fingers. Twenty-five percent off the online price for both, but not worth the trip out.

TIME FOR A CHANGE

COLD WHITE LIGHT sweeps across the house, sucking out any comfort in its path, and crunching gravel has my aching fingers clamping even tighter around the mantel.

This was a bad idea.

The engine cuts out. The car door slams. A silhouette. Footsteps.

Inhale. Exhale. I could hide. Maybe if—

I promise you, Bec, this is the only way you'll be free of him.

Olivia's voice settles me a little, but I feel nowhere close to as brave as in her presence. "Without closure," she told me, "I'll never be able to move forward; I'll always be running."

And God knows I've tried everything else.

His familiar rhythmic rap on the door sets my skin on fire, and all my rehearsed words start tumbling like kicked over alphabet blocks. I walk to the door feeling like I'm going into battle without arms.

I'll be there with you, Bec; remember that. I won't leave your side. None of us will.

There he is—the love of my life.

He smiles his once-powerful smile and raises the bouquet. Never been a flower kind of girl, but I'll take them over a broken jaw any day of the week. My trembling fingers lock around the door handle, the metal feeling impossibly cold.

"Hello, Paul."

"Rebecca, you look amazing."

He leans in towards me, blue eyes all child-like and hopeful, his familiar spicy aftershave wafting in with the gentle breeze, tainting the smell of cooking food and causing my stomach to churn. *Always be running.* A shudder runs down my spine as his lips find my cheek, but I stand my ground, reaching my hand out and imagining Olivia's fingers coiling around mine.

"I missed you," he says, pulling away slowly and offering the flowers, his eyes even more alive with expectation.

People always struggled to understand why I kept letting him back in. They used to look at me as though I was stupid, not quite all there. And Christ, they only knew the half of it, the marks I couldn't cover with high-top dresses, scarves, and long sleeves. But I thought this man was the love of my life. And we were happy once, as content as can be in such an absurd existence. To this day, I can't pinpoint when the darkness consumed him, but as the saying goes, love is blind.

"Wine?"

"Sure," he says, closing the door behind him. "A beautiful night."

"It is. I thought we could eat on the patio."

He eyes the table outside, basking in the glow of a flickering candle. "Stunning place," he says, taking a glass of red, "but a bit off the beaten track. Drove past it twice. Whose is it anyway?"

"It belongs to a friend, a proper country girl." Olivia runs it as a safe place for abuse victims, *Shady Pines Retreat*. Quite often, she'll just let people have it for a few days, a chance to embed themselves in nature.

"Can I give you a hand with anything?"

"No, sit down. It'll be ready in a couple of minutes."

"What a view." He folds his arms, surveying the wooded area at the back. "Smells amazing out here. I mean, the food also, but the air's so fresh and invigorating."

I call this eggshell mode, usually lasting a couple of days after an event but inevitably giving way to darkness. That's how I used to think of it—that there was a demon inside of him, and I was the only one who could cast out the evil—a tumultuous life spent walking a tightrope between love and fear. "It is beautiful," I say, already thinking of the place as a second home. "The pine, the wildflowers, the faint smell of smoke. The simple things, eh?"

"The ones we lose sight of," he says as he pulls a chair out. "How have you been?"

I begin slicing the lamb, my appetite returning. How have I been? How have I been? My bones are fixed, but the scars will remain forever. "Getting there."

"I was surprised." He inhales again, a city boy all his life. "When I got the invitation, I mean."

"Dinner's nearly ready. Help yourself to more wine." But I see his glass already replenished. He's *tried* giving up alcohol before, even booked into an AA meeting once after a particularly nasty *episode*. Just another offering to temporarily appease.

"Don't you get scared out here all alone?" he says. "I didn't see another house for miles."

"It's the safest I've felt in years."

The chorus of crickets seems impossibly loud. He says nothing as he lifts his glass to his lips.

"I hope it's good," I say, carrying his plate through. "Don't usually go to the trouble with it just being me, usually a sandwich or microwave meal."

"Looks great."

I feel his eyes on me as I put the plate down. "There's more if you're hungry," I say. The candle's flame flickers as the gentle breeze blows across, bringing more of his scent and an image of our old bedroom, the extended crack in the ceiling, and the sheer purple curtains. I grasp the back of a chair for support, waiting for the dizziness to pass.

"What am I doing here, Bec?"

"What do you mean?" I retreat towards the kitchen counter, full of doubt once again.

"You haven't replied to my texts for weeks, and then out of the blue, I get an invite for dinner."

Gripping the plate to stop my trembling, I make my way back to the table. *This is the only way you'll be free of him.* "Let's eat before it gets cold."

He smiles and nods. "It's so good to see you."

To anyone who doesn't know our history, I imagine we'd look like lovers at the beginning of our relationship—gentle classical music playing in the background, dining and drinking wine under the light of a glorious full moon. We talk about our jobs and our friends, mutual and new. We smile. We chew. We open another bottle, letting nature's perfume wrap around us. The night has all the awkwardness and superficiality of a first date, but ours takes place on a thin sheet of ice that could crack at any moment.

"I think about you every day," he says, reaching for my hand.

I recoil and pray for strength. "Shall we have dessert?"

"That depends on what's on offer?"

"Baked Alaska. I'll go and—"

"Sit down!" The shadow passes across, the demon leaving just as quickly, softness returning to his face. "Please."

I think this marks the juncture at which small talk ends.

"Why am I here, Bec?"

"So I can move on. So we can both move on."

He says nothing, but from the corner of my eye, I see the napkin crumple under his grip.

"We share a history, Paul, a portion of time that has come to an end. Let's close that book and move to the next."

"What if I don't want to?"

"You just don't have that kind of power over me anymore." I clasp my hands together. "I'm doing this regardless, and I was hoping tonight you'd finally agree to let me go. I know you follow me. I know it's you on the end of the phone." I swallow hard, watching the napkin unfurl as he picks up his glass and consumes the dregs.

"Doesn't it prove how much I love you, though? My heart is breaking, Bec, can't you see that? I'm nothing without you."

Stay strong, Bec; we are with you. "Your heart might be breaking, but mine is just mending." I lift my gaze from the table to his blue eyes. "Some of my bones, too."

His face twitches, a familiar sign he's on the defensive, his offense never far behind. He exhales, leaning back with hands clasped behind his neck, eyes towards the stars. "My parents have been married forever. They never gave up on each other."

"How many times did I take you back. How many?"

"Had their fair share of wars but came out better from it."

"War? Every couple argues, Paul." I lean in towards him, crossing into no man's land. "But no marriage should end in broken bones and blood." I feel the hair prickling on my neck and arms. The air feels charged, like just before a storm. I can almost see the thunder cloud forming around him.

"And I can't apologise enough for that, Bec," he says, all sincerity sifted out by gritted teeth. He leans towards me, hands knotting together, wedding ring on show. "But I've done my time. Had a chance to reflect on my actions, and I—"

"You're what?" I'm taking charge, and it feels fantastic, recipro-cating his advance until our heads are only inches apart. I'm not running anymore. "A different person? A man of God?"

His eyes widen, and his nostrils flare. "I'm not the guy you used to know." He gives me the puppy dog eyes, but I see his knuckles turning white. Always the same lines, same routine.

"I can't even remember the guy I first met." I think back to what Olivia told me, releasing my words with as much dispassion as possible. "He's buried under mounds of tainted soil."

"Why am I really here?"

"I told you already."

"I don't believe you." He settles back in the chair. "You still love me, don't you?"

I look deep into his eyes, beyond the innocence of the blue. "No."

"You're lying." Lines carving their way across his temple, he begins gently shaking his head. "There's still a way back, Bec; I know it." As he lunges forward again, reaching for my hand, the breeze wraps around us, distinguishing the candle and bringing smells of damp tree trunks, moss, and carrion. I try to break free from his grasp, but his fingers coil around my knuckle like a giant's.

"Tell me there's still a way, Bec."

"Let go of me."

"Not until you tell me we can be good again." He momentarily releases his grip, sliding his hand to my wrist and snapping me towards him. "Please, Bec. One more chance. One last chance."

We're here with you. "No."

I feel his elevated pulse on my skin, his grip tightening. The air is heavy, polluted with his aftershave and the smell of rotting meat. "You always were a fucking tease," he says, his sky-blue eyes now loaded with the promise of a storm to end all storms.

"Let fucking go of me, Paul!"

He clamps down harder, his warm smile at the door a fleeting memory, replaced with the demon's leer. "That perfume you know I like, the music, the low-cut dress, eating under the stars—all for what, Bec? Some twisted joke? A way of hurting me?"

I hear rustling leaves. And breathing, heavy and excitable.

"Look at me when I'm talking to you!" He pulls me in, wrapping his other hand around the back of my head. "This is not how it ends!" Glasses tumble, plates clatter as he rakes against my softness, his lips devouring mine, his tongue hungrily searching within.

As I revert to well-practiced numbness, orbs like glowing embers light up the woods around us, moving in time with the music and creating an almost magical display. A fairy-tale romance to the outsider. He comes up for air, resting his forehead against mine. "I love you so much, Bec. We can start again; I'll show you." His left-hand wraps around my waist, his right beginning to slide up my low-cut dress, something I could never wear when we were together for so many reasons. "One more chance."

More ember-like globes appear as he applies his lips to mine with sickening intensity. I hear blood whooshing in my ears. Scenes of violence in my mind melt into the vivid imagery behind my *beloved's* shoulder, each branch visible with impossible clarity, the grass beneath dancing to the breeze.

There's fear, but only of the unknown.

Placing my palms on his back, I bring him into me. He lets out a groan as his tongue gets busier still, his hands squeezing at my breasts. There's a crackle, what I think at first to be the forest carpet, but my skin begins to prickle, and my body flares with pain. More snapping fills my ear, accompanied by explosive pain that has me instinctively grinding our rib cages together. He lets out a muffled rasp as I push my lips harder against his, my sharpness continuing to explore his back. Eyes wide, face red, he flails against me, but there's no give.

The first time is always the hardest.

Every hair on my body stirs as the breeze blows across once more, bringing too many scents to decipher. He continues struggling, trying to force my head back with his hands and sucking air through his nostrils, his tongue finally retreating like a wounded animal.

As though someone is bending my spine like a piece of plastic, pain detonates across my back. I can hear every bone expanding, snapping, buckling. My skin smoulders with impossible intensity as Paul continues offering dampened moans, his eyes widening further still as they search mine for answers. His lips form a scream as my claws pierce his flesh, but I steal it from him, just as he stole mine for all those years.

No more running away!

Refusing to let go, I plunge my sharpness further in, listening as blood pumps violently around a shredded body that now feels puny within my clutches. Fire rages within, skin stretching to accommodate elongated bones. My jaw dislocates, contorts, and enlarges as new teeth cut through the rawness, bringing unimaginable agony.

Instinctively, I clamp down, feeling his body trembling against mine as blood spills down our chins, pure fear in his eyes now.

I'm ravenous again.

Bearing down on him, ready to dine, I catch sight of my reflection within the blue, and I release, recoiling until my back is against the brick. *Embrace it. It's a beautiful thing.* The hair, the eyes, the ears, though. *Olivia, I'm scared! A miracle of nature. We are blessed.* Her voice in my head is like water on my skin, extinguishing the flames until once again, only magic surrounds me, the heightened sounds of the forest and the ever-approaching golden orbs.

With a hand across his shredded lip and blood spilling through his fingers, Paul lets out a garbled cry. In return, I offer a howl of my own, nearly a decade's worth of screams rolled into one.

He begins a delayed retreat, eyes not leaving mine. I see the knowledge in them, though, and can taste his fear now, far more potent than that rancid aftershave. As a chorus of howls return mine, eyes like headlights continuing to close in, his leg buckles, and he crumples to the concrete tiles.

The night didn't quite go as planned, did it, darling?

Olivia said doubt would creep up on me from time to time, but since seeing him through the glass of the door, the pathetically hopeful look spread across his face, and the puny offering grasped in his right hand, I wanted this. Finally, I'll be free of him, no longer frightened to look over my shoulder or answer my phone.

One bite, and it can all be different.

Olivia's first to pounce, launching towards him with a growl, her teeth clamping around his neck, prompting a blood-curdling scream and multiple streams of red that look magnificent against the backdrop of the moon. Writhing and moaning, trying to prise her jaws away, Paul's terror-filled eyes fix on mine, perhaps hoping for a last-minute reprieve.

But this dog has had its day.

I can smell the blood, stronger than before, a coppery bitterness that usually turns my stomach but now only serves to heighten my hunger. He's just prey now. Others begin emerging from the darkness, ready for the feast, teeth bared, snouts frothy with saliva.

The only way.

A series of watery gurgles emerge from his throat as they begin puncturing and ripping at his flesh. They tug at his body like a rag doll, dragging him this way and that until the twitching finally ceases and the light dims behind his eyes.

She was right.

Moving in, I feel free, empowered, about to feed on someone that ate away at me for most of my adult life. And when we've finished eating, picking the meat from his bones, we'll share a glass of wine and toast to new beginnings—a stronger, unified, dependable pack.

We howl in unison, the women of Shady Pines Retreat.

MOUNT PLEASANT HOUSE

THEY CALL this nursing home Mount Pleasant House, but I'll tell you right now, there isn't anything pleasant about it. The place feels more like a prison than a house, too.

Winter sun somehow finds its way through the thick grime of my second-floor window, bringing some relief as it falls across my arthritis-ridden knees. I hear the school bell ring in the distance and the children's faint guffaws and screams. I shuffle across the yellowing mattress, biting at my lip, just managing to catch the last of them flocking to class.

Morning is bittersweet for me, my favourite and worst time of day. It brings a humanising effect, temporarily removing me from the sadistic rituals of the home and an intense feeling of loneliness and alienation from the world beyond these walls. Outside, people will be breathing the air, taking in all the delicious smells and colours that I once took for granted. They'll be laughing, loving, and crying.

They'll be living.

God, I hate this place, the harsh and sterile smell of detergent, the fading yellow paint on the walls, the dirty linen, and loathsome staff. It's a glorified waiting room—housing for the nearly dead.

Visitors are rare. Sometimes weeks pass without me seeing a familiar face. Even then, it's over so quickly; small talk, an awkward hug, and "See you next time." They turn a blind eye to the squalor. The money's gone; nothing in it for them, no reason to stick around.

Edith, the resident from two doors down, is my best friend. She often visits. The last time they caught her in my room, though, they dragged her back to her quarters and gave her one hell of a beating. I heard every blow and cry. It made me sick to the stomach; it did.

Holding my breath, skin prickling, I arch my neck towards the door.

Someone's coming!

As footsteps echo down the corridor, the sun slowly begins to sink away as if as terrified as I am of the woman that walks the halls.

My stomach lets out a groan at the unmistakably slow and menacing rhythm I know to be the stroll of the chief nurse, Rebecca. She moves like that on purpose, like a lion sauntering towards its prey, spreading anxiety and fear among us residents. The other nurses are apathetic, sometimes abusive, depending on their mood, but she—well, she brings an unpredictability that makes me long for my wait to be over.

I hold my breath as the footsteps cease.

Sometimes she does it for kicks, I'm sure of it. That's how Rebecca caught Edith last time—removed her shoes so we couldn't hear her approach. Evil to the bone, she is. Those that have tried to stand up to her have been shut away for days, sometimes until death.

But what can we do? Nobody in the normal world cares. Why would they? We're past our sell-by date, unwanted, with no refund available.

Gripping the sheets, I screw my eyes tightly shut, blood pounding in my ears. I replay the laughter of the children, their joy and lust for life. I imagine the smell of wet mud in the playground and the smoke from the surrounding houses where wood fires burn.

They can never take that away—the scenes and accompanying soundtrack in my head—that's mine.

She would if she could, though.

Sometimes, she stands outside the door for ages without entering. But I always know when she's there. It's as if the air carries a charge, like just before a storm, and in addition to the always present faint smell of piss, she brings something else with her, Devil's perfume, I call it.

It's all just part of the game she plays, how she gets her kicks.

"Alf," she calls out as my door smashes against the wall.

A shiver runs down my spine, and the skin around my skull tightens. One word—just my name—but so much fear. I feel myself trembling. It's suddenly so cold, as though her presence is stealing the remaining warmth. Devil's perfume hangs in the air.

"Look at me!" she barks.

My room is clean; I made sure of it, especially after last time. Nervously, I turn my head towards her, slowly opening my eyes. She's small, wiry, but brings a much larger presence, as though adorned in a heavy and stifling cloak of darkness. At a guess, I'd say mid-thirties, but with a margin of ten on either side. I think she might have even been pretty once, but something bad must have happened to drain the softness.

Her hair is as white as snow. When I first saw her, I thought that admirable, but it soon became just another layer to her iciness. She plasters it down to her scalp with metal hair clips, all with rusty teeth that only add to her wicked appearance. The thick coat of lipstick is blood red, and against her pale skin and stark white uniform, the dark eyes and lips dominate her look. No smile or laughter lines, just a series of deep caverns across her forehead amplifying her rigidity.

She just looks evil.

"You have a visitor," she says, hunched over, sliding her heels back on.

"Who—who is it?" I ask, trying not to show too much excitement. She wouldn't like that. As I swing my legs from the bed, a sharp pain runs down my side but not enough to dampen my spirits.

Without another word, she turns and begins to walk away.

A visitor? My mind begins to race with possibilities, anything better than being stuck in the shoebox waiting for Rebecca to haunt the corridors. Perhaps my family has come for me? I told them last time about what was happening, the bits I could remember, but it's so difficult now, fragments of time disappearing along with my credibility. But I have to hope.

Rebecca is so far in front, most likely strutting in anger, filled with resentment about the visit. *Bitch.*

I follow the sounds of her echoing footsteps, travelling the familiar drab grey corridor and past the other residents' cells. That's what we call the rooms. We're all prisoners. There are no locks on the door, but there are always dire consequences if we're caught outside our cells. Edith's is on the left, just a few yards ahead. She came to me last night, and we spent hours just giggling. We're both losing our minds, forgetting what we're talking about mid-sentence, sometimes before we even begin.

BUT YOU HAVE TO LAUGH.

Rebecca's already out of sight. I know where to go, though. Past the fire exit and to the left. I can't stop thinking about who the visitor could be. My son and his new wife came last month. Surely, they wouldn't bless me with another visit so soon. My sister, perhaps? But she's supposed to be in for a hip operation.

One of the male nurses, Jim, comes out of one of the rooms wheeling a trolley full of meds. The blood starts pumping again, and I quicken my pace, pinching my side to distract from the intense pain shooting up both legs. I know to keep my head down and not make eye contact. My friend Tommy got a broken jaw last week for that privilege. Wary of his eyes on me, I continue to walk, my eyes fixed on the shiny floor. I can almost feel the nurse willing me to look up, any excuse to take a break from mundane duties. Finally,

I'm out of the danger zone, only two doors away from the visiting room. My heart rate begins to slow to just above normal, and I slow my pace, knowing I'll feel that little burst of speed in my joints for the rest of the week.

Kate, one of the other nurses, emerges from the room and holds the door open. She offers an awkward grin. It's the first time I've seen her project anything else but disdain. Warily, I force a smile, crossing the threshold with a flurry of excited adrenaline.

But it's short-lived.

The door slams shut behind me, and I feel the warmth trickling down my leg.

Rebecca stands behind one of the chairs, wearing the same uncharacteristic smile as the others. And a pair of black latex gloves. Beyond the glass window behind her, the world continues obliviously.

"Sit down, Alf. Just a standard dental inspection, nothing to be concerned about."

But there has been no such check in the two years I've been here.

"You said—"

"I lied. Now sit down, Alf. This will all be over quickly."

The room starts spinning, a montage of drab whites and yellows as the surge of fear washes over me. My legs give, and suddenly, I'm falling, landing on the tiled floor in a clumsy heap, agonising pain tearing through my right leg and across the side of my head. I want to scream, but I bite hard into my lip, refusing to show the bitch any weakness.

Rebecca begins her approach. "Oh, Alf. You are a clumsy old fucker, aren't you?"

She threads her arms under my shoulders and lifts me roughly onto the chair.

"Open wide, Alfie. This might hurt a bit," she says before squeezing my jaw tightly. "Open your goddamn mouth, you senile sack of piss!"

The pain is intense. I can't hold out any longer. I open my mouth, grimacing as Rebecca moves her face close to mine. "I hope your little rendezvous with Edith was worth it. She got hers, and now you get yours. My rules don't get broken!"

Pinching my nostrils shut, she forces her black-gloved hand into my mouth. Immediately, I panic, gasping desperately for air, flailing my arms, and kicking against the floor, trying to get traction.

"Sit still, you fucker!"

To a series of high-pitched squeaks, my chair turns slightly towards the window, but it's no good; this is it. My wait is finally over. Head and chest feeling as though they might explode, I let out a series of muffled cries, focusing on the large window and the bare trees swaying gently in the breeze as the clouds roll by. Just another wintry day.

Not like this. Not to her.

My heels continue to squeal, leaving a trail of black on the floor as I wrestle with the nurse's grip. But she's so goddamn strong! More watery gargles emerge from my mouth as flashbacks play in my head, times spent with my wife before cancer stole her, afternoons with my son on the fishing boat, all the stuff we take for granted.

"Was it worth it, Alf? Was it?!" she screams, her cold dark eyes burning into mine and the sickening clinical taste of her glove in my mouth. The pressure in my chest builds, and the black ring around my vision starts to close in. The curtain is coming down.

Edith?

It was, I'm sure of it! I saw her from the corner of my eye.

"My fucking rules don't get broken!"

Just as I put it down to my imagination, I see her again.

With a sparkle in her eyes, Edith puts a finger to her lips and places her other hand on Rebecca's shoulder. The nurse's eyes widen immediately, an understanding that plans are about to be ruined.

"This will give us something to talk about," Edith says.

Rebecca's body begins to jolt as though bolts of electricity course through her. Blood starts spilling down her chin as a lump of her tongue thuds softly against the stark white floor. Her grip on me loosens, and I recoil, desperately sucking in mouthfuls of stale air. I keep my gaze fixed on her all the time, not wanting to miss the show. A series of strange, garbled noises emerge from the nurse's blood-filled mouth as she reaches for her throat, eyes bulging, surrounding skin turning a tinge of blue.

Behind her, Edith slowly begins to vanish; mouth still stretched into a wide smile.

Rebecca's face is the softest I've seen, full of vulnerability and fear. She reaches towards me, clawing at her throat, eyes wider still.

I take in another gulp of air, keeping my stare fixed on her as she approaches the end of her journey. "I guess you got yours, too."

Enjoying every second of her confused suffering, I continue watching her struggle until she finally falls to the floor in a clumsy heap, squirming and twitching until she isn't.

Stumbling painfully back through the corridor towards my room, the other nurses eye me with confusion. I make a point of looking at each of them directly, knowing they'll find out soon enough, but hoping, without their chief, things may change.

Expecting the clatter of the door at any moment, I wait for them in my room, but none of them come. Edith does, though, later in the day. Poor dear doesn't remember a thing. Still doesn't even know she's dead, and it isn't my place to tell her.

How they could have done such a thing still twists at my insides.

I do hope she continues her visits.

JUST A FLY

I CAN'T EXPLAIN IT.

But who can delineate the complexities of true love and its raw power?

I've had similar experiences before—when someone has made me all warm and fuzzy inside. Only it's more than that this time; I feel lightheaded and disoriented, perhaps intoxicated would not be too strong a word. No, I truly can't explain it.

All I know is that I'm in love.

There she is, resting on the arm of the chair in the corner, evening summer light trickling through the hotel blinds, emphasising her vibrancy. I've never seen anything like it. So elegant, so beautiful. Elongated body flowing like an elegant summer gown, shiny as metal but softened by its lilac colour. Mesmerised, I watch a small purple gas cloud emerging from her lower abdomen, momentarily hanging in the air before dissipating into the remaining sunlight. The scent is heavenly, the sweetest of perfumes that makes me ache for more.

Yes, it's safe to say I'm smitten.

"Bloody insects," Stacey says, pulling the covers away as she reaches down for her skirt. "They need one of those zappers in here." Drawing her arm back, she readies to launch the clothing towards the chair.

"Wait," I say, snatching at the hem of the skirt. "It's just a fly. It won't kill you."

She shakes me off and hurls the skirt with vigour. "Dirty little fucker."

Heart in mouth, I watch the makeshift weapon fall well short, landing in a heap near the chair leg. As *she* takes flight again, my love creates a hypnotic melody that works its way to my bones. My skin tingles as though her wings are fluttering against each layer, setting off a chain reaction of hyperactive nerve endings as I squirm with delight between the sheets. Such grace. Such speed. Stacey didn't stand a chance. Yes, the melodic hum of my love's wings epitomises the essence of summer. And that scent!

Perfection.

Is it a she? Why do I assume that?

"Fucking thing!" Stacey screams, dampening the moment. Naked, she pushes herself from the bed and inelegantly stomps over to the chair. Bending over and giving me an eyeful, she snaps at the skirt before twitching her head in line with the insect's movement. Together, we watch my love finally come to rest on the wall, only a few inches from my head. Even without the touch of light, she looks so beautiful, almost jewel-like, similar to something you might find at the centre of an expensive collection.

Stacey looks at me and smiles with an I've got this look. I have seen it in her eyes before; she won't rest until her body is just a smear.

"Stacey, it's just a fly. It won't kill you."

But she's already halfway across the room, teeth clenched, everything jiggling as she swings her skirt wildly through the air. Thankfully, my love is long gone before the fabric hits the wall. "I hate them!" Stacey yells, continuing her assault, her fleshy imperfections highlighting her lack of grace relative to the display of beauty effortlessly outmanoeuvering each attack. "Fucking hate them."

"Just a fly, Stace."

Offering another war cry, Stacey strikes again, the buzzing stopping well before she reaches full stretch. "Where did it go?" There's a wildness behind her eyes now, cheeks rosy red, teeth still clenched. "Where did the little fucker go?"

Nerve endings sing in my wrist, and I look down to find my love, eyes ruby red and as perfect as the rest of her. My skin tickles as she makes her way up my arm, finally coming to rest on my upper bicep. Staring straight up towards me, she fires another spray of that alluring purple haze, the enigmatically intoxicating scent immediately filling my nostrils, the perfume cloud increasing in size, gradually morphing into the shape of a heart before vanishing without a trace.

I'm going to call her Jade.

"How can you bear that, Patrick? Filthy fucking insect!"

I study Stacey's naked form as she stands in front of me, cursing and holding the fabric weapon in her right hand. No, she could never be as elegant as Jade, the way she manoeuvres gracefully in the air, her gentle stride across my skin, the hypnotic shimmer, the beautiful music she makes when in flight.

"She's just a fly," I say.

"She?"

Without warning, Stacey swings her arm back and brings it violently down towards my arm, the sting instant as the zip catches my skin.

"Hey!" I yell, but thankfully, there's no sign of my love as Stacey lifts the skirt away. Frantically searching between the creases in the covers, I pray I'll not find my love's remains. *Please. Please. Please.* My heart sings as I hear my love again, the volume of her flight fading in and out as she circles the room.

"Damn it!" Stacey says, aimlessly flicking the skirt in the air, following my love's sweet music. Eyes wide, her breathing heavy and erratic, Stacey's on the hunt again. She performs a spin, her forehead creasing as her gaze lands in my direction. "What the hell, Patrick?"

"What?"

"That!" She aims a finger towards the small tent near the centre of the duvet. "If I'd known the sight of me running around in my birthday suit, swinging my skirt above my head, did it for you, I'd have done it more often."

"Oh." But that isn't for you, silly. "Oh, yeah." No, that's an aching to bask in the vibrancy of my beloved next to me, to transcend human form somehow and lose myself in wave after wave of euphoric green as we make love to her sweet music.

Stacey brings the skirt behind her right shoulder, snapping her head left and right. "As soon as I get rid of this fucking fly, we can christen the room. Start putting the spice back in our life. What do you say?"

"Sure." A burst of that beautiful music draws my attention to my chest. And there she is, blessing me with her touch. My skin, a composition of excitable nerve endings, marks her path as my enchantress slowly and elegantly graces me with a close-up of her exquisiteness. "I love you," I whisper.

"Aw, I love you too, Patrick," Stacey says, aggressively delivering my name as she flings the skirt across my chest, causing a light rush of air and immediate panic. Frantically, I pull it away, again searching the dark crevices of the duvet. "What the hell, Stace?"

"Did I get it?" she says, looking positively jubilant. "I think I got it."

The silence is deafening.

No struggle. No flutter of wings.

I pull the duvet all the way across. Nothing. I search the floor, the table, and even under the pillows, but no sign.

My beautiful Jade.

"Yippee-ki-yay, motherfucker!" Stacey yells. "Now, let's see what we can do with that, shall we?"

Just as I lose hope, my heart breaking, eyes filling with moisture, I hear her beautiful melody again, the undulating volume of her flight as she soars above our heads.

"Goddamn," Stacey says through gritted teeth. She reaches down for her skirt again, head snapping around the room like a zombie as she follows the rapturous symphony.

Silence falls once more.

It takes me a while to catch on, but as a series of strange and garbled noises emerge from Stacey's lips and she begins stabbing at her throat with a finger, all I can think is I've lost *her all over* again.

My wife's eyes start to bulge as though they're trying to force themselves from her head. She staggers across the room red in the face, heaving and rasping at the floor, her mouth so wide it looks unnatural. Fingers in her mouth, she releases a series of horrific gags, strings of saliva extending towards the bland carpet. "I swallowed it," she finally manages to say. "I swallowed the fucker."

"It's just a fly," is all I can think to say. But she was the love of my life.

Stacey scowls at me, eyes raw and watery. "Hate the fuckers," she croaks, making her way towards the bathroom. "Fucking, fucking flies!"

I know I should help, but I can only think of Jade. Heaviness washes over me, paralysing grief as though I've lost my one true soulmate.

And I did nothing. Nothing!

As my wife aggressively brushes her teeth between spasmodic bouts of retching, I feel lost, empty. I can't stop thinking about her; I should have protected her, and now she's dead. I could have stopped it. The way we looked at each other, the way she made me feel inside. A magical connection, yet I did nothing, just passively observed as Stacey attempted to spread her guts. Such beauty, a miracle of nature. The sound of her wings in flight sent tingles down my spine, and her colours were so impossibly vivid and seductive. And the feel of her dancing across my skin created an inexplicable desire that I imagine could never be quenched.

My Jade.

I don't understand any of it, but she made me feel more alive than ever before. Her scent somehow ignited feelings evading human words, an inexplicable, immeasurable level of emotion. But now she's gone, and only memories of her exist now and will until my dying day.

"I'm sorry, my darling."

"Huh?" Stacey emerges from the bathroom, looking a little worse for wear but slightly more composed. "Wow, even after all that, seeing me at my worst, you're still up for it? Where's all this passion back home?"

I shrug, my love's scent still in my nostrils. "Stacey, we don't have to do—"

"Nonsense."

As Stacey approaches, passing through the filtered moon rays of the hotel room window, her skin momentarily appears to take on a green tinge. A projection of my loss, perhaps? A trick of the light? She slips under the covers and wraps her hand around my length.

I don't want this. I want Jade.

As my wife plants her lips on mine while straddling me, visions of Jade being inside her fill my mind. I let them take me, plunging me into soft, moist layers of velvety-green ecstasy. I feel closer to her, agonisingly so. I get harder still, reminiscing about Jade's elongated abdomen, the glossy red eyes that burned into me, her music, and her touch on my skin. I'm on top, suddenly hungry, consumed by the moment.

"Jesus Christ, Patrick, where have you been all this time?"

We moan, groan, lick, bite, our sweaty bodies slipping and sliding against each other in animalistic harmony. It's the first time we've made love for weeks; that's what the holiday was for, somewhere as far as possible away from all the entrapments of life, but not in a million years would I have thought I'd find the love of my life. But this isn't her; my love is gone, dead, our fleeting love affair over.

"Yes, Patrick!"

I swear her skin just shimmered.

"Don't stop, Patrick!"

Yes, there it is! Once again, imagining it's Jade underneath me, I drive harder into her.

"That's it, Patrick!"

I put a finger to her lips. Stop talking, will you? She writhes underneath me, her skin undoubtedly beginning to change colour. Is this all in my head?

Holy shit.

Her body—something's happening—stretching, glistening. Skin taut over her ribs, she grips the headboard, moaning, whimpering, the veins in her almost translucent arms pulsating like sleeping serpents. She opens her eyes, offering me a flash of red.

I'm close, I can feel it, but I don't want it to be over. Her eyelashes begin to flutter, gently at first but with ever-growing intensity, until they mimic my lost love's melody.

Please don't talk. Please don't talk.

She opens her mouth, but thankfully nothing emerges.

Our bodies glide against each other as close as two people can be, but it still doesn't feel like enough. I want more. I want to feel Jade properly, not just through my wife. I thrust harder and harder, but it's an itch I can't scratch. She stretches and twists underneath me, her body shifting through colours so rich, striking, evocative, and—shit, I'm going to come. No, no, no, not yet!

Between flutters, I see her eyes burning red again. Jade's in there; I know. We see each other. Understand each other in this moment of exquisite passion. Impossible love, orchestrated by fate.

I'm lost in her world.

But as I finally orgasm, observing Stacey's face beneath, eyes wide and back to brown, her skin sunburnt red, I feel so dramatically underwhelmed and, again, consumed by grief. Just Stacey. No elongated body, no gleam, no grace.

No Jade.

She pushes me off and rolls to her side. "What the hell, Patrick?" Her voice is quavering, suddenly vulnerable.

"What?" I say, drenched in sweat, taking in mouthfuls of warm air. "That was amazing, the best we've had."

She begins to cry, curling up into a ball.

"Stace."

Swatting my arm away as I try and console her, she inches to the edge of the bed. "You were looking right through me."

"I was—in the moment."

"I asked you to be gentle, but you carried on."

Couldn't hear you over the beautiful music. "Sorry, Stace. I thought you were enjoying it."

"I was at first. But—"

"But what?" I feel my anger rising. "What do you want from me, for Christ's sake?" She calls me prudish back home, unwilling to experiment, yet here and now, I gave everything, and it's still not good enough.

"Never mind," she says, bringing the sheets over her, even though it's stifling. "I'm tired."

"For fuck's sake. I wish you'd make your mind up." I turn to face the other wall, feeling lousy but at the same time free-falling into sorrow's oblivion.

We stay as far away from each other as the bed will allow. Now and again, I think I hear the light flutter of wings and look for *her*. Inevitably, though, I settle back into my damp pillow, resuming my restlessness, enduring Stacey's familiar snore.

Hours pass as I stare at the crack in the ceiling, reminiscing about *our* time together, and just as my eyes begin losing their fight, Stacey's snoring stops. Seemingly asleep and unaware of her movements, she starts twitching, causing the entire mattress to shake.

"Stace?"

I turn towards her to see a faint ripple across her skin. And another. And another.

No way.

Thinking it might be my eyes playing tricks, I trace a hand across her back, feeling the skin raise beneath her fingers, observing the shades of green and purple.

There's just no way.

But everything's far too well-defined to be a dream. I feel the damp sheets, can smell the residue of sex, and see the room as a series of sharp lines, moonlight splitting across my wife's ever-transforming flesh.

"Jade?"

There's an urge to wake her, but I fight it, watching the illuminated parts of her flesh take on that shimmer again. Holding my breath, I follow the network of dark green veins working across her back.

This is happening.

My skin prickles and my senses heighten. Anxiety, excitement, fear, euphoria—a cocktail of emotions all loaded into a single dose and injected into my bloodstream.

Her body jolts, side to side and up and down, and I ride the vibrations, watching with excitement as the skin around her shoulder blades begins to split.

"No fucking way."

But as the skin continues to break, sending blood cascading onto the sheets, I see the white bone beneath. Continuing to jerk and twitch, my wife(?) lets out a whimper, and deep within, I hear things snapping, popping, ripping. Colour spreads, the top half of her back now almost entirely purple. As her body splits from the shoulders down, I recoil slightly, watching as bone gives way to something else.

Holy shit.

Following the tearing flesh, I lift the covers, only to see her body tapering off, legs melting into a single lower abdomen. More splitting, popping, cracking, and finally, the wings break through, twisted folds of vein-ridden translucence tarnished by smears of blood.

The twitching stops.

I remind myself to breathe, wondering who this is in bed with me.

As one of the wings awkwardly creases against the sheets, a high-pitched scream rides up my spine and explodes in my ears. Pained, desolate, otherworldly, it chills me to the bone but intrigues me just the same.

"Jade?"

She begins to turn over, and I ready myself, fingers coiled around the bloody duvet.

There's only a semblance of my wife, cheeks covered in tiny hairs, eyeballs now a collection of ruby red cells extending beyond the edge of her face. A small fleshy tube emerging from her purple lips flops onto the blood-saturated pillow.

A hybrid, but one that is so obviously dying.

"What can I do? What can I do?"

The mouth stretches as the wings move again, but only a croak emerges this time. She raises an arm, still human-like but covered in more tiny dark hairs, and with the back of her hand, she strokes my right cheek.

"Tell me what to do," I plead.

Her thin lips contort into a silent scream.

Unable to move, I stare at the creature in front of me, a twisted mess of flesh, bone, and wings. Helplessly, I watch as her mouth continues to shape her pain until her arm finally falls to the sheet.

She is still.

She is gone.

I feel my adrenaline dissipating, my heart rate slowing.

The high is fading.

The metallic smell of blood fills my nostrils and, like a powerful dose of smelling salts, begins dispersing the fog, lifting the veil of this dream-like world. It's my turn to scream as I run my eyes over this bloody mess that was once my wife.

"Oh, God. Oh, Christ!"

My stomach churns, and I dry hack into the blood-drenched sheets. This thing, this vile creature I was making love to only moments ago. Those horrible eyes, the dull green skin, the disgusting tube that extends across the pillow towards me. What the hell? What the fuck?

Unable to tear my eyes away from the monstrosity next to me, visions of our intimacy forever engrained into my mind, I bring the pillow to my mouth and gag some more.

I hate flies! I fucking hate them, always have. Even more than Stacey does. *Did.*

Just as I begin sliding towards the end of the bed, thoughts of getting as far away as possible, I feel something on my legs.

Cold. Wet.

Blood pounding in my ears, eyes screwed half shut, I lift the covers.

The spray of vomit comes without warning—no muscle spasms, no doubling over, just a violent projectile of orange. And as my stomach performs a series of after tremors, I finally scramble from the bed, brushing frantically at my flesh, studying with disbelief the patch of uncovered maggots on the blanket, a solid disgusting ten-inch circle of writhing bodies.

"Jesus fucking Christ!"

Desperately, I reach for the wall, still brushing at my skin.

There must be thousands on the bottom sheet, squirming, floundering. Still, they continue leaking from *her* new lower abdomen, an impossible and sickening sight, the linen a writhing sheet of nastiness. My back connecting with hardness, I watch the wriggling slow until the bodies harden into a shiny emerald-green shell.

Impossible.

But I just fell in love with a fly.

And as I reel against the wall, a sick thought crosses my mind that the squirming mess on the bed is my offspring.

"Oh, Christ, no. Please, no!"

But they are; they're opening—the cocoons—fully formed insects emerging, the room beginning to fill with a raucous and unbearable buzz.

Can't think. Can't fucking think. That noise!

A piercing scream draws my attention to the window. Through the slats, I make out the lit-up balcony opposite—someone waving their arms, impossible to tell they are male or female, body covered head to toe with flies, and a tornado of them circulating above in an almost predatory formation. A more muffled scream quickly fades as they launch themselves over the railing.

No, this isn't happening; it can't be real. What the fuck is going on?

A sharp sting at the back of my neck jolts my body erect and still. "The hell?" And another on my lower back. "Jesus fucking Christ!" Other random patches of skin scream in protest until my entire body is on fire.

"Fuuuuuuuuuuck!"

A moving wall of filth awaits as I turn to the door, but it's my only option. My limbs suddenly feel leaden and uncoordinated, my right leg sluggishly dragging behind. "Help! Somebody help!" Grimacing through the pain, I continue hobbling towards the door, the flies covering my face, a series of stings setting my cheeks on fire. I manage to swat some away, but relentlessly they attack, sharp bursts of agony internally exploding as the flies saturate my chest.

I can't see. Daren't breathe, afraid of swallowing one of the fuckers.

Blindly reaching along the wall, searing pain continues ripping through me, their bites like little knives cutting into my flesh. And that buzz. That hellish buzz feels like it's trapped inside my head. They're all over me, a moving blanket of legs, wings, and sharpness that brings me to my knees, not a single part of me untouched by pain. *Come on! Come on!* Fingers immersed in layers of flies, I finally find the wall again and begin frantically searching for the door handle.

They're in my ears, the incessant and voluminous fluttering no longer harmonious but rambunctiously cruel. And my eyes. My fucking eyes! As though someone holds a flame to them. I swipe at my face, connecting with some but still—just blackness. I'm blind. And deaf to anything but their relentless buzz.

More flashes of pain run up both my arms, and as I futilely brush at their filthy bodies, I feel the sticky indentations in my skin. It dawns on me—they're no longer just biting; they're feeding.

Where's the fucking handle?

And just as the tip of my finger connects with something solid, my body gives, pain swelling as my cheek bounces off the carpet, darkness temporarily replaced with an explosion of white light.

I'm cocooned, wrapped in carnivorous filth.

What the fuck is this? A fucked-up science experiment? Nature's fucking revenge?

I feel them working their way into my flesh, my mind conjuring images of them vomiting on my skin, sucking up my liquefied flesh through their tubes. And as I try and rub at my eyes, I'm greeted only by more stickiness that squelches on contact, sending pain flares down to my toes.

Fuuuuuuuuuuuck!

Body screaming for me to give up, I drag myself back to the blackened wall and prop myself against it. I can't die like this; I won't! This time, as I lift my impossibly heavy arm, my palm finds metal almost immediately. I snap my fingers around the handle, heave the door open and like a maggot, squirm and writhe across the threshold.

Unable to hold onto my scream any longer, only a garbled croak emerges as the flies begin to fill my mouth and work their way down my throat. Wings beating against my larynx, I taste their foulness as I cough and retch, my skull vibrating as they begin busying themselves in the sockets of my eyes, working their way inwards— eating at me. Around me, above the frantic fluttering in my ears and the buzz inside my head, blood-curdling screams escape through the walls.

I'm so sorry, Stace.

It's only a matter of time before they'll begin feasting on my brain. As the pain starts to numb, I know it's over, that this is how it ends. And as I pray for it to be quick, I can already hear some of them leaving, no doubt on their way to find more victims they can seduce.

It's just a fly, I tell myself.

OLD TIMES

THROUGH THE WINDOW, I watch the taxi rolling to a halt. The feeling of helpless spiralling is already washing over me, the knot in my stomach tightening.

"I'm off then," Jacqui says, face caked with makeup and the smell of perfume hanging in the air. "Do I look okay?" she asks, patting her dress down.

"You look amazing, love." I want to cry, and I hate myself for it.

She gingerly moves to the hallway, heels impossibly loud against the wooden floor, each step a painful blow to my self-worth. As soon as the clicking stops, I imagine her preening herself in the oval mirror.

I think she's cheating; I've suspected it for a while. She seems so distracted these days, even more than usual, and recently, she's been leaving the room to use her phone. I'm not proud, but I've followed her occasionally, observing the frantic button-pushing between rooms. Been through her text messages, too, but I think she's wiping them.

Christ, I hope I'm wrong.

"There's a load of washing to go in. And don't forget to empty the trash, okay?"

"Okay, love," I reply.

"Mustn't forget the trash," Jed says, waving his finger and smirking at me from the other side of the room.

I haven't slept for weeks, my mind a simmering pot of anxiety and jealousy. Perhaps, I'm just being paranoid. Regardless, I feel like I'm slipping back to the darker times.

"I'm not sure what time I'll be back," she says. "Don't wait up."

"Behave yourself!" Jed shouts as the door slams, thrusting his middle finger in the air.

"Shut up, Jed," I say through clenched teeth, watching her down the path.

"Why do you let her speak to you like that?" he says. "Ordering you about while she goes out gallivanting. I wouldn't stand for it."

"I love her." I arch my neck, watching her step into the taxi. "I wouldn't expect you to understand."

He's not been around in months, and quite frankly, that was just fine with me. Rocking in the chair, legs tapping frantically, he looks agitated, volatile.

"What's wrong with you, anyway?" I ask.

"Bored. Want to get wasted?"

"I've been sober for months, Jed. The last time you were here was the last time I had a drink, and we both know how that ended."

"Come on, just a little one," he says, reaching behind his back and presenting the bottle of golden liquid. "She's out having fun; why can't we have a little drinky?"

"Haven't you got anywhere else to go?"

"Don't be like that, Paul." He twists off the cap, making a big deal of holding the neck of the bottle near his nostrils and inhaling deeply. "Ah, that smells mighty fine."

"I'd like you to leave, Jed. I'm not really in—"

But the bottle's already on the table in front of me.

"Go on, Paul. It will help you relax a little, take the edge off."

"I promised her, Jed; said I'd never drink again. She said she'd leave if—"

"She really has got you by the balls, hasn't she? How is all that obedience working out for you anyway? Whose fucking life are you living, for Christ's sake?"

I push myself from the chair and walk around the room, pausing at the mirror above the fireplace. The dark circles under my eyes are emphasized further in the subdued light.

"Look what she's doing to you, Paul. You look like shit!"

"And what's your excuse, Jed?" I say, snapping my head towards him. "Anyway, what do you know about it? I've not seen you in over a year! You don't know anything."

"Paul, how far do we go back? This isn't you. You've lost your spark; she's sucking you dry and not in a good way!"

"Look, can you just fuck off now, please."

"One drink for old times' sake, then I'll go. You have my word."

"One drink."

"One drink. Promise."

I want him gone. I want to wallow in self-pity and worthlessness, and he's fucking it all up. "Okay, but we do it the civilized way." I march through the kitchen.

He claps his hands together. "That's the way, Pauly."

I collect two tumblers from the cupboard, filling each half full of ice. There's a crooked photograph of Jacqui and me pinned to the back of the refrigerator door. It's five, maybe six years old, and none have been added since. She looks happy, but how do you ever truly know?

"One drink," I say, sliding the glasses across the coffee table.

The sound of whisky filling the glass is heavenly, and even without taking a sip, I can feel its warm blanket already wrapping around, protecting me. Ice begins to crack, and its melody is hauntingly beautiful.

"To old times," Jed says, lifting the glass.

"To old times."

As I pick up the glass and inhale the whiskey, a shudder rattles through me—the fear and excitement of being in a place I know I shouldn't be. Thoughts rush through my head as I swirl the golden liquid around the glass, foreboding visions of the future. Regardless,

I take the first sip, sending a network of hot prickles and warmth through my body. One drink. My gums tingle as I hold its silkiness in my mouth, enjoying the sensation before finally letting it slide down my throat. It's so good—smooth and balanced—evoking just the right amount of burn as it slides down. Already, it's dissolving the knot in my stomach, freeing me of all of it. I take another sip, and it begins to drown out the thoughts, turning down their volume.

Jed smacks his lips together. "A fine drop," he says. His leg has stopped shaking, the whisky no doubt working its magic.

"It is good," I concede.

"Refill?" He rests the neck of the bottle against my glass.

"We said just the one, Jed." But we both know the words are merely a formality, a half-hearted objection already forgotten. One is never one.

He fills the glass and smirks his smirk. "Why don't you just leave her?"

"Can we talk about something else?"

"It could be you and me again, just like old times. She's stifling you, got you wrapped around her little finger. She'd be better off with a little fucking lapdog."

"It's just a rough patch." There, I said it. "We'll work it out."

"Oh yeah, I bet she's working it out right now, talking to all the fellas about how much she wants to work on her marriage. Even when her mouth's stuffed full of cock, I'm sure she'll still be yapping about how much harder she's going to try."

I offer a scowl before knocking back the whisky and crunching down on the ice. "I hate you, Jed."

"Just jesting." He pours himself another glass and knocks it back. "Another?"

"Yes. We've been happy before."

"Can't say I've seen it." He slumps back into the leather, taking another generous sip. "All the time I've known you, it's been like this. You used to be fun; now you're nothing but a shadow."

"I don't want to lose her."

"Never mind her, Paul. You're losing yourself. What even makes you get out of bed anymore?"

"Fuck off, Jed." The whisky no longer burns, but his words do, hitting hard as only the truth can. "You're just jealous."

He leans forward and tops us both up. "We used to go out on the town every week. The world was our oyster. Why did you have to get yourself tied down to that skank?" His words are starting to slur into each other. And I know that tone; good things never follow.

"Take that back."

"I'm just saying—you're obviously not happy. We could do it again; the old team reunited. There's an ocean of pussy out there, and you're just playing it safe in the shallow end."

"Jed, I'm not interested in that. I don't want to talk about this anymore."

I lift the glass and tip its contents into my mouth. Jed fills it up as soon as it comes down.

"I care, that's all," he says, tone changing to a drunken and patronizing melancholy. "She doesn't."

The temporary comfort blanket of the whisky is slipping, leaving me vulnerable and exposed once more.

"She doesn't give a fuck, Paul; you know that. When was the last time she did anything for you? When was the last time you made love? Hell, when was the last time she even asked how you were doing?"

"She's got a lot going on."

"Don't we all, goddamnit!" He brings his fist down onto the coffee table. "You need to stop being such a fucking pushover!"

Fingers squeezing the glass, I swallow the whisky. He's getting to me. This is what he does—even more manipulative than her. Anger rises, not just with him, but with it all.

"It's your own fault. You let her get away with it," he continues.

My hand shakes as I pour another.

"You're just shit on her shoe, Paul. She just wants to control you. That's why she's always on at you to take your pills. She's part of the system."

I drink the contents and refill the glass. He's right; I know he's right. That's why it hurts. Each day, I hope for it to get better. "I love her, Jed." I don't want much, just to be seen.

"I know, Paul, but it isn't mutual. It's you and me against the world. Always has been, always will be. I'm the one who's been there from the start. Only I know what you went through as a child—the abuse, the trauma—nobody else will ever truly understand. How could they?"

I still have nightmares—hunched over in that small space, wet from my own urine, shaking at the sound of creaking floorboards. Christ knows how long they used to lock us in there, but it was a damn sight safer than being out in the open; I still have to bear those scars. We were only ever let out to clean and do the jobs they didn't want to, and God forbid, the work wasn't up to scratch.

It was our neighbours that made the call, just a few years too late. The authorities found us locked in that cupboard, almost starved to death, filthy and terrified. I was ten years old.

Our so-called mother and father were sent from hell; I know that now. They'll rot in prison for what they did, hopefully. I also know that being fed scraps underneath the door and being brought out for random beatings isn't the usual childhood experience. To this day, I still walk with a hunch and wince at the sound of a squeaking floorboard. I wanted to get carpets put through the house, but Jacqui wouldn't let me, even though she knows what I've been through.

Jed's right. He's the only one I really trust, the only one I can rely on to be there.

"I'm going to tell you this for your own good, Pauly," he says, his face creasing with seriousness.

"Go on."

"I fucked her, too."

The words don't make sense at first, as if they're not in the correct sequence. "W—what?" The night turns darker still, the room starting to feel slightly off kilt, everything seeming a little less sharp.

"More than once. She's an animal, Pauly; I'll give you that."

As I dig my fingers into the arms of the chair, the room begins to spin. I feel disoriented—present, but not—as if out of my own body. I close my eyes and take several deep breaths, finally coming back and landing with a thud.

"And I have to wonder how many dicks she's wrapped her hands around tonight."

Rage consumes me, liquid splashing over the rim as my grip tightens on the glass.

Is that a sneer on his face? Just like Father's.

Unable to hold it in any longer, I let out a roar, bringing the tumbler into his cheek and whipping his head to the left. Glass shatters, sending shards to the floor but leaving some in his flesh, streams of fresh crimson running down his cheek. He growls as we rise, and almost immediately, his fist connects with my chin, sending me reeling backwards and bringing an explosion of white light.

Time seems to slow until the shrill in my ear finally dampens.

"How could you?" Spittle sprays ahead as I reach for the marble bookend. "I trusted you!" I bring it down hard onto his nose. "I fucking trusted you!" The pain in my head is off the charts, my ears still ringing, but I'm filled with uncontrollable fury as I continue smashing the paperweight into his face.

The sucker punch knocks the wind out of me, doubling me over. I flail my arms wildly, but he plunges another fist into my side, prompting a tiny bit of vomit onto the floor beneath. "She's no good for you, Paul," he says, wrapping his hands around my throat. I kick out, gasping for air, the pressure in my chest and head already unbearable.

I can't fucking breathe!

I'm back at our old home, Father's big hands around my neck, scolding me for not taking the trash out and taking too long to clean the toilet. I can smell the alcohol on his breath, even feel the stubble against my cheek. Christ, my throat feels like it might snap. Darkness draws in, and now I'm back in the cupboard, swallowing the mustiness. Let it end, please. Just let it fucking end!

Finally, the pressure relents, and I suck in air, clutching at my neck.

"I had to tell you, Paul. You need to know these things."

Still doubled over, I stagger towards the kitchen.

"That's it, run! You never face up to anything; that's the problem. That's why she walks all over you in those big porno heels!"

But I have no intention of leaving things like this. I'm raging, adrenaline flowing, my mind exploding with hate and revenge. I reach for the knife block, pulling out the one I know to be the sharpest.

"Oh, shit," Jed says as I return to the lounge. "He's got a knife, everyone. Pauly's balls have finally dropped!"

I make my run, offering a strange and garbled war cry as I whip the knife across his defenceless face. He smiles, putting a hand to his cheek, studying the blood as it drips to the floor. "Fuck you, Jed!" I swing again, this time catching him in the chest, inducing a satisfying cry.

"Yes, Pauly. That's it! Let it all out."

"Fuck you!" I scream. Fuck you! Fuck you! Fuck you!" I hit him in the leg this time, yet still, he puts up no fight. Bottled rage and hate unleash into every strike until I feel nothing, disconnected from his pain, marshy sounds distant and other-worldly. I finally relent, only as Jed drops to his knees, his hands reaching towards me, tears rolling down his cheeks.

I freeze, my blood-smeared hands shaking.

What have I done?

"Oh God, oh God, oh God. I'm sorry. I'm so sorry." I collapse to the floor in a heap, reaching out for my best friend, the only one who truly knows. "I love you, Jed." Holding hands, we squirm side-by-side, painting the tiles red. "I love you, too."

"PAUL!"

The voice seems distant and distorted.

I open my eyes, my head pounding and full of thick fog, my body singing with pain as I try to move.

"Paul, it's okay; the ambulance is coming." Jacqui's eyes glisten as she leans in. "What have you done to yourself?"

I look down to find my grey shirt saturated with blood. "Where's Jed?"

She looks at me, saying nothing, eyes wide with fear.

"Where's Jed?" I repeat.

"I'm still here, Pauly." He lets out a moan as she pushes himself to his elbows. "The tears—just guilt—you know that. Don't let her fool you."

"I know. It's just you and me forever, Jed; I see that now."

"You haven't been taking your tablets," Jacqui says. "And"—she swallows hard, a tear running down her cheek— "you've been drinking."

"It's her who should feel guilty, Paul. I can smell those other men on her," Jed croaks. "Their sweat and cum. Hell, they were probably laughing at you while they were doing it."

"Oh, Paul, remember you told me about Jed?" She says softly, crouching and stroking the back of her hand against my forehead. "How you made him up—to get through those days locked in the darkness."

"She's full of lies, Paul. They're all against you. Every last one of them."

I no longer feel alone.

I'm glad he's back.

"Don't worry, Pauly. She won't get away with it. If we make it through, I'll sort her for you." Jed seals the promise with his familiar smirk. "I'll cut her up real good."

TIME TO REFLECT

There's a bittersweet point in our childhood when we stop believing in ghosts and monsters. I guess it's roughly the same time we find out there's no Santa, tooth fairy, or a chance we'll be swallowed by quicksand at every turn, holding onto a branch for dear life until the crows begin sweeping, trying to peck our eyes out.

I was at that stage on that cold and wet Friday October evening, leaning back against the rusty and graffiti-covered *Rail Trail* sign, trying to convince my friend the shortcut was a great idea. Josh still had some way to go.

"No way. Uh-uh. No way."

"Ten minutes and we'll be watching *Who's the Boss* in front of the fire," I pleaded, resisting the urge for chicken impressions as I observed the fear in his eyes. "Don't be a big baby."

"I'm not a baby!"

"Alright, alright, don't get your nappy in a twist."

I hate to admit it now, but in a world becoming larger and ever more complex, his vulnerability gave me a sense of superiority, some level of control. And with that power I had yet to name, I applied a different kind of pressure. "Come on. We'll be back in time for dinner. Your mum will go apeshit if you're home late again."

"It's not her I'm worried about." He placed his reddening hands in his pockets and ducked his chin under his zip collar. "Why do we have to hang around with him anyway?"

I shrugged. "Max is okay."

Max was a moron, the class clown, though the association meant a free pass from torment. "Tomorrow, it's just you and me, all day. I promise! We can stack up at the milk bar and rent some movies. If we don't get grounded, that is."

He lifted his gaze towards the overgrown foliage and let out a sigh. "I don't know."

Offering a smile as I blinked away some of the water, I rested a hand on his shoulder. "Have I ever let you down?"

I was more scared for my own skin, truth be told. My mother was wired to the mains back then, high on a cocktail of pink and yellow pills prescribed for *her nerves*.

"Come on, wingman. Ten minutes."

He dragged an arm across his face and squinted into the rain, finally returning his gaze towards the trail. "Mum said people sniff glue down there and that someone approached a kid just three weeks ago. And what about that boy that went missing?"

"That's rubbish. They just want to scare us; make sure we always do as we're told." I take a step into the opening, nodding for him to follow. "Besides, it's pissing it down. What idiots, apart from us, are going to be out in this?"

"I'm sorry, Will," he said, hands raised and beginning to back away, screwing his face up as his right sneaker plunged into a puddle. "I'm sorry."

"Sorry?" And suddenly, he looked pathetic to me. "Sorry for what?"

"I can't, Will. I—"

"You don't still believe the place is haunted, do you?"

"No, of course not, but—"

"That was playground talk from years ago. Just kids' stuff." I was angry at him and felt let down. My comrade in battle, suddenly a deserter. "You still think the boogeyman is down there, don't you? Sniffing glue and killing time, waiting just for little old you in this pissing rain?"

"Stop it, Will!"

"Bet you still have a teddy for the dark, don't you?"

"I don't!" he shouted. "But Mum said—"

"Mum said! Mum said!" I began to laugh, doubling over for dramatic effect. "You pussy! You loser." I could hold onto the chicken impersonations no longer. *"Puck-puck-puck."*

"I'm sorry, Will," he said, turning and launching into a sprint.

"Yeah, run home to Mommy! Hug that teddy real tight tonight, Josh! *Puck-puck-puck.*"

And he was gone. And I felt like a prick.

I turned towards the trail and swallowed hard, feeling far less brave without my friend. Heavy, too, not just from the rain, but with the responsibility of knowing I had to see it through. After one last glance behind, noting the torrent of water beginning to rush along the edge of the street, I pushed off from the sign, scanning the water-soaked concoction of gravel and mud ahead. Doing my best to ignore the overwhelming compulsion to take off after my friend, I planned my first few steps and set off.

Only thirty or so feet in, I already felt like the loneliest kid in the world, only the rustle of foliage and the heavy patter of rain against my clothes for company. I would have likely turned back any other time, but I was twelve, and it felt like a critical time, one of those moments I'd read about in some of Stephen King's novels. Overgrown shrubbery on either side blocked my view of anything beyond, and grey clouds above made the day appear much later than it was. Every part of me wanted to turn back at that point, thinking nobody would know.

But I would have known. I would have.

My pace started steady, nothing more than an amble as I planned each step, mostly keeping to the grass verge to stay out of the boggier ground. Perhaps a hundred yards in, I even started gaining confidence, thinking of the stories I could tell at school on Monday, that even Max would likely be impressed I tackled the infamous trail alone. As for Josh, he could go and get screwed.

But the bravado was short-lived as the rain picked up its pace and the clouds above brought further darkness. My feet plunged into ever softening ground, the puddles becoming deeper and more abundant. Wisps of breath peppered the air ahead with ever-increasing frequency. My clothes clung uncomfortably to my skin, chilling me to the bone. It's safe to say that at that moment, I hated Josh more than anything else in the world.

Josh's words invaded my head then. *Someone approached a kid just three weeks ago. What about that kid that went missing?* Scenes from Creepshow and late-night movies awaited in every direction. I began to imagine the spiky undergrowth creeping onto the path, wrapping around my legs and snapping me into oblivion.

I was a mess, full of regret, suddenly missing my father so much it hurt. "Man up, Will!" I mumbled into the cold, thrusting my chest out and lifting my head high.

Ahead, rusty tracks veered to the right, disappearing behind more of the sharp-looking shrubbery. Along the verge, trees reached out towards me, skeletal branches twisting around each other, evoking more nightmarish images.

Man up. Man up. Man up.

Staying dead centre of that track as best I could, I noted the ditch on my right, just a boggy trench on entry, looking to be a quarter full. I tried my best to keep fear at bay, alternating my glance between the ground and the trees ahead, but then I saw something, a dark stain on the horizon. My pace slowed, and my stomach dropped. A case of fight or flight, and I wanted to run like the fucking wind.

I continued edging forward, eyes scrunched and chewing on my lip, surprised at my bravery and that my legs were even moving. "No such thing. No such thing. No such—" As my right foot slipped from beneath me, I balanced for my life—legs spread, arms outstretched, eyes remaining fixed on the dark object ahead.

Waiting just for little old you in the pissing rain.

At that moment, I was sure if I were to fall, I would die; that somehow, in the pelting rain of that cold Autumn evening, someone knew that I would take that route, and they were just waiting for the right time to strike. Blood relentlessly whooshing in my ears, I sucked in the cold air as best I could. "No such thing as boogeymen, Josh," I said for my own benefit.

I felt weak right then, my mind filling with a vision of Mum's concerned face at the bay window; my chocolate lab, Barnie, waiting next to her, tail down. A lump swelled at the back of my throat as I edged forward once more, not a drop of saliva in my mouth as I listened and watched, expecting the darkness to rush me at any second.

The dark stain was still there, waiting just for little old me.

The ice-cold wind wrapped around me as I made slow progress, the ground beneath my feet becoming softer still, hardly any parts not covered with water. I snapped my head around, momentarily thinking I heard a whisper on the breeze, but only the sight of the ditch being almost a third full greeted me. I was losing it fast, my body just a collection of raw nerve endings being prodded and poked by nature. Unsure how far I had already walked and how far was left, it took everything in me at that point to keep my tears at bay.

Only as I caught sight of the tree limb ahead in the middle of the path, the source that triggered imminent thoughts of death only a few yards back, did I let my guard down a little. I even let out a nervous snigger when I saw the crumbling paint of the dilapidated old station shed on the right, floor to decayed roof wrapped in spiky bramble vines resembling barbed wire. I was close to being halfway.

"I told you, Josh. I told you."

With a renewed spring in my step, numb to the coldness of the brown water splashing up my legs, I started to imagine the heat of the fire and Barnie's excited pants as I rubbed at his belly. I was going to make it through, live to tell the tale. I wouldn't get to spend the day with my friend, who would likely get grounded, but I'd be on home soil with unrestricted access to the snack cupboard.

But then I saw the swirling vortex of thickness perhaps sixty yards ahead that swallowed everything beyond it.

I stopped dead, ego deflated, listening to the low hum of the frogs and hoping for nothing more. That smell, too; heavy, more than petrichor, more than rotting vegetation.

Nothing good ever happened in the movies where mist was involved. That's what went through my head, and I could do nothing to dislodge images of monsters and zombies lurking within the smog. *The boogeyman.* I kept telling myself it's just water in the air, just like Mrs. Penis-fingers had said in class last week. But as I approached the cloud, my fear of all that could not be seen returned, my stomach folding in on itself, squeezing the air out of me. I was the kid again, gripping the duvet, searching the darkness.

Just mist. Just mist.

I kept the chant going, hoping the cloud would begin to disperse when I neared, but it remained even as I stopped just ten feet short. It wasn't moving with the breeze; it was dancing to its own tune.

I took a few steps closer, occasionally glancing over my shoulder and into the foliage on either side. The ditch was well over half full, and the rain showed no sign of easing. *Just mist. Just mist.* But as I reached the distinct edge of the fog, extending my arm and watching the greyness swallow it to the elbow, I'd already convinced myself it was anything but.

Sucking in the damp air with water dripping from every part of me, I'm not entirely sure how long I stood there trying to summon the courage to move forward. Perhaps I was waiting for the mist just to fall away as quickly as it had seemed to appear.

Finally, I decided I would get my head down and pelt it, hoping like hell momentum would stop me from slipping on my ass. After three, I told myself.

Three.

Two.

One.

I went through the sequence four times until I finally made my move, blindly running forward, arms outstretched to keep the zombies at bay. I remember it feeling impossibly cold, as though I was running through the corridors of a giant fridge. My feet kept sliding, but I was moving at speed. Hell, it wasn't pretty, but I was doing it.

"Over here."

My skin tightened at the softly spoken words, a renewed feeling of hopelessness washing over me. It sounded like the voice of a child, but I'd seen those types of tricks in the movies. *Not real. Not real.* That was my new mantra as I planted my feet down with even further intensity, my lungs filling with icy cold air. I wasn't going to stop for anything. Not a fucking thing. Head tucked into my chest, I ran for my life, feeling sure I would stumble and for whatever it was in the darkness to come and collect.

Not real. Not real.

Water crashed either side and into my brand-new sneakers as my feet slapped against the mud. *Slap. Slap. Slap.*

"Hey, you! Over here."

My stomach dropped again.

"Here. Over here."

I ran hard and fast but couldn't seem to escape the voice. I kept telling myself it was impossible and that it must just be in my head.

"I just want to talk."

"Go away!" I screamed, tears finally beginning to work their way down both cheeks. "I just want to go home."

Darkness returned, the clouds above turning on me, gathering around for whatever was about to happen. The rain intensified, stinging against my cheeks.

"Quick! He's coming," the voice said. "I can show you the way."

Slap. Slap. Slap.

I couldn't feel my toes at that point. Each breath became painful.

"Just want to go home!" I began to sob; my tears quickly washed away by the faster than ever rain.

Patter. Patter. Patter. Slap. Slap. Slap.

When the whistling started, I came to a cautious and slippery stop, thinking my heart would explode there and then. The tune was coming from all around, the volume the same no matter which direction I turned my head.

"Please! I just want to be home." No longer sure which direction I was facing, I turned on the spot, around and around and around, but there was only greyness wherever I looked. And the whistling was getting louder.

"I told you. Come here."

I could no longer see or feel my legs. "Where are you?"

"Over here."

Using the drenched sleeve of my jacket to try and clear my vision, I managed a couple of steps forward.

"That's it; just a little bit closer."

"Where?"

"Closer."

The whistling grew louder still, travelling up and down my bones.

"You're getting so warm now. Just two more steps."

I played the game, grimacing in preparation, lifting a foot from the ground and placing it down slowly and dramatically as if it was the first step on the moon. "I don't see anything."

"One more."

I inhaled sharply, screwed my face up even tighter, and took another step.

"Down here."

As I crouched, staring into the rippling puddle and at the distorted face of the child wearing a smile, I had to remind myself to breathe. I could feel my skin tightening around my skull and imagined that's how people would find me—just a kid with a shrunken head sprawled across the mud. I was a believer once again. Ghosts.

Monsters. Things beyond a world that drove my mum to take colourful pills.

The rain was pelting down too hard for me to get a good look at the face, but I would have said the boy was perhaps a year or two older than me, a dark shadow lurking over his top lip. "Who—who are you?" I was amazed the words formed as I felt my throat continue to shrink.

"A friend. Listen to me. He's coming. You have to run."

"Who's coming?"

"Father. You have to run. Now!"

With urgency in his eyes, the boy extended his arm and gestured with a finger. And then he was gone.

"Wait. What do you—" *Shit. Shit. Shit.* I got to my feet and obediently ran in the direction he pointed. Not sure how long for, but time seemed to stand still in that grey cloud.

"Oy. Over here."

A different voice, higher pitched, from directly ahead. "Hello?" I croaked.

"Yes, here!"

Again, I slowed my pace, shifting my gaze from the greyness to the ground immediately ahead.

"Three more steps."

"The whistling's getting louder," I muttered. "Please help me."

"One more."

I saw her then in the small pool of murky water. At least the outskirts of a much younger face, the huge unmissable gap between her two front teeth and another further back. "Who are you?"

"A friend. He's so close now. You have to run."

"Which way?"

She extended her right arm straight above her, and I followed her finger towards the greyness. When I looked down, she was gone.

And I ran. *Slap. Slap. Slap.* Muddy water enveloped the entirety of my sneaker with every step.

"Here!"

It was barely audible over the blood in my ears, but I was accustomed to the game now and darted straight towards it, desperate to escape the ever-increasing bone grating whistling.

"Where?"

"Three steps left."

The kid would have been ten at most. "What are you doing down there?"

"Ain't nothing to do but stare at the clouds. Run!"

I followed the direction of his arm, but only for the whistling to get louder still.

Then I heard it, a little to my right above the sound of my beating heart and the intensity of rain against the volume of water —unmistakably my voice.

"Over here. Quickly, he's coming!"

It always made me cringe, but the sound of it that day made me feel like my insides were freezing over. A strange, garbled croak emerged from my throat as it seemed to shrink further, and I doubled over, gasping for breath, willing my legs not to give way. "I want my mum. I want my dog."

"Just a little more. Come to the edge."

Arms stretched out, dragging my feet through the mud like a zombie through the mist; I made slow ground until finally, I reached the edge of the ditch. Looking for a face but hoping not to find one, I stood for a while before the voice beckoned me.

"You have to crouch."

And as I squatted towards the cold and wet ground, head jutting out over the water, I saw my distorted face appear, impossibly vivid through the otherwise muddy obscurity. "I'm scared. What's going on?"

"It's okay. We get a daddy again!"

"What? What do you mean?" The subsequent gust elevated the sound of the ever-approaching whistling. Rain came down harder, my rippling face sinking back into distorted murkiness until it was no longer visible. "Wait! Come back!"

And then I saw their petrified faces.

Two boys submerged under the water with hands the size of dinner plates wrapped around their necks. I could hear their dampened cries and see their air bubbles appearing on the surface of the brown water. "Stop!" I screamed, but with wide eyes on me, they continued their struggles, flailing at thick arms that kept them pinned. I grimaced, plunging my hands into the water but only managing to distort the scene further. "Help! Someone help!"

"This never had to happen," a man's voice spoke from my right shoulder, but only grey mist and the smell of liquor greeted me when I turned.

For seconds, I continued splashing in the water, futilely scraping my fingers against the muddy banks, listening to their death cries, until finally, only the sound of heavy rain remained. Breathless and shaking, I watched their lifeless faces sink back into the muddy oblivion from which they appeared.

"It's not real. It's not real." But my mantra felt weak—lead bullets against a werewolf.

I sensed it before it happened, could feel the presence that hadn't left, the smell of the pub lingering on the cold air, giving me a flashback to when Mum tried to get on my good side by letting me have a shandy.

And then I saw the reflection of the darkness wrapping around me.

"Please let me go."

"She had it coming," the man said. "They all do."

As meaty fingers wrapped around the back of my neck, I imagined Barnie diving into the water, tail going like the clappers, big pink tongue hanging from the side of his mouth.

The water was strangely warm.

I kicked, clawed, and splashed as much as I could, but the pressure on my throat and chest became unbearable. It felt like my lungs were on fire, but at the same time, as though my veins were full of ice. Memories flooded my head, mostly bad ones, but I still wanted more than anything to be back at home with Mum.

All would be forgiven.

My movements slowed, my body shutting down, but I could still hear him above me, shouting his distorted barrage of anger into the mist.

Then silence—nothing but an overwhelming peacefulness and serenity, a strange, undramatic cocktail of contradictory sadness and contentment as I sank into the darkness.

Into oblivion.

Thoughts of never seeing my mum or friends again would inevitably hit explosively hard, but at that point, relief at escaping the mist and *him* more than outweighed any sorrow.

But I never did—escape him—that is.

You see, this is my home now, along with the others; this little stretch of overgrown trail, giving off the scent of pine and wild-flowers in summer, but something far more potent than decaying leaves in autumn. He makes us call him *Father*, and we always do as we are told. If we don't, he hurts us, puts his hands around our necks, and drowns us in the darkness for as long he cares to. Some-times, when he gets angry, he does it anyway.

It's the loneliness that's the worst. He used to visit us when the mood took him—teach us things—perhaps out of guilt or just for someone to talk to other than his boys. But there's only so much one man knows, and when he's done teaching the latest member of his extended family, he goes looking for the next.

I couldn't tell you how long it's been since I decided to take that shortcut. While our bodies don't age, our minds do, and I've lost track of the countless seasons that have passed. It's horrible here: damp, wet, dark. I can't imagine any place worse, that's for sure.

I have two bits of advice. Number one: don't dismiss everything you hear on the playground. Thomas Flynn took both his boys for a quiet Sunday autumn stroll, promising ice cream when they got to the other side. Drowned them both in that ditch just out of revenge for his wife leaving. Justified taking us, too, so they'd "have company."

Secondly, always take the long way around whenever possible, especially if you're alone and it looks like rain. Nothingness most year-round is enough to drive a person insane, but when the clouds come, so do we.

And so does he.

If you see the mist, it's likely too late.

If you hear the whistling, it is.

THE BEDROOM WINDOW

As EDDIE LOOKS over to where his brother's bed used to be, he feels a rush of overwhelming sadness. He thinks he could have done better, been a better brother.

"Sorry, T—Tommy," he whispers.

This house has always scared him; something about it, besides just being so old. It reminds him of the ones from the old horror films his dad used to let him stay up and watch when they were close. Remote, timber with faded and cracked white paint, and far too big to ever feel finished. When the wind blows through, the house voices its displeasure through a series of creaks and crackles that would keep any child from a restful sleep, himself and Tommy included.

Their bedroom—his bedroom—is on the third storey, and as the wind shakes the moonlit canopy of trees in the distance, whistling its tune through the rickety window frame, Eddie waits for his brother to appear as though carried on the breeze. Still no sign.

He loved him. He hated him.

Tommy was simple; that's how most people referred to him. Eddie always thought that a strange term to use for someone that made his family's life anything but. Tommy turned it upside down and some. He was nine when he died, four years Eddie's junior, but mentally he was always a toddler. It's fair to say Tommy gave them their best and worst times.

He and his brother used to have a daft little game they would play. He can't remember how it started, but one of them would place their hand against a glass window or door, and the other would place theirs on the other side. They used to pretend Tommy could transmit his thoughts through the glass. He would think of a number between one and ten, and Eddie would try and guess it. Sometimes they did it with words, too. So silly, really, but it always put a big goofy smile on his brother's face, one that would stay for hours if Eddie guessed right.

Now, when Eddie sees his brother's docile face on the other side of the glass, his wide eyes and the awkward smile that isn't quite right, he needs to remind himself to breathe. He knows Tommy must be a figment of his imagination, but it doesn't stop his body from prickling with fear each time he appears.

His dad found him first, lying in a twisted heap of limbs on the concrete path directly below their bedroom window. It was the first time Eddie ever heard a man scream, and he'll never forget how it made him feel inside. When he stuck his head out the bathroom window to see his dad holding Tommy in his arms, bawling like a child, it was as though his brother's eyes were staring directly at him. The knot that subsequently developed in his stomach is still there, and he's not sure it will ever go away.

From that moment, he knew things would never be the same again. Every day feels identical, and he doesn't know how many weeks have passed.

Time hasn't healed at all.

His mum isn't Mum anymore. She stays in bed, staring at her bedroom window.

Perhaps Tommy visits her, too.

The house feels even bigger now without his brother, even scarier. It used to be the dirty piles of clothes, the closet, or the shadows that made them both afraid, but it's Tommy that haunts him now. Tucking his knees tightly into his chest, he wraps his arms around them, anxiously waiting for his face to appear. He breathes quietly but erratically, pulse racing and eyes fixed on the glass.

In his head, he begins to count by threes. Three, six, nine, twelve, f—fifteen—

A garbled shriek of surprise leaves Eddie's lips as a hand slams against the glass, sending the whole window rattling thunderously in its frame. He jolts upright, bringing his knees in even further, locking them tightly with his arms until it begins to hurt.

Never like this before.

Usually, Tommy's face appears but vanishes before he can blink, and there's no connection with the glass.

Please go away. Please go away.

It's his brother's hand, no doubt, covered with scar tissue from when he put his palm down on the blue flame of the oven hob. Curiosity was not his brother's best friend.

Please go away.

But his brother's hand remains, the uncuffed sleeves of the red and black chequered shirt fluttering in the wind, the same one he was wearing the day he died.

He knows this can't be real, but still, *why won't it go away?*

He continues with the sequence, making it to thirty-nine, but the hand remains. It's all beginning to feel too real. He wants to run, but where to? His parents' room? What would he say? It would be all too much for his mum.

"P-Please go away, Tommy," he stutters. "I said I was sorry."

He glances quickly towards the lava lamp and back to the glass, but still, the hand floats impossibly outside of the third storey window. The sound of his breathing seems unreasonably loud. He tries to control it, slow it down, just in case he misses something—a noise, or—

The window rattles in its frame once more.

Eddie tries to make himself smaller. Beyond the glass and the sleeves of his brother's chequered shirt, he can make out a tuft of blonde hair gently wafting in the breeze.

What do you want from me, Tommy?

And it clicks.

His brother wants him to go to him. He wants him to play the game.

It seems like an age before Eddie summons the courage to release his legs and drop them over the edge of the bed. Feeling the cold wood floor beneath his toes lends more frightening realness to the situation. A bolt of pain shoots up his right thigh as he squeezes at a mound of flesh, but he's still here. And so is Tommy.

Slowly, he begins to edge towards the window, each squeak of the floorboards filling him with dread. He hangs onto the thought that this must end at some point, that Tommy will disappear and that he will be alone once more, that sleep will finally come.

Eddie sees his brother's face. It's just as he remembers—smiling —always smiling. And he looks so excited. He used to spit his words out with so much enthusiasm as though they were the most important thing ever to be orated.

The face lingers as Eddie draws closer, each step shorter than the last. He's frightened to exhale, just in case it sets off a chain of events. Tommy's mimicking him, his face turning red as he hovers in the air. Finally, Eddie releases, observing as Tommy does the same and as breath fogs the glass between them.

It's not possible. It's just my head playing with me.

Warmth spreads across the front of his pyjama bottoms and begins to run down his legs. Hairs across his body prickle their alarm, but he can't move, wrapped in oppressive fear that squeezes at his chest. The house creaks again as the wind rushes through it, weatherboards moaning as if an extension of his terror.

Stop it, Tommy! Stop it!

With a combination of dread and anger, he marches towards the window with a raised hand, his brother's face lighting up, eyes almost popping out of his head. He loved him. He hated him. And as soon as Eddie's fingers touch the glass, Tommy's voice fills his head,

"I lub you." And just like that, his brother vanishes, as does the cloud of breath.

As if he was never there. As if he never existed.

"I said I was sorry," he says, rushing to his bed and throwing himself across it. He begins to cry uncontrollably into the sheets, remaining like that for some time, until his eyes are red raw and his throat desert dry. Drained of everything, he finally settles into his pillow, longing for the brightness of morning to take some pain away.

BREAKFAST IS ALWAYS THE SAME, MOSTLY EATEN IN SILENCE. HIS DAD tries, but it's forced. How's school? Soccer? But he doesn't listen to Eddie's answers. Eddie feels for him; his lines have grown visibly deeper, and there's an irreparable sadness in his eyes. It's cruel to think he has so many years left ahead of him still.

Eddie preferred the arguments, how it was before Tommy died. At least it wasn't fake. There were so many of them, almost always revolving around the same subject: Tommy. The school, the money it cost to send him, the bullies, the amount of care, endless worry and concern that spilled over into slammed doors and broken plates and glasses. Eddie copped a lot of it, and that never seemed fair. All the time, Tommy would be laughing and clapping through the entire episode, serving only to fuel the fire.

He knows how much his mum adored Tommy, more than she ever loved him. The two of them had a bond, and it was all-consuming. She had nothing left for anyone else, not even his dad. It's worse now he's gone, though, as if she's unable to look at Eddie these days.

She hates me; I know it.

"How did you sleep, Ed?" his dad asks. He doesn't call him son anymore, and Eddie guesses that's for his mum's benefit.

"Okay, Dad. Yourself?"

He looks across at *her* and nods, smiling a smile that isn't.

"What's on at school today?" *Always the same order of questions.*

"Dad, it's Saturday."

He gives no reaction as he gets to his feet to take the dishes across to the sink, but as he leans against the bench, his body stiffens, and Eddie can tell he's trying not to cry. His mum continues to sip from a trembling cup, tea running down her fingers towards the multiple gashes in her wrists. Accidental, according to his dad, but Eddie knows better. Next week she's going to stay somewhere else. His dad didn't say where, but he said it would be safer. Eddie's not quite sure what he means by that.

He can't remember the last time he saw her hair brushed or in one of the dresses she sometimes liked to wear. The tablets used to help, but she stopped taking them.

Before Tommy died, and on the nights the house kept Eddie awake, he often used to earwig their conversations from the top of the stairs. Sometimes Tommy would join him, his entire hand in his mouth to stem the giggles. Eddie remembers hoping they would mention him -just once- but Tommy always monopolised discussions.

Sometimes, he sits in the same spot wishing for a sign they loved him, the son that was still here, alive, but Tommy's still number one, even when dead.

It wasn't long before his dad talked about selling the house, moving on, restarting, but his mum said she could never leave him, told him that Tommy was still here and could never abandon him.

Now they don't talk at all.

He excuses himself from the breakfast table and runs up the stairs back to his—their room. Beyond the glass, there's a blue sky with a handful of rolling clouds, treetops gently dancing in the distance. He unlocks the sash window and pushes upwards, the sweet smell of spring filling his nostrils as the warm breeze rushes in. He ducks under the wooden frame and swings his legs over the windowsill, looking down towards the soft patch of grass beyond the concrete path. "I could probably jump and not break a leg," he remembers boasting to Tommy once. But Tommy fell on his head and split his skull open.

Why did you have to die, Tommy?

He remembers that day so well. It was just like any other, but he was so over it, stretched to his limit by merciless abuse. He let them get to him. He was weak. All the comments at school, on the bus home, there was no escape. Even at home, the texts, emails, and posts came non-stop.

Does he still wear nappies?

Is it contagious?

"Tommy gives retards a bad name!

It's in the blood.

That's been Eddie's life mostly, a relentless barrage of Tommy-related insults. So, when he came home that day and found him trying to catch butterflies while perched across the window ledge, he just snapped. Walked over and gave him a hefty push.

He'd just wanted to hurt him, to make him feel some pain for what he was putting the family through. Tommy was always so oblivious to trauma—what Eddie went through—what their parents sacrificed for him. It was bottled rage, a momentary lapse of control. He didn't want Tommy to die, though.

When Eddie peered over the edge and saw his brother's arms and legs arranged at impossible angles, eyes looking straight up towards him, he panicked. After his brother's legs finally stopped twitching, he ran to the bathroom and waited, anxiously rocking back and forth on the cold tiled floor, his body trembling. It didn't seem real. Regret was instant, but he knew there was no way back. He stayed in the bathroom for what felt like an eternity until his dad eventually came across the body.

Perching on the window ledge, Eddie lets the warm breeze wrap around him, momentarily taking comfort in the quiet and hypnotic movement of the trees. But looking down, he sees Tommy's face again—those eyes, dead but knowing—and the familiar knot in his stomach returns with gusto.

"It's 'kay, Ed," Tommy's voice comes from behind, loud but soft. "I still lub you."

Eddie's legs immediately stop swaying. He swallows hard. He dares not to turn around.

Something clamps onto his right shoulder as though—a hand—but there's nothing there. Below, the ground looks much further away. Another hand coils around his left shoulder—he can feel fingers pressing into his flesh as though—

"Come wiz me, Ed. Pweeese."

Eddie curls his fingers around the edge of the windowsill. "No, Tommy. I'm sorry, but I—"

The pressure stops, and he holds his breath. Nothing apart from the blood pumping in his ears and the distant song from a bird. *Four, eight, twelve, sixteen, twenty, twenty-four—*

A loud clap punctures the silence. His ears begin to ring. "You come with me, Eddie!" The voice is so close he can feel the breath on his right cheek.

"I—I can't."

More frantic clapping breaks out around him, followed by Tommy's familiar blubbering.

"But, it's so lowenly here—Eddie, pweese."

"Tommy, I'm so sorry. I didn't mean for you to die. I was just angry—"

"See, Mama!" he bawls. Clap. Clap. "See!" And he's gone.

Eddie turns to see his mum standing in the doorway, a look across her face that chills him to the bone.

"M—Mum."

She begins walking slowly towards him. "I put my hand to the window, and he told me everything."

He sees the handle of the knife sticking out of her dressing gown pocket.

"I just wanted to hear it from you, Eddie," she says, her face pale, eyes cold.

"Mum, please, it was just a—"

"Eddie, he's so alone. He needs you now more than ever. It's only right, after what you did." She wraps her fingers around the blade of the knife. "My baby needs his big brother."

"Mum, no!"

Stomach twisting, Eddie looks down towards the soft grass beneath. Suddenly, it seems like an impossible jump.

Floorboards creak as she continues her approach. The clapping starts again. "Fwy, Eddie, Fwy!" Tommy screams.

Three—two—one—

MAKE ME SHINE

For Susan.

Tedium drove me. Ego, too. And I begged for the chance.

Michael Joseph fucking Siddharth.

I sat behind the wheel for some time, almost talking myself home at one point, before I finally summoned the courage to grab my pad and leave the comfort of the car. I knew the article would never be as good without offering the reader something more authentic, above and beyond what I could deliver from the confines of my small office. Trembling, I was, standing outside those walls, feeling like a child about to stand up in class for the first time. "Here we go." After flashing my press pass to the guards and trying my best to appear as nonchalant as possible throughout all their protocols, it wasn't long before things started to get to me—the echoing footsteps, the jeers, metal on metal. I bit down hard on my lip and walked as tall as I could through those corridors.

When we finally arrived at the cemetery itself, my shoulders dropped. Standing amongst the evil dead on a chilly September morning, swallowing the damp air and surrounded by the ghostly mist did nothing for my nerves. Without Frank and Tony standing behind me, I might have turned and run back to the car.

"Air feels more charged than usual," Frank said, leaning back against the stone. "Probably excited. Don't get many visitors."

"Which one is Michael's?"

"Six rows down, fourth one in, Mr. Farland," Frank replied.

"James, please," I said, already on my way.

"Be careful," Tony shouted after me. "He bites."

The words already sounded distant, as though the mist had a tangible thickness. When I anxiously turned, only their silhouettes were visible. "You hear me, guys?"

But nothing. I asked them later if they were fooling, but they just looked at me blankly, as they would, I suppose, if it was a private joke. The mist only seemed to get thicker with each step, its movements more aggressive. *Air feels more charged than usual.* The words bounced in my head.

I think I'd counted five rows but couldn't be sure.

Then I heard it. Or at least I thought I did, what sounded like an inaudible whisper carrying on the breeze.

"Guys?"

And another, dry and throaty, as if someone was trying to find their voice.

"You got me, guys. I give in, okay!"

I followed the husky whispers through the mist, finally catching sight of *his* gravestone. There was nothing unusual about it, a slight lean, but nothing to set it apart from the others. At least that's what I told myself. I could feel it, though, the pull. Something else, too, a stale, putrid smell that made my stomach turn.

Another whisper.

Closer.

That's what it sounded like as I approached as if Mr. Siddharth himself was beckoning me. "Come on, guys," I said, my tone much firmer. But there was nowhere for them to hide unless they were in the ground with him. Blood thrummed in my ears, and my heart pounded.

Closer.

Less than three feet from the white cross, I came to a stop, still chewing at my lip. Dewy droplets covered my clothes, and I felt cold moisture on my eyelids, but sweat dripped down my back.

Closer.

I snapped my head from side to side, but only wisps of fog awaited. Likely less than fifty yards separated me from the guards, but it felt as though I'd slipped into a different realm.

Closer.

Up until stepping foot in that prison, I would have laughed in your face if you'd brought up the subject of ghosts. But as I edged forward towards the grave of Michael Joseph Siddharth, I felt like a child braving the darkness of a long hallway.

"Guys! Come on; this isn't—"

I saw something then, weaving between the wisps of fog, darkness within the grey. "Hello?" Breath held; the silence created even more of a charge. A storm was coming; I felt it in my bones.

"Is someone there?"

Michael Joseph Siddharth. Serial rapist of men and women. At least twenty-six victims, all of whom had their throats slit afterwards. Some so young.

"Hello?"

I felt like I was right where he wanted me to be. I tried not to blink, afraid I might miss him coming at me. Feeling heavier, weighed down, as though the mist, no longer swirling, was falling across me, layering me with guilt never claimed, I almost threw up as a hand clasped around my left shoulder.

Make me shine.

I snapped my head around to the voice.

Nothing but mist.

My heart was pounding so fast; I thought I might keel over there and then.

Laughter began shortly after, interspersed with those three words—*Make me shine*—this time delivered without so much as a crackle, as though the owner had finally found his voice.

Menacing, taunting laughter swallowed me.

"Help!" I shouted. "Help!"

The howling intensified. Shadows moved within shadows. Shades of grey in every direction.

"Help!"

Impossibly cold, I staggered forward, managing only four steps before another stone brought me to the ground.

Make me shine!

Close to tears, remaining bravado out the window, my body trembled.

"Help!"

I saw a silhouette coming towards me through the mist. Scrambling backwards, I desperately kicked my heels into the ground. I wanted out, to get as far away from Fairgate Prison as possible.

"Help!" I sobbed.

Only when I had a crystal-clear view of the wrinkly face and the prison insignia on the ruffled shirt did I stop lashing out.

"Easy," Tony said, hooking his arms under my shoulders. "Easy."

"He was here," I said. "Michael."

"We okay?" Frank's voice came from behind Tony's concerned face.

"Yeah, we're all good," Tony responded, dragging me to my feet and offering a wink. "Only our friend, James Farland, claims he just had a one-to-one with Mister Siddharth."

Frank nodded. "This place can do things to you. Chills the soul just thinking about what some of these monsters did."

"You need a coffee and a nice sugary bun," Tony said as he started towards the exit. "I'd keep this to yourself, friend, if I were you. If word gets out that you're talking to the dead, it won't be long before you find yourself somewhere similar, only with thick padding lining the walls."

"Did you ever meet him?" I said to both, feeling foolish and shaken.

"Know someone that did," Frank said. "I'll give you his number on the way out. Getting on a bit now, but he ain't in nappies just yet."

I said my goodbyes, and with no word of a lie, as soon as those double doors closed behind me, I felt a free man, as though emerging from years of incarceration. I had that coffee and sugary bun and felt a lot better for it, too.

After getting home and almost convincing myself I'd just got carried away with events, I rang Frank's contact, Gerald. The nice old man gave me some gems, and by the time my wife, Susan, arrived home, kids in tow, I'd written nearly a thousand words. By the time we'd put the children to bed, had a couple of glasses of wine, and decided to retire ourselves, I'd doubled that. I printed two copies, one for my personal file and one to read in bed to ensure it was flawless. Superstition, habit, call it what you will, but that was my routine. After re-reading twice and knowing it was the best thing I'd ever written, my finger still hovered over the laptop a good few seconds before I finally hit send and put the laptop away.

"Are you going to tell me what's wrong?"

"Nothing, love." But the reflection in the bathroom mirror told a different story. A sense of burden still shrouded me, my skin taut and pale, and my eyes sunken. I splashed some water on my face and climbed back into bed, knowing the interrogation wasn't over.

"You're not you, James." She put her book down, and I felt the burn of her stare. "What happened up there?"

Eyes lingering on my notepad, a lengthy list of the worst of the worst, I must admit, I felt a momentary urge to spill all. But I knew how that would be received.

"Prisons aren't the most uplifting of places, love."

"If it's going to hit you like—"

"Susan, I'm fine. Just tired, okay?"

"You're just like your father."

We kissed, turned out the lights, and by the time sunshine leaked through the side of the blinds, I guessed I must have had no more than two hours sleep, haunted by shadows and voices in the mist. Squinting against the light, I threw my legs out of bed, offering a sharp inhale as I noted the circle around the name on the notepad next to my bed. Thomas Butterworth.

Trying to think back to the night before, I remained there for some time. During nights of broken sleep, I would often write things down by phone light, notes for some of the more creative stuff I was working on. Illegible and useless most of it, but now and again, there was a golden nugget waiting for me. I took the circle as a sign, prioritising Thomas Butterworth as my next project.

"Where did you put the copy, Susan?" I asked.

"Haven't touched it, James."

After breakfast and giving my wife and kids a kiss goodbye as they went about their day, I snapped open the laptop.

James, this is magnificent. Next-level stuff. Take the reins on this one and go wild! James Farland is going to be a bloody household name!

Gut-instinct and moral fibre, easily overridden by a few nice words and a bit of ego-stroking. I guess that's the definition of narcissism.

That first article changed everything. The weekly, never getting more than a few letters at the best of times, mostly the bored or elderly pointing out errors, was flooded with praise. People wanted more, and we were about to give it to them.

Anyhow, within five minutes of reading my editor's praise for the third time that morning, I made arrangements to see Thomas Butterworth's gravestone on the other side of the region.

All prisons look the same, and even with the prettied-up name, Sanctuary Lakes, it didn't stop the chill riding through my bones as my tyres crunched the gravel of the visitor car park. I took some time in the car before I made the walk again, adamant I wasn't going to lose it like the time before. Likely late fifties, a warden called Trevor was waiting for me, and if truth be told, I didn't care for him, and I know the feeling was mutual.

"Don't approve of people like you glorifying what they did," he said as he took me to the graveyard. "Ten down, four from the right." Eyes remaining towards the ground, his baton pointed towards the vicinity of the intended stone. "And don't dither as I've things to do."

I didn't get the same feeling as last time: no eerie mist, no charge. Marching towards my target, shoulders back, chin up, I felt a mixture of relief and disappointment, anxious I wouldn't be able to duplicate the atmosphere of my last piece.

"Did you know him?"

"I don't want anything to do with what you're writing, sonny," Trevor replied. "Keep my name out of it."

As I continued my approach, I was half-hoping for a blanket of mist to fall, for the whispers to begin. Even as I stood, perhaps three feet from the final resting place of Thomas Butterworth, 1975-2014, the only thing I felt was Trevor's eyes burning into the back of my head.

To this day, I still don't know what made me reach out to touch the cold roughness of that gravestone.

Felt like a million volts shooting through me.

Got a story for you, the voice spoke in my ear.

I can't explain it. All I know is what I saw.

From the moment I spied the reflected face in the rain-spattered patio window, watching that family laugh and play, I knew what was in store. I could have likely snapped my hand back at that point, but my ego was as smooth as a pebble, and I wanted to keep that *shine*.

Don't get me wrong, I was terrified, but curiosity and fame formed a potent potion.

I remember Sinatra was playing. Flickering lights on the Christmas tree and countless presents underneath, I guess Thomas Butterworth felt he had a right to their happiness.

Tap. Tap. Tap.

"Is that Santa, Daddy?" the blonde-haired boy said.

"Call the police, Denise. And get the kids upstairs."

They didn't even make it to the hallway before I—Thomas—was inside, barking instructions and slicing at the Christmas air with a knife. "Really should be more careful, folks," he said. "All sorts of night creatures out there." He made them swap presents first, rocking back and forth with excitement, watching them untie golden ribbons, and tearing off the expensive wrapping paper. "Isn't it all so damned cosy?" he said.

While the little ones wailed and the wife begged for Thomas to let them go, he helped himself to some brandy. Even started dancing and singing along to the tunes. Swear down; I could taste the liquid at the back of my throat.

"Come on; let's have a dance."

Sobbing, the wife shook her head, withdrawing further into her husband's arms.

"Come on, love," he said. "You only live once."

It was then I felt the pressure on my arm.

"Sonny!"

And just like that, the scene was gone, and I was left squinting into daylight, the same whooshing in my ears and heart thumping.

"I ain't got all fucking day."

During the drive back, I contemplated how far I would have let myself go; what would have been my threshold? The thought terrified and intrigued me.

Once home, I followed the web trail. It came as no surprise to read Thomas Butterworth killed every member of that family. Put both kids back in their beds and filled their stockings with—well, some things are best left unwritten.

It took me just shy of three hours to put everything together. I printed two copies, as usual, one for my file and one for reading in bed. Felt pretty good about it, too, what with that genuine thread of fear running through the entire work. Shook off the nastiness that little bit quicker, too.

"I don't know how you do it," Susan said, once the kids had left the dinner table.

"What do you mean?"

"Surrounding yourself with all that carnage."

"And that's coming from a teacher," I replied. "Look, it's only for a while. I can't spend the rest of my days rambling about different types of pasta. I'll go bonkers."

"What were the kids talking about at dinner?"

"Huh?"

"The thing that happened at school today. You were nodding as Jessica was telling you about her day."

"I'm too tired for your tests, Susan." Seeing the sting in her eyes, I lowered my tone. "Look, just a few more weeks, okay. I've already had an e-mail from a couple of newspapers. And that job at the university."

"You're not here, though, James. Every conversation I try to initiate, you're driving it towards the finish as quickly as possible."

'I'll do better; I promise." I place my palm across her wrist. Her words ring true, though. Fear has turned into an obsession, and I'm ready for my next fix. "I just want more than a page in the local rag, Suse."

"Don't you remember how happy you were when you got that job?"

"I know, love. I just want to"—*Shine*— "make you proud, that's all."

She offered a sigh. "Go and spend a couple of hours with Jessica and Arty, okay? Take an interest."

"For sure."

I never did get to see the children that night. Instead, I stood outside their bedroom door, reading the printed copy of my latest article. Things like that get to me now, the assumption there'll be other days, hindsight having razor-sharp teeth. Shortly afterward, I flopped onto our bed, letting the manuscript fall to the floor. I closed my laptop after hitting send, and my eyes soon followed.

Yet another night of broken sleep ensued, dreams of making it as a prize-winning journalist, stunted by visions of blood-filled savagery. I woke to find the manuscript gone, afraid that Susan would shortly deliver another lecture on having such material in the house. But it was the name circled on my pad that stole my attention. Leonard Tamms. I didn't question it this time; I just assumed that my journalistic instincts were reawakening after being dumbed down for so long.

Another outstanding article, James! We can't wait to get this out to the public. Bravo!

Squinting into the artificial light of my laptop, I clicked off my e-mail and refreshed myself on the legend that was Leonard Tamms, a serial killer made even more infamous by his appetite for human flesh. Two hundred and sixty-seven pounds of pure evil. Made the arrangements shortly afterwards to see his grave.

There was no mist that day, no build up as I approached the stone. But I do recall the smell of rotting flesh on the breeze and the feel of warm breath against my neck.

They don't know about all of 'em. Got some more for yer!

I took out my notepad there and then and started writing names down. It turned out these people were all missing, dating back for decades.

Fan mail, hate mail, people trying to shut us down, we couldn't get to it all quickly enough. Even had to hire a legal department. And we couldn't print the weekly quickly enough, flying off the shelves it was.

The circling of the names carried on, too, bringing me to the resting place of more monsters, each more evil than the last. Hard to think they once walked the streets, passing themselves off for normal. What scared me more than anything, though, was my developing numbness to it all. By the time I was on my way to visit the circled name of the week, Clive Durrell, I reckon I'd seen more carnage and bloodshed than any man alive. It seemed like my threshold for violence increased each time, too. Sometimes I carried it around for days.

Susan and I grew more distant, and it got to be so the kids didn't even try to engage me. I was slipping, consumed by the darkness, with a hunger for more.

But things were about to change.

Shortly after I finished my final piece on Clive Durrell—printing the usual two copies—we sat down for dinner. Another awkward one, the clatter of cutlery impossibly loud against the silence, the kids were now well attuned to it, their faces wearing angst before their years.

"I got it!"

She looked at me, offering a gentle shake of her head.

"The job at the university; I got it!" I lifted my phone to her confused stare.

"Oh, thank God," she said before breaking into a sob. It looked, at one point, as though she might pass out with relief.

The air immediately felt less *charged*.

"What are you doing?" Susan said, cosying up to me in bed later that evening, her face renewed with hope, that smile I hadn't seen for so long. "We need to celebrate."

"I just have to—"

"No," she said. "You don't have to." Her face changed then, the look in her eyes severe and the tautness returning. "Prove you're finished with all of this, James."

I laughed, not realising what she was asking. "What do you want me to do? I've spent three days on—"

"Tear it up. And delete the e-mail." She pushed herself to her elbows, the vein in her forehead beginning its bulge. "We're done with this!"

"Love, I just—"

I didn't know how to react as she snapped the manuscript from my grasp and began ripping it into pieces, tossing it around the room like confetti. I let out a snigger, but internally, I wanted to lash out and scream at her. The laptop was next, her eyes darting across the screen until she found the delete button.

"No, love, I—"

"There!"

And it was gone. From deleted items, too. Into oblivion. All that was left was the copy in my file downstairs, and I knew that if it ever saw daylight, my marriage would end. She even made me write an e-mail to Claire there and then, telling her I was done, that she wouldn't be getting anything else from me.

We made love that night. For the last time.

I couldn't tell you what time it was when I woke up to the sound of scratching. Momentarily, I thought it might be rats in the walls, but the smell fell across me like a noxious dose of smelling salts—

burnt meat and incense. Waiting for my eyes to adjust, I just stared at the ceiling, the sound of my breathing becoming gradually faster.

I slowly leaned over the edge of the bed, fingers clinging to the duvet, knowing what was making the noise but praying I was wrong. But there it was—a hand—the bony fingers pinched around my Parker and scribbling across my notepad.

Blood pounding in my ears, the grip on the duvet tightening further, I watched with inevitability the almost skinless and charred limb slowly and jaggedly continue scratching my name across the bottom of the paper. I tried to call Susan's name as the hand started to circle my name, but any immunity to fear I'd thought I'd developed deserted me, and once again, I felt like a child in the darkness, unable to summon a voice.

"They said you'd make me shine," the crackly voice said from under the bed.

I opened my mouth to reply but still couldn't find anything.

Between the manuscript fragments, the bony fingers clamped down onto the wooden floor, a loud groan emerging as the top of the head came into view, a sinewy mess of twisted flesh and skull. "I came all the way back from Hell. Wrote my name on your pad, just like they said."

Beside me, I could hear Susan's quiet whistling as she continued her peaceful sleep.

"I'll fix it," I finally managed to say. "I'll write it again tomorrow. Even better, you'll see."

"Too late." The body crackled and popped as it continued to make its way out, the almost meatless and blackened bones scraping against the timber. And then the head spun around. "I came all the way back for my copy." Something dark and shiny poked out between the exposed teeth, falling to the floor with a squelch and scuttling back under the bed.

"I'll make another," I say, voice croaking as I stare into the two blackened eyeholes of Clive Durrell.

"My legacy litters your floor."

"Please come back tomorrow; I'll have it for you. Please!"

I felt the iciness of his grip. "Begging did none of them any good." Impossible pressure around my throat; I tried to call out once more but knew then I was as good as dead. "Not to worry, James Farland. You will get to write my story." He began to laugh, bones crackling as he squeezed harder on my neck until the tidal wave of darkness appeared on the horizon. Feeling those fingers clawing within, I offered my sleeping wife one last glance before he dragged my soul under the bed.

"We'll both shine down here."

NEXT TIME YOU'RE STANDING WITHIN THE GHOSTLY MISTS OF A cemetery, look out for my gravestone—James Farland—last name on that list.

Not a monster, just a writer.

THE CANDLE MAKER

"KEEP WALKING, JODY," Seth says. "Head down and don't make eye contact."

They're tantalisingly close to the relative safety of the food section, the sickly but oh so sweet smell of fried food cutting across the waft of scented candles.

"Shh," Jody hisses. Her pace slows, and she alters direction—going, going, gone—lost in a haze of colours, ribbons, and mood cards.

"But I'm hungry," he offers weakly, eyeing a young boy through the gates, one hand locked to his mother's and the other around a hot dog that is losing the battle against gravity.

"Are they all homemade?" she chirps to the lady at the table wearing the black veil, who has been watching them for some time.

"Of course they are, darling."

"Fuck's sake." Seth drops his shoulders and follows, four paper bags already full of handmade crap and randomness rustling against his legs. With a mixture of pride and foreboding, he watches his wife smile her smile, the one that indicates she's found yet another kindred spirit.

"I love your veil," Jody says, that sparkle in her eyes.

"Thank you."

"Let me guess," Seth comments. "Homemade?"

She nods and flashes a wink.

"It's so pretty," Jody says. "Why buy bulk when you can have something so incredibly unique?"

Because it's a quarter of the bloody price, Seth thinks to himself. "We've got so many candles already, though, Jodes. If the house ever caught fire, our street would become a lake of wax, a perfumed catastrophe. I mean no offence to you—"

"Patricia," the veiled lady says, offering a wry smile and her hand. Automatically, he reaches for it. "Seth."

"What's your favourite smell, Seth? The one that takes you away; the one that brings you peace?"

"Food," Jody volunteers.

"There's just no room," Seth persists. "I opened the cupboard in the hallway yesterday and had to chase some of the buggers down. If you both know about an upcoming apocalypse, please let me know, so I can at least ring my mother."

"They make me happy, Seth," Jody says, voice slightly raised. "You like your food, wine, and I like my—things."

"I know you do, Jody, and that's great, but don't you think we have enough—things? The candles all smell the bloody—"

"Seth!" Jody snaps, her face turning a shade of red. Seth's not sure if it's anger or embarrassment, but he knows it's time to bail either way.

"You two are adorable," Patricia says. And oddly enough, she means it. They remind her of a time before loneliness, the comfort of being in a relationship with no heirs or graces. She's developed an eye for such things. The man looks at his wife in the same way George used to look at her, with a resigned submission to love. And how they behaved before—the playful nudges, the inhibition to share their affection in public. She lets herself believe they could be the ones.

"He likes travelling," Jody says. "Hiking. You know, the smell of the forest."

"I was fitter a couple of years ago," Seth jumps in, unconsciously breathing in. "Work means I don't get many vacation days these days, and as Jody said, I'm running on heavy fuel at the moment."

Patricia laughs. "My late husband loved the forest—said it took him away from all the bustle, made him feel like a child, full of play and imagination. You remind me of him, Seth."

He's almost falling for it. She's drawing him in with practised patter, and he can feel his defences dropping.

"And I agree with you," she continues, "most of them do blend into the same noxious explosion of perfume. Let me assure you, though, that these are very different." She reaches underneath the table and pulls out a coarsely cut piece of card with *Patricia's Candles* scrawled above a dull orange flame. There's no e-mail address or social media tags, just a landline number. "If you're ever dissatisfied."

As Seth takes the card, Jody's already on her fourth candle, closing her eyes and inhaling the magic. "Oh, this one's lovely. Tropical Sunset. Smell this one, Seth."

"Where's the forest one, then?" he mutters, knowing the battle is lost; too many words exchanged now to run.

"Patience, Seth. What about you, Jody? Where do you like to go?"

Jody looks across to Seth, eyes already glistening.

"She likes anything that reminds her of her mother," Seth answers.

The veiled lady nods as though this is secondary information. "She's no longer with us," she utters, not phrasing it as a question.

Lifting the hem of the tablecloth, she reaches under and brings out a small ornately carved box. The catch gives a satisfying snap as Patricia pulls back the lid and brings out the second and fifth candle from the selection.

"I like you both a lot. And I think you'll like these. Unlike the rest, they're both one of a kind, not made in batches like the others. They're made with even more care, love, and an extra special bit of magic."

The word sets Seth's tolerance waning again. As if on cue, his stomach churns, reminding him he's being hustled without the comfort of any snacks. He reaches for the green candle, but Patricia snaps it back. "Close your eyes," she says.

He contemplates arguing the case but figures it will only delay things. He does as the veiled lady commands.

"Breathe in," she adds to the order.

And with a sniff, he's there, babbling stream in the distance, fern giving to the warm breeze, and undergrowth crackling beneath his feet. All thoughts of greasy food fade quickly, making room for the earthy smell of life and death: vegetation, moisture, soil, and decaying plants. His legs buckle, forcing him to open his eyes and reach out for the edge of the table.

"Holy—"

"You're not funny," Jody utters.

He opens his mouth to speak, but Patricia beats him to it. "I'll bag that one up for you," she says, holding the black candle towards Jody.

Jody goes in, eyes closed, a strange and garbled moan leaving her lips. Seth watches his wife begin to sway from side to side, feeling all warm and tingly as her smile develops. He's always loved her smile, but unlike the one that has naturally moulded over time, the one spreading across her face breaks the boundaries of adulthood—unrehearsed, spontaneous—full of hope. It reminds him of the smile she gave when he proposed.

Bringing her in close, he wipes the fresh tear away and kisses her forehead. "I was in Mother's house," she utters, eyes now wide open. "I saw her, Seth. I saw Mum."

"Scent can conjure many things," Patricia says softly. "People underestimate it, think of it more of a secondary sense, but it can conjure vivid memories, joy, sadness, and hope. It's what brought me here in front of you."

Jody feels exhausted all of a sudden. "You're very talented."

Patricia smiles and puts her hands behind her back. "Wait until you light them."

"How much?" Seth says, rifling through his wallet.

"Jesus, Seth! Way to ruin the mood."

"Adorable," Patricia comments, dismissing the sight of his wallet with her hand. "As I said before, I like you both. It's like going back in time. Let's call it a late wedding gift, eh?"

"You sure?" Seth comments.

"Just knowing they're going to a good home is enough for me." She bows her head slightly and raises an eyebrow. "I do hope they don't just get shoved into a cupboard, though."

Jody reaches across the table and embraces Patricia as though she's an old friend. "We promise they won't." She wants to know more. She wants to talk about how the candles were made, what happened to the lady's late husband, and how she could even have one, spying flawless skin through the black lace. She wants to share a coffee with her, perhaps a glass of wine, and bask in their love of craft and all things homemade. Her friendship group is solid, but they often mock her fetish for such things.

"One last thing," Patricia offers them. "Will you honour me with a promise?"

At this point, Jodie would promise her life savings in exchange for another brief encounter with her mum. "Of course."

"Will you light both candles at the same time? I know it's an odd request, but I love the thought of you enjoying them together."

"We can do that," Jody replies.

"Just not in the same room," Patricia adds firmly. "If the smells mix, it won't have the same effect."

"Of course," Jody mutters.

"Well, it's been a strangely awesome encounter," Seth says, offering his hand before Jody can say another word. He means it, though. What he thought would be just another awkward stand-off of rattling bags and wishing Jody away from another *crazy* turned out to be a rather pleasant experience. Truth be told, he's looking forward to settling down in his favourite armchair with a tumbler in hand and his new gateway to the forest. His stomach lets out another grumble, reminding him of priorities.

"Thanks so much," Jody shouts as they slowly begin to back away. "I hope you sell thousands."

"Just one might be enough," Patricia responds.

She waits for them to turn and uses her veil to dab at the fresh tears, hoping that one will indeed be enough. She didn't think it would be so difficult. She knew love once—real, selfless, all-consuming—thought she could spot it a mile away, but appearances have proven deceptive. Real love, the genuine die for you kind, seems incredibly rare. This could be her last shot—all those torturous and solitary years, for what?

THE CANDLE'S FLAME FLICKERS AS SETH PLACES THE PEPPERMINT TEA on the edge of the bath. "Are you sure you don't want me to scrub your back?"

"I'm sure. Oh, shoot, can you take that tea back down with you?"

"You only just asked for it."

She smiles. "I know, sorry, but it's such a strong smell and—"

"Ah, of course. Mustn't let the smells mix. What about the bubble bath?"

"Unscented, smart arse."

"Touché. Are we supposed to do a countdown or what?"

"I don't think that's necessary," she says, tentatively dipping her toe in the thin layer of foam. "We can if you want."

"That looks so nice." He watches her slide into the bath. "Are you sure you don't want company?"

"As sure as shit."

She only started using the term after her mum, Vanessa, died. It was one of many sayings she adopted since her passing—a long and arduous battle with cancer. One of a kind, a force to be reckoned with apparently, but one that he never got the chance to meet. That said, it still feels like he lost a family member, and as far as he's concerned, anyone that Jody nurtured so much love for is an opportunity stolen.

He picks up the tea and winks. "Okay. See you on the other side, I guess."

"Thanks for a lovely day," she says on his way out. "And thanks for letting me indulge my crafty side."

"Nothing but crafty," he says, descending the stairs quicker than he usually would, hot tea spilling across his fingers. He places the cup on the kitchen counter, empties some ice from the freezer into a heavy tumbler, and whistles his way into the living room. *Bourbon time.* He opens the cabinet, rubs his hands together with anticipation—a habit picked up from his father—and fills the glass half full. He can even hear his father's voice in his head as the ice begins to gently crackle.

Day done, places been, people seen, now time to relax with a glass of Jacks.

At this point, Seth would usually throw a vinyl on and dance his happy alcohol dance, but secretly he's been getting excited for this moment. Hairs bristling on his neck and feeling slightly silly about the unmistakable adrenaline prompting an elevated heartbeat, he grabs the lighter near the small cigar box. Momentarily, he considers lighting one up but recalls the lady's—Patricia's—advice about mixing scents.

Settling into his armchair, he sips back a generous gulp of gold and flicks a flame, applying it to the wick. He kicks off his shoes, knocks back the rest of the glass, and closes his eyes, waiting for the forest to come.

JODY SCOLDS HERSELF FOR THINKING ABOUT WORK, KNOWING IT TAKES more than its fair share without having to steal extra. She lets her head fall back and closes her eyes, expecting to feel the tickle of foam but recalling the lacklustre effort of the scentless soap.

She breathes in deeply, inhaling the intoxicating heaviness.

And just like that, she's there.

The garden path is as neat as she remembers, not a weed in sight.

Her mum was always so fastidious when it came to appearances, even more so when *Dad* left for someone half her age. It's an old house with crumbling brickwork and scars from where clematis once grew, but it's still pretty.

Everything is so impossibly vivid, the faded blue paint of the front door, even the familiar cracks in the pavement. And as soon as she opens the front door, a thousand memories carry on the cocktail of scents. The musky sweetness of the hallway, the smell of baking from the kitchen mixing in with perfume that her mum used to wear, the one that always reminded her of candy, fills her with contrasting melancholy and happiness.

"Mum?"

She can see the open kitchen window down the hallway, two pies resting on the sill, creating a film of steam. Just a normal Sunday evening from eons ago.

She prepares to step across the threshold, filled with excitement and unease. She looks behind and to her sides, but the rest of the world is just a blur, not part of the story, not part of the experience. The scents are getting stronger, taking hold, putting her doubts to bed.

"Mum."

Unable to resist any longer, she steps into the hallway, her dress wafting behind as the breeze travels down the corridor, slamming the front door shut and causing her to jolt.

"What did I tell you about leaving that door open?" her mum's scolding voice floats across from the kitchen.

"Sorry, Mum," Jody instinctively replies as steam begins to pour into the hallway, stretching towards the ceiling.

"Not to worry. I made two blueberry, one blackberry, and the cherry's still in the oven."

She just ate a healthy serving of Seth's apple curry, but Jody's stomach lets out a deceiving growl. Nothing beats Mum's pies —*made with love.*

It's surreal, disorienting, each grain in the wooden floor, the texture of the wallpaper, the click from the old-fashioned phone as she spins the dial with her finger. The scene is playing out as vivid as some dreams, yet it offers so much more.

The smell.

She wafts her hand, sending a wisp of grey smoke spiralling, but more replaces it. She can no longer see into the kitchen now, her vision distorted by the ever-thickening film.

Observing her reflection in the condensation of the hallway mirror, she edges forward, surprised not to see a younger version of herself, one that took everything for granted. "I miss you, Mum."

The dress she's wearing in this—whatever it is—was her mum's favourite. It should be far too small for her these days, but the image shows impossible perfection. Cold to touch, she runs a finger across the glass, writing the same message she did for months after her mum died. *Are you there, Mum?*

There's a cough from the kitchen, weak and filled with agony.

"I'm coming, Mum."

The explosion drops her to her knees, shards of glass spraying against the wall and floor with deafening impact. She curls into a ball, body violently trembling, soft fingertips scraping against the fragments in her hair as she puts her hands to her ears to block out the sound. But it feels like the glass is trapped in her head, scraping against her brain. She remains in position, waiting for the fragment to her right to stop spinning and fall to its side.

Silence.

The bitter taste of blood layers at the back of her throat, and the stinging begins to ramp up. She inhales sharply, running her fingers across the segment of glass lodged in her cheek, and with her tongue, she finds the other end, prompting a liquidy croak. Fragments of glass glisten in her skin, streams of bright red running down the sleeve of her dress and creating the only colour in the now very grey hallway.

"Mum."

As the ringing in her ears begins to subside, she slowly stands, pulling glass from her arm and brushing herself down. She leans in towards the mirror, futilely waving at the smog. On the piece of glass that remains in its centre, impossibly unsupported, the word *No* is written underneath the question that she could have written with her eyes closed.

Her breathing feels far too loud. Saliva rattles in her mouth, but she's too afraid to swallow.

A creak of a floorboard snaps her head to the right.

The glass that littered the floor around her is gone, as is the searing pain in her jaw. Another creak prompts her to hold her breath and freeze. There's a scratching sound, as though someone is dragging something along the walls.

"I know it isn't you," she cries.

She takes a step back, blindly reaching her hands into the fog, noting the now untarnished mirror and her smoky full-length reflection. The word *No* still plain as day, though. She begins to panic, reaching to her left, praying to find the door's handle.

Another creak.

She tries to scream, but nothing emerges.

FRUSTRATION OVER CURIOSITY FORCES SETH FROM THE CHAIR, THE scratching sound infrequent and gentle but enough to irritate and demand his attention.

A washout.

He can smell the forest, but it's faint as if carrying on his clothes from a previous camping trip—nothing like the experience from the lady's stall, where a mere sniff conjured a majestic canopy.

He ambles towards the source, his legs feeling heavy and his brain cloudy. Perhaps sleep would have stolen the experience anyway. He can try again tomorrow.

Mouth falling slightly ajar, he drops his shoulders and freezes, letting out a grunt. He arches his neck to see if the imagery holds from a different angle and takes an excited step forward.

Window fogging as he draws in, he begins to inspect the jungle that has taken the place of his manicured front lawn. Darkness only allows him clarity of the first few layers of vegetation, but shadows moving on shadows suggest the denseness extends well beyond where his petunias used to be.

"Jody!"

The smell is stronger than ever. Through the gaps in the window that Jody always moans about in winter, the bitter earthiness begins to fill his nostrils with nostalgic wonder.

"Fuck me."

Expecting the foliage to disappear at any moment, he edges towards the hallway. Inhale. Exhale. He coils his fingers around the front door handle, not taking his eyes from the window. Thick vegetation continues its dance, brushing against the house with a quickening tempo.

Afraid to open the door in case the illusion fades, he remains in position, skin crawling with excitement.

Three, two, one.

So many smells seep through as he pulls the handle, the warm breeze even leaking some dead leaves onto the carpet and causing his shirttails to flap.

"Holy Shit."

He inhales the spiciness, savouring the thickness at the back of his throat. Such a smell often reminds him of the greenhouse from the old house. His dad never used to let him play in it, but the one he sneaked into anyway. It's been too long, and he knows he ought to call.

The wind blows through again, a stronger gust this time, carrying more forest debris into the house. Full of childlike awe, he steps outside onto damp leaves and closes the door behind him.

A fucking candle, for God's sake.

But here he is, standing in an impossible rainforest, only a few feet away from his whisky.

He reaches out, caressing the soft ferns with his fingers. How is it possible for a single sense to evoke the others in such a powerful way? Thoughts fade as he allows the forest's sights, scents, and feels to seduce him. He's captivated, breathing in nature's sweet perfume—in his good place—where magic lives.

ALL THE CRAP JODY HAS BROUGHT HOME IS FINALLY WORTH IT. HE wants to show her, to go back and get her but knows it's not possible. This is a solo experience, and no doubt she is in her own personal heaven, basking in the nostalgia and smells that make her weak at the knees.

Almost stumbling as the gust wraps around him, he stretches out his arms and begins to laugh, harder than he has for some time, raw and explosively, until it finally becomes a tear-inducing rasp. "In-fucking-sane." His breathing slows, and he begins to wipe the moisture away with the back of his shirt sleeve. *Totally fucking insane.*

As he begins removing his socks for further immersion, he spots something ahead between the flashes of foliage, at least he thinks he does through his cloudy and obscured vision. A cross? He takes another step forward, squinting into the semi-darkness, but the wind drops quickly, and the wall of green is back.

Enjoying the feel of nature beneath his toes, he begins to move, sliding aside the moist vegetation. He glances back a few steps in to make sure he can still see the house, prompting another laughing fit, albeit shorter and slightly more self-aware. He thinks the experience absurdly terrific, even beating those mushrooms from college.

Something *special* in the wax. What other explanation is there?

With more confidence, he strides forward, still giggling as he pulls back vines and swats at mosquitos that are starting to appear. But laughter bluntly stops as he steps into the small clearing, observing the man nailed to a makeshift cross, eyes removed, intestines spilling from his abdomen.

His skin tightens. His stomach churns.

Two names are etched on the man's right arm, either side of the blood-encrusted heart-shaped wound: Seth and Jody.

And just like that, the forest feels darker, meaner, the smell of death layering at the back of his throat, dread replacing awe and wonder.

Breathing quickly and erratically, he shrinks back into the relative safety of the foliage, his eyes darting left to right, tracking every moment of the forest. A wave of nausea doubles him over, and he bites at his lip, trying to fight it, trying to rid the vision from his mind. And each step back, the vegetation feels sharper and the ground softer.

"Jody!" he screams as loud as possible, hoping it might snap him back into reality.

His heel catches against something hard, and he looks down to find a grey bone emerging from the soil. To his right, he spots another. And another.

"Jody!"

He turns and runs, wincing as the forest begins tearing into his face and limbs. Beneath him, the ground becomes increasingly marshier, his feet slopping against dampness and exhausting him far too quickly.

Where's the house? Where's the fucking house?

Grimacing and brushing away the vegetation he longed for only minutes ago, he prays for a glimpse of paintwork, but as foliage finally gives, he stumbles into another clearing, another makeshift cross, and another man with most of his insides missing, the same sinister declaration of love carved into his arm.

Fuck!

Vomit finally explodes from Seth, landing inches before the cross and next to something that once belonged inside the man's chest.

"Jody!"

He takes off again, his feet squelching into the boggy ground that feels like it wants to swallow him.

Which way? Which fucking way?

The explosion crackles across the forest, stopping him dead in his tracks. *A gunshot.*

Holding his breath, blood whooshing in his ears, he remains perfectly still.

He waits.

And waits.

Nothing.

Impatience and fear win over, and more cautiously, he's on the move again, ducking and swerving to avoid the claws of the jungle. Ahead, foliage gives to the wind, revealing the outline of another cross and another lolloping head.

"I want to go home now. I want to go home." As though the chant is the secret to being back in his comfy chair and sipping his whisky.

From his left, there's a rustling. Not a breath of wind, though.

He sprints in the opposite direction, pumping his arms and legs in sheer desperation, rain splashing across his forehead and running down the back of his neck as he forces his way through. He gasps at another explosion, this one overhead and even louder, followed by a flash of lightning that bathes the forest floor in white, highlighting the abundance of bones and glistening innards littering its dampness. He carries on, blindly forcing his way through to God knows where and hoping for an exit from whatever hell this is.

"I want to go home!" he screams.

Lightning disappears into the canopy not so far ahead, and the subsequent thunder is surrounding and deafening. He pushes on, legs heavy, fighting against the ever-softening ground. Thoughts turn to Jody. Only now is it crossing his mind that she might be having a similar experience, holed up in some twisted and induced nightmare, alone and terrified.

He stumbles through into another clearing, but this one with a line of crosses stretching for as far as he can see, each with a body nailed to it, skin slashed, innards pulled out. The wind gifts him the stench all at once, forcing him to dry retch towards the ground, nothing left in his gut.

With a garbled scream, he's on the run again, not caring where he's heading, just as long as he puts distance between himself and death. He runs as fast as his tired legs allow, praying he's heading in the right direction, praying that Jody won't be suffering a similar ordeal.

Through the foliage ahead, he sees a flash of drainpipe and his trusty cycle leaning against the side of their house. *Oh, God, yes!*

WAKE UP, JODY. FOR FUCKS SAKE, WAKE UP!

Confused but mostly terrified about what lies behind the fog, she runs her hand across the door, finally finding the frame with her palm.

The smog makes it almost impossible to see, but she knows *it's* close—the rattling breathing growing louder with each creak of the wood.

It isn't her. It isn't Mum.

Blindly and urgently, she feels her way across, a ripple of relief washing over her as her fingers finally clasp around the handle. Something foul is diluting the air now, sweetness and perfume replaced with rotting meat.

She yanks down hard on the handle and begins to cry.

Locked.

"Jo-dy." The croaky voice rattles from behind.

"Please, no. Please, stop this."

Something darker moves behind the grey as she yanks at the handle again, but there's no give.

As coldness clasps around her left shoulder, she screams.

THE STENCH IS PUTRID, MAKING HER INSIDES TURN. THE FLOORBOARDS creak again, and now she can feel its breath, warm against the back of her neck, each hair bristling its warning.

"Seth!" she screams as she eye's her husband running up the driveway, all torn up and bloody. "Seth, help!"

Iciness falls across her right shoulder, bony fingers pressing into her skin.

As she's pulled back into the fog, their eyes briefly fix on each other. "Sorry," she cries. "We had enough candles."

"JODY!" SETH SCREAMS AS HE WATCHES HIS WIFE DISAPPEARING INTO grey. He throws himself against the door, but it hardly moves. Again. And again. "Fuuuuuuuuuuck!"

She's gone.

Drawing blood from his lips as he thunders his fists against the door, he looks across to the window and makes a move but only manages two strides before the vines wrap around his legs and pull them from beneath him. He hits the ground hard, the wind rushing out of him. "Jody!" he croaks. Muscles screaming, he forces himself to grab onto the synchronised serpents, trying to wrestle them away, but this is their territory, home soil, and they only coil even tighter.

The warm breeze turns cold, and the soft rain feels hard. His body slides easily across the ground as the forest begins dragging him into its depths, away from the house, away from Jody. Futilely he digs his fingers into the softness of the earth, turning his attention towards the rustling to his left. "Help," he screams towards it in desperation.

Emerging from the wall of green, gun dancing in the air and uniform stained with darkness, the soldier glances at Seth but continues running, eyes wide with panic.

"Help us!" Seth calls again, but the soldier pays no attention, continuing his run towards a house no longer made from weatherboard but brick. Helplessly, Seth watches the soldier lean his gun against the side and crouch down towards the plant pot, sucking in strained breaths.

"Help!" Seth cries. "Please!"

There's just enough time for him to see the soldier push the door open before the man with sharp fingernails and fireflies for eyes steps out of the green, greeting him with a crooked smile.

PATRICIA HEARS THE RATTLE OF THE KEY, AND HER HEART SKIPS. SHE lets herself hope, but—

Footsteps.

Nervously, she taps her fingers against her thigh and swallows loudly before rushing over to the mirror to fix her lipstick.

All this time. But she won't believe it until she sees his face.

She had no plans to fall in love with an American. She cried for days when he got drafted. She'd seen all the movies, had boyfriends before, but until that moment, never believed in love at first sight— the kind that hurts, twists at your stomach with a yearning, the kind that puts you off food and imprisons you in your room with only books and music to see you through until you can see *them* again.

Her skin prickles as the stairs begin to creak.

Only the same pure love could bring him back from the dead; that's what the man with the long fingernails had said. She dismissed it as snake oil at first, laughing and giggling along, but when he grabbed her hand, she saw things in his fiery red eyes, otherworldly things that no human should be privy to. "It has to burn," he had said, "like love."

And that's when she knew the stranger could bring him back.

At what cost? How many souls had she needlessly cast to him over the years? And down to her last couple of drops, she had almost given up hope.

Was it worth it? Blood on her hands. Decades of loneliness, drifting through endless days without companionship, without love.

She turns to find George standing in the doorway. Beaten, bloody, but hers.

Yes, it was worth it, she thinks.

She lifts her veil, ready to kiss her husband for the first time in over fifty years.

ABOUT THE EDITOR / PUBLISHER

Dawn Shea is an author and half of the publishing team over at D&T Publishing. She lives with her family in Mississippi. Always an avid horror lover, she has moved forward with her dreams of writing and publishing those things she loves so much.

D&T Previously published material:
    ABC's of Terror
    After the Kool-Aid is Gone

Follow her author page on Amazon for all publications she is featured in.
    Follow D&T Publishing at the following locations:
    Website
    Facebook: Page / Group
    Or email us here: dandtpublishing20@gmail.com

MARK TOWSE

Mark Towse is an Englishman living in Australia. He would sell his soul to the devil or anyone buying if it meant he could write full-time. Alas, he left it very late to begin this journey, penning his first story since primary school at the ripe old age of 45. Since then, he's been published in Flash Fiction Magazine, The Dread Machine, Cosmic Horror, Suspense Magazine, ParABnormal, Raconteur, and many other excellent mags.

Mark's work has also appeared on many exceptional podcasts such as No Sleep, Creepy, Chilling Tales for Dark Nights, Tales to Terrify, The Grey Rooms, to name a few.

2021 saw the release of his debut novellas, 'Nana' and 'Hope Wharf,' and early 2022 saw his novella 'Crows' take flight, and his most recent novella, Nature's Perfume from JournalStone in March.

There's Something Wrong with Aunty Beth by Mark Towse

Edited by Jamie LaChance

Cover art by Ash Ericmore

Formatting by J.Z. Foster

There's Something Wrong with Aunty Beth by Mark Towse

Made in the USA
Monee, IL
24 June 2024

60572566R00151